PEOPLE LIKE US

Chris Binchy is a graduate of Trinity College Dublin, has been a chef and is now a full-time writer. His first novel, *The Very Man*, was a bestseller. He lives in Dublin.

'There is a wonderful authenticity in his dialogue and this fine debut brims with the true atmosphere of Celtic Tiger Dublin as the bubble started to burst' Dermot Bolger, *Evening Herald*

' . . . there is a strong sense of place, and the energy and essence of social life in Dublin are well captured . . . this debut is likely to be the start of a long and fruitful career . . . *The Very Man* slips down as smoothly as a Baileys' *Irish Examiner*

'A razor-sharp portrait . . . But it's not just Rory's antics or his ambivalent take on the city in all its grubby splendour that make *The Very Man* such an enjoyable read – it's Binchy's writing' *Irish Times*

'Binchy writes like a younger, Irish-er Nick Hornby, with an uncanny ability to get into the human mind, and in particular the male mind' *Sunday Tribune*

'It makes for a sad but at times hilarious story, and an impressive debut by Binchy which brings alive a world usually seen through a bar or car window' *Sunday Independent*

'Darkly hilarious' *Sunday Independent*

Also by Chris Binchy

THE VERY MAN

CHRIS BINCHY

PEOPLE LIKE US

MACMILLAN

First published 2004 by Macmillan
an imprint of Pan Macmillan Ltd
Pan Macmillan, 20 New Wharf Road, London N1 9RR
Basingstoke and Oxford
Associated companies throughout the world
www.panmacmillan.com

ISBN 1 4050 4162 5

1 3 5 7 9 8 6 4 2

A CIP catalogue record for this book is available from
the British Library.

Typeset by SetSystems Ltd, Saffron Walden, Essex
Printed and bound in Great Britain by
Mackays of Chatham plc, Chatham, Kent

For Siobhan

Acknowledgements

Thanks to Marianne Gunn O'Connor, Imogen Taylor, Cormac Kinsella, David Adamson, my parents, Sarah and all my family and friends for their help and support.

1

At a curve in the high road there was a viewing point with enough space for a couple of cars to park. At night the orange lights of the city spread below, north and south as far as could be seen and east to the edge of the water, the curve of the bay marked by bright white street lamps along the coast road. Planes circled above. Boats and ferries floated, islands of coloured light, towards the port. The towers of the power station rose together from the blackness of the sea. Across the bay was a peninsula, dotted with the occasional lights of houses, and above the highest house was an area, barely discernible, that was darker than the night sky above it. If you knew the city, you could fill in the gaps and make sense of it. You could say what was water and what was land, what was industrial and what was housing. But if you didn't, it was just a mess of darkness and light.

The viewing point was paved up to a grass verge marked by a fence. If you stood on the verge and looked down, you would see that the ground fell away and fifty feet below was a scrubby field, half of it dug up. There were six lorries and two JCBs parked in a row beside a Portakabin. Away to the left was a road and there were large hoardings facing the traffic, advertising the new development, selling the houses and apartments, when the foundations had yet to be dug. Straight ahead, beyond the lorries and the disturbed earth, beyond what was left of the field was a wall, lined on the far side with a row of trees. They were tall enough to be seen, but not yet thick enough to block the view to the backs of the houses behind the wall, transplanted while still saplings for the older estate, to mark it, delineate it and to hide it.

The name of the estate was painted in Gothic script on a flat, two-foot-square piece of wood attached to a large rock and was visible from the main road. That rock stood on a green area in the middle of a circle of sixteen houses, ten years old. All of them were the same when built, the same size, same number of rooms, detached, painted white, wide at the front, two storeys high and each with their own driveway. All came from the same plan. They were built when space was cheaper, when living out here on the edge meant that the owners were missing out. Unserved at the time by a proper road or shops or transport or schools. A small community away from everything that was happening until the city spilled out and sprawled around them. A wise investment, the residents said to each other now, as if they had known all along that it was coming. As if they had been waiting for the rest of the world to catch up.

Three boys, two girls, aged about fifteen or sixteen, stood around the rock and one boy, who looked older than the others, sat on it. They were all dressed the same, tracksuits and hoodies, same colours, like they were playing for the same team. The boys were talking. The girls were watching.

'. . . and that other fucking muppet,' Tim said. 'That clown. What's his name?'

'Which?' Alan asked.

'Dean's brother. He's in sixth year but he's tiny. I'd box him around too.'

'In your arse,' Liam said.

'I would. I swear to Jesus. He's the same size as me but he's real scrawny.'

The others laughed.

'So what are you?' Alan asked.

'I'm bigger than that. I'm nearly as big as you, you wanker. And, anyway, have you seen him? He walks like a girl. He's a faggot.'

'Dean would kick your arse. He'd give you a hiding.'

'Yeah, but not his brother. I know he's older but still. And not Dean either anyway. Not Dean.'

Alan and Liam looked at each other. Alan grabbed the cap off Tim's head and ran backwards away from him.

'Come on, big man. Come on, tough guy. Let's go.' As he spoke he tripped over his feet and fell on the ground laughing. In a second Tim was on him.

'Give it back,' he said, slapping Alan's face, half-messing, unsure. If the girls weren't there he'd have known what to do. Before he could think Alan pushed him off and stood up, like he wasn't there.

'Give me the hat,' Tim said after him and Alan threw it on the ground.

'You couldn't beat Dean's sister,' Alan said to him as he walked back to the rock. 'She's eight,' he explained to the girls, who were looking at each other in silence. Tim's face was burning.

'We're going to go,' one of the girls, Orla, the better-looking one, said.

'You're what?' Robbie said. He jumped down off the rock and stood beside them. While the others had been messing around and talking crap he had been playing with his mobile, not looking up, not speaking. 'Why?' he asked, staring straight at her.

'It's getting late,' she said. 'Aoife has to get back.'

'It's only half-nine,' Tim said.

'So let Aoife go,' Robbie said. 'You can stay out a bit longer, can't you?'

Orla looked at Aoife, who just shrugged and turned away. Orla blushed.

'I better go,' she said, looking at the ground in front of him.

'OK,' he said. 'See you after. Tomorrow night or whenever, yeah?'

'Whenever, yeah.'

The two girls walked off together, linking arms and leaning into each other talking.

'Goodnight, girls,' Alan called after them.

'See you,' Liam said.

'Bye, girls,' Tim shouted, too loud. Orla and Aoife looked back and the boys could hear them laughing as they went.

'Nice one, Tim,' Alan said. 'Smooth.'

'Fuck off.'

'You're a plank, Tim,' Robbie said quietly. 'You're a fucking child.' He jumped back up onto the rock and took his phone out and started texting. The other three stood, not looking at each other, their hands in their pockets, and they waited.

A car drove into the estate past the boys and pulled up outside a house across the green.

'There he is,' Liam said.

'Wanker.'

'Scumbag.'

Robbie watched as Joe Mitchell got out of his car. As Joe locked it, he stopped and stood staring over at the four of them at the rock.

'What's his problem?' Tim said.

'Is he coming over?' Liam asked.

'He won't come,' Robbie said and as he spoke, Mitchell turned and walked up the drive to his front door. Without saying anything, Liam picked up a half-empty plastic Coke bottle and threw it hard into the air. By the time it bounced off the roof of Mitchell's car and landed in the flower bed beside the front door where Joe was standing, Tim, Alan and Liam had scattered, disappeared, gone.

Things speeded up. Robbie was sitting on the rock on his own. Mitchell was walking across the green shouting.

'What the hell are you doing? Are you insane? You could have killed me.'

Robbie was laughing at that as he jumped down. The space of fifty feet was closing fast. He saw a flash, felt the rush of adrenalin and let it go. It was a feeling between joy and fear.

'What's this?' he shouted. 'What's this?'

Mitchell stopped where he was. He raised his shoulders and made himself as big as he could.

'You threw that bottle.'

They stood ten feet apart.

'I threw nothing,' Robbie said. 'You want to watch what you're saying. I threw fucking nothing.'

'Yeah, right. You're a classy one.'

'What's the problem, Joe?' Robbie kept his face straight but he was loving it.

'Don't call me Joe, you. Who threw that bottle?'

'What bottle? What are you talking about? I was just sitting there.'

'You or one of your apes. Your little monkeys.'

'Who? I'm on my own and I threw nothing.'

Mitchell looked at him. There was disgust in his face which Robbie could see, but there was a powerlessness there too and that was more important. He wasn't going to do anything. Robbie was in charge.

'One of you threw it,' Mitchell said, 'and it's not on. I'll get the guards on you.'

'Get the guards, Joe. Go on. Get them. You're seeing things. You need your eyes tested. I'm on my own and I threw nothing.'

Mitchell turned away and walked back towards his house, shaking his head. He turned when he got to the gate.

'I'll be talking to your father about this.'

'Do what you want, Joe,' Robbie called as he followed at a distance. 'He'll get you an optician. You blind fucker.'

Mitchell went into his house and closed the door behind him.

'Yeah. Go home, Joe. Go to bed.'

Robbie looked down towards the entrance of the estate. The two girls were still there. They stood looking back at him.

'He's a wackball,' he called to them, pointing at his temple. 'He's doesn't know what he's doing. He's a lunatic.' He shrugged and waited. Aoife said something to Orla and they walked away and turned the corner out of the estate.

Robbie ran across the green to the wall at the back. He launched himself at it, got a hand to the top and then pulled himself over. He landed in the soft mud on the other side and saw the others. They were leaning against the wall behind Alan's house, smoking.

'I was just saying,' Liam said as he approached them. 'I reckon that Orla one fancies you. I think you're in there . . .'

He paused. Without speaking Robbie walked up to him and punched him hard in the stomach, the soft spot between his ribs. He knew where to hit him. Liam fell on the ground. Robbie grabbed him by the hair and spoke into his ear.

'If you ever do that again, I will fucking break every bone in your body. You hear me?' Liam lay gasping, tears running down his face. 'Do you hear me or what?' Robbie asked again.

'He can't talk, Robbie. You knocked the wind out of him.'

'The same goes for you two chicken-shit bastards,' he said turning to them. 'You don't leave me on my own like that. You don't run unless I run.'

'What happened? Did Mitchell get you?' Tim asked.

'Mitchell didn't get me. He didn't get me. He's only a bollocks. I don't mind him. But this prick,' he said, pointing with his foot at Liam, 'he's got to learn. It's not on. Is it?' Liam was on his knees. Robbie kicked at him. He shook his head.

'I wasn't thinking,' Liam said. 'It was only a laugh.'

'Yeah, for you. But I had to deal with Joe and he's going to go to my dad because you want to have a laugh. We're not fucking kids you know.'

'I'm going to go,' Alan said.

'Where?'

'Home.'

'You stay,' Robbie said. 'And give me a smoke.'

Alan handed him the packet and sat on the ground. He leant back against the wall of his own house and hoped that his mother couldn't hear them.

Paul was moving faster and faster towards the door and then he was outside and his father was behind him on a bike and he was saying something to him. Paul couldn't hear him and then he realized that he was running and the old man was behind him trying to catch up. Paul tried to get away and then his father was standing in front of him, talking fast. When he listened, when he tuned in, he could hear him and it mattered what he was saying but he couldn't understand and then he thought I've got it and he was awake.

It was the noise of the television coming through the floor that had done it. Paul lay there and worked it out. It was Sunday. It was one of the kids. He sat up. Ruth was still asleep, her face a foot away dug into the pillow.

'Turn it down,' Paul shouted. He felt the buzz in his chest as he called. There was no change. He rolled over and hit the floor with his clenched fist three times.

'Fin?' Nothing. 'Fin?'

'What?' The boy's voice came from the room next door.

'Tell Louise to turn it down. The telly.'

'Lou,' Fin called without leaving his bedroom. 'Lou,' he shouted again.

'What?' she called from below. Paul could feel her voice vibrate through the floor.

'Turn it down,' Fin said.

Louise walked out into the hall and shouted up.

'What?'

'Turn it down.'

'It's not loud, I have to hear it.'

'Dad says turn it down.'

'Where is he?' she asked.

'Dad?' said Fin.

'It's only quiet,' Lou called up.

'Turn it down,' Paul shouted.

'I have to hear it.'

'Just do it. Now.'

He could hear her muttering to herself as she went back in. The volume faded away and for a second it was quiet. Then he heard Fin's door open and the thumping down the stairs, then the muffled conversation as the two of them started.

'Christ,' Ruth said, her eyes still closed.

'All right?'

'Why are you shouting?'

He lay beside her and pushed her hair back off her face.

'The television woke me,' he said.

'You woke me,' she said, her eyes opening.

He draped an arm over her waist.

'How are you feeling?'

'All right.'

He moved his hand along the curve of her hip, into the dip of her waist and up along her side.

'Are you tired?'

'I don't know. What time is it?'

'Half-eight.'

'Then I'm tired.'

His hand moved back down along the outside of her thigh and rested in the crook of her knee. He pulled her leg forward and she rolled onto her back.

'You can try,' she said, 'but you'll have to be quick.'

'I'm always quick,' he said and she laughed. The fug of the bed lay over her, morning breath and sticky eyes. The metallic taste of his own mouth sweetened as he kissed her. She yawned. He nuzzled into her neck and pulled at her T-shirt, trying to prompt her to sit up. She lifted the T-shirt over her head and dropped it on the floor beside the bed. She lay back waiting and he pushed himself up and lay on top of her. She reached down and guided him into her. He moved gently, kissing her ear.

'You smell great,' he said.

Louise screamed in the living room. Then there was a bang and they could hear her shouting at Fin. Then more banging and she screamed again. The television got louder and louder and then went quiet.

Paul and Ruth waited, silent.

'It's not going to happen,' she said.

'Hang on,' Paul said.

'Mum,' Louise called, 'Fin won't give me the remote.'

'She won't let me watch,' Fin shouted.

'Mum?' Louise called again and then they heard her crashing up the stairs. Paul rolled away and Ruth pulled the duvet up to her shoulders. Louise knocked on the door once and then came in.

'I was watching first and he came and took it off me.'

Fin came into the room, the remote control in his hand.

'She's seen that video ten million times. I'm allowed.'

'Let her watch it,' Ruth said.

'But she's always watching it.'

'Give her the remote now and let her watch it.'

'That's not fair. Dad?'

'Give it to her,' Paul said. 'And get out, the pair of you.'

Louise tried to take the control out of Fin's hand. He held it above her. She reached up to try and grab it from him.

'Give it,' she said.

'Why does she get to watch what she wants?' Fin asked.

'Just give it to her,' Ruth said.

'But I'm always letting her . . .'

'Fin. Give it.'

Fin dropped the control on the ground and walked out, his face red.

'Hey,' Paul shouted after him. 'Get back here.'

Fin turned round and stood in front of them. Louise didn't move.

'Pick it up and give it to her,' Paul said. 'I swear to God, Fin.'

Fin looked at him, raging, and then bent and handed it to Louise without looking at her. She skipped off out of the room and downstairs.

'Come on, Fin. She was there first.'

'You always take her side. It's not fair.'

'We don't,' Ruth said. 'You can put whatever you want on at half-nine.'

'That's an hour.'

'So let her watch it for an hour, then you can have it, OK?'

The music of Louise's video echoed through the house.

'Look, you can watch the match this afternoon,' Paul said. He felt Ruth move on the bed beside him. Fin walked out shaking his head, leaving the door open behind him.

'He's supposed to wash the car this afternoon,' Ruth said.

'He can do it before.'

'When? After lunch? He won't have time.'

'OK. It's all right. I'll get him to do it.'

'When?' she asked.

'I don't know.' He banged on the floor. 'Louise.'

She called up from the living room. 'What?'

'Turn it down.'

Ruth got out of bed and put on the T-shirt.

'Are you getting up?' he asked.

'I am up,' she said and she went out to the bathroom.

At a quarter to eleven, he called Louise.

'Are you ready?'

She was upstairs on the landing.

'Clare won't get out of the bathroom.'

He waited for five minutes, trying to ignore the banging and the shouting.

'You'd better go up,' Ruth said.

Louise was sitting, her back against the bathroom door.

'She's been in there for ages and she won't come out, she's not even doing anything.'

'Clare? Are you all right?' he said through the door. He was about to ask again when she spoke.

'I'm fine.'

'Can you get out? I have to take Louise to Mass.'

'In a minute.'

Nothing happened. He listened at the door and heard nothing.

'What are you doing?' he asked.

'Jesus,' she said from inside. The toilet flushed and the door opened.

'I was using the toilet,' she said. 'Would you like to know which number?'

'Shut up. You were taking ages. Louise has to get ready.'

Clare walked by him.

'Bet you'll be glad when it's over. Only a few more months.'

'Enough,' he said. 'Leave her alone. She'll do what she wants.'

'I wonder what that'll be. Cartoons or Mass? Oh, I don't know.'

'Go away. And stop being so cynical.'

When they got back from Mass Clare and Fin were on the floor in front of the television watching wrestling.

'What are you doing?' he asked. Neither responded.

'Clare?'

She looked up at him, smiling.

'I'm watching telly.'

'Shouldn't you be studying?' Paul asked.

'It's great stuff,' she said, ignoring the question. 'They kill each other. It's compelling.'

'Is it?'

'Yeah. I never realized it before. It's quite artistic. It's choreographed, you know? I always thought it was for complete morons. Like Fin.'

'Yeah, well you're watching it,' Fin said, staring at the screen.

'I'm being ironic, you dope.' She slapped the back of his head.

'Don't hit me.' He grabbed at her arm but she was too strong for him. She twisted it behind his back and pushed him face first into the living-room carpet. Paul tried not to laugh.

'Get off him, Clare. And go and do some work.'

She stood up and walked to the door.

'You're the dope,' Fin called after her.

'Yeah, right. But I kicked your arse,' Clare said.

'Balletic,' Paul said as she swaggered by him.

'What?'

'I'm being ironic,' he said. She shook her head and smiled as she went upstairs. He felt like an idiot.

'Car. Later. You,' he said to Fin.

'After the match.'

'It'll be dark. Do it after lunch.'

'I've got homework.'

'So do it now.'

Fin looked at him for the first time, outraged.

'You said I could watch this. You said if I left Lou watch the video—'

'Let Lou watch,' Paul said.

'What?'

'If you let Lou watch. Not left her watch.'

'Whatever. You said—'

'I know what I said.' Paul was trying not to get annoyed. 'I know what I bloody said. I don't care. Just wash the car and get your homework done and stop being such a pain.'

Fin looked at the TV. As Paul closed the door he heard Fin whisper something to himself. He stood outside for a moment and then went back in. He walked over and turned off the television. When Fin looked up at him he could see the fear in his face.

'What did you say?' Paul asked.

'Nothing.'

'When I was going out, I thought I heard you say something.'

Fin shook his head and blushed.

'No. I didn't say anything.'

Paul stood in front of him, staring at him. He could see that Fin was scared to look away, that Fin knew that anything he did could send Paul into a fury.

'OK,' Paul said, calmer. 'But just watch it, you understand me? Don't get too smart. OK?'

'OK,' Fin said.

Paul left and went into the kitchen. Ruth was sitting at the table reading the paper. The radio was on in the background and the windows were steamed up from saucepans simmering on the hob. He sat at the table and held his head in his hands.

'They're doing my head in.'

'Who?'

'The kids. I thought I was going to throw Fin out the bloody window just now. Wasn't he nice once? I'm sure I remember liking him at some stage.' He was trying to smile.

She held his hand.

'He's still nice,' she said.

'I know,' he said. 'When he's asleep I find myself warming to him.'

'He's not that bad.'

'He's not. He's not bad at all, but Christ, he knows how to wind me up. And Clare as well. When she shakes her head in pity. Does she do that with you?'

'Not really. But I get a whole load of other stuff. So what do you want to do?' she asked. 'Send them back?'

'If we could. We could keep Lou, though.'

'Give her two years, she'll be the same.'

'Oh no, don't.'

'Do you remember Clare at ten?'

He smiled. 'No. Was she all right?'

'She was lovely. And she still is.'

'I do remember,' he said. 'Our little angel.'

'Do you want coffee?' she asked.

They sat for an hour reading the papers. The house was quiet. Lou was watching telly, Clare was studying and Fin was doing homework in his room. At half-one he got Lou to set the table.

They ate in near silence. Fin wouldn't look at him, though Paul tried to make peace with him. 'Are you nearly finished your homework?'

Fin looked at Ruth before he spoke.

'I was going to do it this evening. After I do the car.'

'OK,' Paul said. 'I can give you a hand if you want.' Clare was looking at him. He stared back and she looked at her plate, half-smiling as she chewed.

'It's OK. It's not much,' Fin said.

'All right.'

'You could help me,' Clare said. 'I'm having a bit of trouble with the binomial theorem.'

Paul looked at her smiling.

'I don't know,' he said. 'I think maths were different then.'

'You must remember,' she said. 'Pascal's triangle and all that?'

'I wasn't there the day we did that,' he said, 'or maybe I've forgotten after twenty-three years.'

'Maybe you did pass maths,' Clare said. Ruth was smiling now.

'Isn't it lucky then,' Paul said, 'that you're the one doing the paper in twelve months' time and not me?'

He smiled. The kids were laughing at Clare.

'I'm sure I could explain it to you,' she said. 'I'm quite a good teacher.'

Paul was annoyed. He didn't show it and he kept any edge out of his voice but he felt it.

'I'm sure you are,' he said.

'I probably get it from you,' Clare said and he flashed a look at her. He waited for her to laugh, or smile or sneer but she did nothing. Her face was blank when she caught his eye. And then she smiled. He thought she was genuine, defusing the situation. She had enough subtlety at this stage to see that she should back down and not push it.

'I doubt that,' he said. 'Your mother's more patient than I am.'

The conversation picked up after that. He stayed out of it, happy to let it flow around him. When Ruth tried to involve him he said what he had to and then dropped out again.

'Are you all right?' she asked him when he was making tea and she was scraping the plates into the bin.

'I'm fine,' he said.

'She didn't mean anything bad.'

'I don't think she did.'

'She didn't,' she said again.

'But we both noticed,' he said.

At ten o'clock they were in bed. Ruth sat up in bed reading. He lay on his side facing away from her. He tried not to think of the morning, of the gloom of the Monday morning alarm and the silence of the house as he left for the train. He thought that for once he would like to go to bed on Sunday night less tired than he had been on Friday. The weekend took more out of him than the week at work. This seemed to him a depressing thought as he fell asleep. His mind began to race and he took up his normal dreaming viewpoint. He was standing in the window of the staffroom smoking, looking out on things that happened. Beside him Ruth heard his breathing, regular and deep. She turned off the light.

2

It was called a town centre but there was no town. It was an enormous shapeless red-brick block floating on a still lake of parking spaces. It was a Monday afternoon. The boys, the four of them, were sitting in the middle of it on a wooden bench, drinking Coke and smoking. High above them was a glass-domed roof. Up there the sky was still bright, but the light didn't reach them, bleached out by fluorescence that seemed to come from nowhere. It was noisy, different music from each shop mixing in the corridors into a disorientating mass of sound. The boys had to shout at each other to be heard.

'What are we going to do?' Tim asked. 'Because I'm going home if we're not eating.'

None of the others said anything. They sat looking around at the people passing. Girls in groups and women and foreign families wheeling trolleys. It was boring but something might happen if they watched. They wouldn't miss anything.

'Let's go to a film or something,' Alan said.

'What?' Liam asked.

'A film. Jesus, are you deaf?'

'What film?' Liam asked. 'That's what I meant, you fucking gimp.'

'Anything. I don't know. Something. Are you on for it?' Alan asked Robbie.

'Fuck it. Yeah. Let's go.' He stood up. 'Are you coming?' he asked Tim.

'I don't know. I can't go to a film and eat.'

'You're always bleeding eating, you.'

'I'm growing,' Tim said smiling.

'I don't know where,' Robbie said.

They stood and walked through the crowd towards the cinema.

'Can anyone lend me a fiver?' Tim asked.

'Not me,' Liam said. The others shook their heads.

'If I get a child's ticket I can get a meal as well.'

'You can't get a child's ticket for an eighteens' film,' Alan said. 'Are you thick?'

'Well I don't know what we're going to see. What are we going to see?'

'I don't know,' Alan said. 'We'll look.'

'If it's not eighteen—' Tim said.

'Will you shut up?' Robbie said.

They stood outside the cinema looking up at the digital listing above the cashier's. A crowd walked by them going in, their own age, five guys and three girls. Alan and Robbie standing beside each other watched one of the girls as she passed.

'Did you see that?' Alan said. Robbie laughed. The four of them looked after her as she went. One of her group, a boy, turned and saw them.

'What did you say?' he said stopping. 'You.' He pointed at Alan. 'What did you fucking say?'

'I said did you see that prick?' Robbie said walking towards him. 'So what?'

Everything else around them disappeared. No one said anything. Robbie stood face to face with the one who had spoken, the same height, bigger than the others.

'You're the prick,' he said and Robbie slapped him. He didn't wait. He didn't bother. It was going to happen. Then they were all at it.

Nine of them swinging and kicking and grabbing. The girls stood out of it, shouting and screaming. Around them a circle opened, people stopped, watching. Parents grabbed their kids and dragged them off, away, anywhere. Security guards and bouncers were in among them in twenty seconds and tried to pull them apart, trying to work out who was who. No logic to it. They all looked the same. It was arms around throats and dragging them in different directions. Alan and the others were pushed through glass doors and thrown out onto the ground outside. The security guards stood above them, waiting. Inside the others were still fighting. More bouncers were arriving.

'Fuck off,' one of the security guys said to the four of them.

'He started it,' Alan said. 'We did nothing.'

'You're all barred. If I see any of you in here again, you'll get the shit knocked out of you. I won't even ask.'

'We'll get them when they come out,' Robbie said. 'Tell them that. We'll be waiting.'

'You can wait,' the guard said. 'But I'm calling the cops now. They'll be here in two minutes. It's up to you.'

He went back through the doors and stood inside with five others looking out at them. Behind him the other group were being dragged off in the opposite direction.

'Pricks,' Robbie said. 'I had him. That one. I would have had him.'

'What are we doing?' Liam asked.

'Let's go,' Alan said. 'Fuck it.'

They walked off towards the bus stop. The adrenalin was going and Robbie's left eye was aching now, beginning to swell.

'We would have had them,' Tim said to him. 'They were fucking shite.'

'Arseholes,' Liam said.

They stood in a line waiting to get on the bus that was waiting.

'Hang on,' Robbie said, looking back at the entrance. The three others turned. A group of people were coming out.

'Not them,' Alan said. 'Come on. Let's go home.'

Paul had gone to work early. He preferred to leave the house at seven and get a seat on the train. It was a fifteen-minute walk from the station to the school. If he left later, there would be pupils in front of him, looking over their shoulders and laughing at him, running by, shouting as they passed.

That morning he was able to walk in peace, taking the longer route through the park. The smell of damp leaves and earth, the tarry pond and the broken and graffitied benches in the morning calmed him. He sat there for ten minutes. He watched people as they passed him carrying cups of coffee and brown bags. He watched two women jogging together, their breath visible in the morning air, Americans from the hotel that backed onto the park. Three young office guys stumbled in silence together in the direction of the bank centre, bleary-eyed and sullen at the prospect of another day. They were scarcely older than his pupils, only a year or two of work behind them, but he felt the same way. All he wanted was to go back to the station and get on an empty train back out to the suburbs. He stood up and went to school.

There was no point. There was no way you could change them. They were less than three months away from their exams, the exams which, no matter what their parents or gentler teachers might say, would determine where they ended up, and still it was the same.

When he walked into his classroom nothing changed. The same level of noise. The same squirming mass of awkward smelly bodies. The air already dying.

'Shut up,' he said. For a second they stopped and looked around waiting for something to happen. Then Brophy started. He covered his mouth and coughed the word wanker. Paul ignored him.

'We left it last time on page two forty-seven, factors influencing elasticity.'

'Wanker,' Brophy said again, clearer this time. The others began to snigger.

'Are you all right, Brophy?' Paul asked.

'Something in my throat, sir. I've got a bit of a cough.'

'Maybe you'd like to go outside until it clears up.'

'Me, sir?'

'Yes, you.'

One of the others spoke up.

'That's not fair, sir. You can't put him out for coughing.'

'Shut up, Farrell. I'm not interested in what you think. Brophy, get out.'

'I think it's cleared up now.'

'Just get out,' Paul shouted. The boy sat unmoving. Adrenalin rushed through Paul at the thought that he might do something. Grab him by the throat and drag him into the hall. Throw him against a wall. Brophy smiled to himself. He waited as if he knew Paul's limit and then stood up. He walked slowly to the door. As soon as it closed behind him, a spate of coughing broke out across the classroom. Paul stood up and watched them. When it died away he spoke.

'Any of you who want to join him outside can do so now. You can go and cough to your heart's content or whatever. And in six weeks' time you can fail as well. I don't care. Some of you, I'm sure, want to pass this exam. To the others I'm telling you get out now.'

He looked around the room and waited. None of them looked at him. None of them spoke.

'OK. Can we get on with it, then? Farrell, start reading from page two hundred and forty-seven, chapter nine.'

There was the sound of books opening, flicking back and forth to the right page.

'We have already discussed the impact—' Farrell began.

'On your feet,' Paul said.

'What?'

'Stand up.'

Farrell stood.

'We have already discussed the impact—'

Paul walked into the staffroom at ten o'clock. He had an hour free. The sun shone through the window from the garden beyond casting beams through cigarette smoke and dust. He put the kettle on and sat at the table beside Sweeney.

'Hi, Eoin,' Paul said.

'Where are you coming from?' Eoin asked.

'Economics with sixth year. With Brophy. Outside in two minutes.' He shook his head.

'Acting up?'

'He was out before I even began. First class. Monday morning. You'd think maybe he'd try and behave like—' He paused.

'A normal person?' Eoin suggested.

'A human being. I don't know.'

'He just doesn't think,' Eoin said. 'He's a clown. He's all bravado and the big man now, but he'll fail and repeat. It's a waste of time. He's going nowhere.'

'He won't be repeating here,' Paul said.

'Of course he won't.'

'You look at guys like him, the ones who'll never do anything, and they're the ones that the others imitate and try to impress. Why are they so susceptible to that kind of stupidity? Even the bright ones?

There are guys there who can argue with you about the Civil War and they know what they're talking about. Then ten minutes later they're making monkey noises.'

'They're kids,' Eoin said. 'They shave and they're taller than you or me, but they're still children. I was the same leaving school. I'm sure you were.'

'I don't know. Probably,' Paul said. He had never been like that. He was certain of it.

Every year it was the same. There were idiots and brains. Workers and messers. The proportions varied but the dynamic was always the same. His time and effort were spent trying to limit the impact of the messers. There was no point trying to teach them, never enough of them to matter. Even most of the idiots wanted to work. Nice middle-class boys from the nice middle-class areas were afraid of their parents. They were controlled by expectation and a fear of shame. They got what was expected of them or they repeated until they did. Their parents would happily sacrifice them for another year to get the A1 in maths that was needed to become an actuary. He heard the boys talking in the corridors and on the way to the station. They spoke of what they were going to do, where they were going, about drink and girls and nights out with a lust for the freedom that college or work promised them. But the road they would take was already paved for them and only a few would stray from it. He had spent fifteen years watching them leave and was no longer surprised by lack of imagination or innovation. Forty per cent straight to college in Dublin. Twenty per cent to a grind school to repeat. Thirty per cent straight to work and ten per cent would drift. It wasn't surprising, he thought, that the process of forgetting them started when they walked out the door. In a year he wouldn't remember Brophy's name.

As the years passed the only thing that came as a surprise was how little they knew by the time they reached him. How intelligent pupils could pass through the educational system for twelve years, through the world for eighteen years, and absorb so little en route. How suggesting background reading to them was like suggesting voluntary torture, their faces distorted in horror at the idea of gaining a deeper knowledge. How they valued rote learning over understanding. It was getting worse. At a time when information came at them twenty-four hours a day in more ways than ever before, they seemed to try and avoid its impact entirely. He thought of Clare, who at seventeen was sharper than the brightest of the current sixth year. But girls were different.

Maybe the boys weren't so bad. They could be friendly and warm and funny. They made him laugh sometimes. But their unpredictable nature, their ability to shift from civility to a pack mentality in which he was the quarry, made no sense to him. He watched their alliances form and shatter. The jockeying for power, the struggle for popularity and the fear. How some of them were players and some victims and the majority happy to be bystanders, biddable. It was an unsophisticated group dynamic and even after fifteen years he didn't know how to control it. All he knew was that it was as much a mystery to them as it was to him. They could never have told him why sometimes they rioted and sometimes they submitted.

He sat looking out across the garden. Through the trees beyond the railings he could see the road, cars gliding by slowly, all heading in the direction of town.

'Do you think it's pathetic playing mind games with eighteen-year-olds?' Paul asked Eoin. 'Taking pleasure when you win?'

Eoin looked up.

'It would be, if that's what it was,' he said after a moment, 'but it's not. You're trying to do your job and it's hard. It is for all of us.'

'I know. You're right. Yeah. Fair enough,' Paul said.

'You know what's going on. You know what it's like.'

'I should. Shouldn't I?'

'Yes, you should,' Eoin said. 'You've given whatever it is, fourteen years, to education. There's nothing pathetic about what you do. Most people couldn't do it.'

'They wouldn't want to,'

'No, they wouldn't. But you have.'

'I suppose I have,' Paul said.

'And you must remember that teaching is still a very respected profession,' Eoin said. They both laughed at that.

When he got home from work that afternoon, Ruth was sitting in the kitchen. Clare had stayed on in school to study, Fin was at rugby and Louise was at a friend's. The radio was off and the house was silent.

'What's up?' he asked as he sat beside her.

'Everything's fine. Don't worry. Are you all right?'

'I'm grand.' He looked around the kitchen for a clue. There was nothing.

'What's going on?'

'I was thinking that rather than go on holiday this year, maybe we could do something else.'

'Like what?'

'Like moving house.'

Afterwards it occurred to him that his reaction must have been comical, but she didn't laugh. She just sat there and waited. It took thirty seconds for what she had said to sink in.

'Move house?' he said eventually.

'Yeah?'

'Sell here?'

'Yeah.'

'Where would we go?' he asked.

'I don't know. Somewhere else.'

'In Dublin?'

'Yes, in Dublin,' she said. 'Of course in Dublin.'

'Don't tell me of course. I don't know what you're thinking.'

'It's simple, Paul. I'm just talking about it. It's nothing to worry about.'

He didn't even hear her.

'We can't afford to move,' he said.

'Of course we can. You can buy a lot for the value of this house.'

'Not around here.'

'No,' she said. 'I'm not suggesting we move next door. I'm saying we get somewhere bigger.'

'But I don't understand,' he said. 'Why do you want to move?'

'It's not like we haven't talked about this before, Paul.'

'I don't remember. You're not talking about before Lou was born, are you? Back then? Because that's the last time I remember us even considering it.'

'We talked about it then.'

'That was eight years ago,' he said. 'You'll have to forgive me for forgetting. We looked at it for about five minutes and then decided against.'

'I know. But I think it might be worth checking it out again.'

'And you want to buy now? When houses are more expensive than ever before?'

'And sell now. It works both ways.'

He sat back in the chair and rubbed his face.

'OK. Tell me why. Are you not happy here?'

'That's not it at all. But I was thinking about it. This place has been great for us, we've had no problems. It's a lovely area and all that. The kids are happy—'

'But? What's the but?'

For a second she looked too embarrassed to say it.

'It's too small,' she said. 'The two girls are sharing, which I don't think is fair on either of them. Clare's nearly eighteen and she's sharing a room with a seven-year-old. Lou is going to be going into the whole teenage thing in a few years. It would be too much for both of them. Fin's room is a box. They're all on top of each other and on top of us and I think that's why they fight so much.'

'Kids always fight,' Paul said.

'Yeah, but it's easier if they have their own space. Get Fin a portable TV for two hundred pounds, he'll leave Lou alone and we might be able to have a conversation.'

'But Clare will be going to college in just over a year,' he said. 'She might move out then.'

'She's not going to move out, Paul. How would she? She'll go to college in Dublin and unless you want to pay for rooms or a flat for her, she's going to have to stay here.'

'Well, it'd be cheaper than moving house.'

She smiled.

'Rental and support for a year would be up near fifteen thousand. And that money's just gone. If we sell here and take three hundred thousand . . .'

'How do you know all this?' Paul asked. 'Have you been planning this for a while?'

'Of course not. Jesus, Paul.'

'Well, I don't know. I'm just asking,' he said. 'I didn't mean anything. Sorry.'

'Of course I haven't been planning it,' she said. 'I just read the paper. You remember when the Devlins sold. You know there's a boom on. Everybody talks about it. You don't know how much your own house is worth?'

'I'm not interested. You know I find that conversation so bloody tedious. Everybody talking about how much they might get, but nobody is actually moving so what's the point?'

'The point is that it's nice to know. And loads of people are moving. That's why there's a boom. I mean did you imagine that we were going to stay here in this house for ever?'

He had to think. He struggled to remember what he had thought about before this conversation had started.

'I don't know. I think I thought we'd be here until we retired and then maybe go to the country.'

'The country?' she said. 'You couldn't live in the country. You'd go mad.'

He smiled. 'I know. But I think that's what I thought. I wasn't planning on going anywhere before Lou leaves home.'

'That could be twenty years.'

'She'll be twenty-seven in twenty years.'

'Well, you never know,' she said.

'I've really never had a problem with living here. It's just never crossed my mind.'

'I don't have a problem with it either,' she said. 'I'm just putting it out there as something to talk about.'

'Right.'

'So what do you think of the idea?'

'I don't know. I'd have to let it settle a bit.'

They sat in silence for two minutes.

'Are you happy?' he asked her then.

'What?'

'Are you happy? With me, with the kids, with your life?'

She picked up his hand.

'Of course I am, Paul. You know I am.'

'You'd tell me if there was anything?'

'Oh Christ, what have I started?' she said. 'There is nothing wrong. I would tell you if there was. I was just thinking about the money that we would spend on a holiday because it's a lot and that we might put it towards something. That's all. There's nothing more to it than that.'

'So why a house? Why now?'

'Jesus, Paul. You're like a kid. Why? Why? Why?'

'So why?'

She thought about what he was asking. She knew she had to wait. She thought for long enough to make him uneasy and then she said, 'Because we need space. For all of us. I think a bigger house would suit us now. I saw you at the weekend and it was like watching a kettle trying not to boil. You just about kept it together. We had ten minutes alone together over the whole weekend when we weren't asleep.'

'And you think a bigger house is going to solve it all?' he asked.

'I think it would help.'

'So what do you want to do?'

'I don't want to do anything. I want to talk with you about it and think about it and see whether or not we can afford it and if we can't then we won't. But if we can then we can think about it.'

'Right. OK.'

'Is that all right?'

'Yeah. It's fine,' he said. 'But if you find out that we can't afford it, you're not going to be upset or too disappointed?'

'No. No. But if we can afford it, will you be disappointed?'

'No. If we both agree then it's fine.'

'Exactly,' she said. 'It's no big deal.'

He felt more relaxed.

'Did you find that conversation scary?' she asked him, joking now.

He smiled. 'I just wasn't expecting it.'

'It was hard work,' she said.

'For us both.'

'So I'll start checking it out,' she said, standing up. 'Just looking at it.' She went out to the washing machine.

It was when she said casually that she'd look at it that Paul began to worry. Until then, he'd assumed that this was something that had just occurred to her and that she had been working it through in her head.

But when she said she'd look at it, he knew it was more than a random rogue idea that had just shown up unexpected. Because this was how she did things. She got things done. Ruth was methodical and went about things in sequence and the stage after thinking about something was looking at it. She did not go out and buy a new couch. She talked, looked, compared, talked some more and then bought. His contribution to the process was as a sounding board for her ideas, nothing more. If he was against an idea of hers, she would negotiate, suggest, bargain, and if he didn't shift and she thought he was being unreasonable she would push her agenda until he snapped and found himself shouting.

Then in the changed environment that resulted, in a house where the children whispered and meals were eaten in silence, he would feel isolated and desperate until he saw that it was stupid to pollute the whole atmosphere over something as inconsequential as a couch and he would apologize, make peace and together they would buy the couch.

All of this would be harder were it not for the fact that she was right. His arguments against her suggestions, whether motivated by money or time or practicality, came to seem as nothing given that every decision she had made had been the right one. With the house, the children, their lives. She knew how to do things and he recognized it. And while his objections might have seemed pointless, they mattered to him because he wanted to remain involved. He would rather argue for two days about whether they really needed a new washing machine and then apologize and a week later sit in the kitchen with her and tell her that she'd been right all along and he was glad that she'd thought of it. He'd rather go through this ridiculous dysfunctional routine with her because without it he played no part. She ran the house. She knew how to deal with the kids in a way that he never would. She organized the holidays, the parties, doctors and dentists. Every aspect of their lives was orchestrated by her. He went to work and provided the money.

He loved her and was good to her and fussed over her. She was happy as far as he knew. He was comfortable and satisfied with his life. He was. So when she talked about looking at moving house, he felt that the decision had already been made. That no matter what the financial implications, however much difficulty and discomfort might be involved, if she wanted more space, more space was what they would get and that, somehow, some way, he would find himself in six months' time in a new living room looking out the window at a new garden and beyond to a new area with unknown people. He found this idea without merit and, he was surprised to discover, quite terrifying. He was at the mercy of her vagaries. The inevitability of it was unsettling. He didn't know where they would end up.

He liked where they were. It was near everything. There were parks and you could see the sea and there were restaurants and bars and shops where they called you by your name. Or they would if you wanted. They smiled vaguely at Paul in the butcher's and the vegetable shop as if they were supposed to know him, which was the way he wanted it. Free-range eggs and organic beetroot and beef from a farm in Wicklow. Their own farm. In the supermarket, where the girls on the till knew Lou and talked to her, they looked at Paul like he must be great. One hundred types of cheese. The smell of bread and coffee and the deodorant of the happy kids sweeping the floor in front of him, waiting in case he needed them. There was the train into town or buses for the kids. There were cafes with girls from the area working on Saturdays, all nice vowels and talking to each other about hockey matches and how drunk they got the night before and how they were so hungover. Shiny eyes and fresh skin. They never looked tired. There was a newsagent's where the paper that Paul read sat on the counter by the till for the convenience of people like him. Where the magazines that he wanted were in a row on the shelf, one after the other. There were bookshops and hardware stores. A Garda station where they would sign the photos for your passport without even asking if you were who you said you were because you wouldn't be there if you weren't. Not someone like you. They stopped cars at checkpoints on the main road on Saturday nights looking for drunks. Protecting their own from other people passing through their area on the way to somewhere else. Somewhere different.

There were pubs for the sailing-club boys, the rugby-necked shouting young fellows with Volkswagens and blonde girls and striped shirts. People who knew where they were going, never too far from here, and nobody was going to say no to them on the way. Sitting at tables outside in the summer in big hissing groups. Laughing. Drinking pints. Sunglasses and watches and phones and Marlboro Lights for everybody. There was nowhere else that they wanted to be. Everybody they knew would pass by some time. Lofty and Dunnie and Hugh. All the boys.

And away from it. Only ten minutes. Across the main road and up along by the big houses with cypresses and Land Rovers and gravel, around the corner onto their road where the houses were smaller but not small. An avenue between two side roads. Paul knew that they were built in the 1930s and before that the land had been a part of an estate, the one they named the shopping centre after. But the road felt like it had been there for ever, the trees as big as the houses, the houses settled and grown into the street, like a living organic unit. As if it would die if you changed it. Solid, grey- and red-brick houses with bay windows. Small front gardens with driveways. A road that was for people to live on. No traffic ramps because nobody ever came down here too fast. They couldn't. It would be rude.

Neighbours who knew just enough about each other. Enough to be polite. Never prying. A respectful distance maintained always. The same conversation every time that Paul met one of them on the road.

'How are you? And how is—?'

'Ruth?'

'Ruth. Of course, Ruth. How is she? And the children?'

'They're fine.'

They were always fine. Everything was always fine. Because this was not the kind of place where things went wrong. Nice people living their lives quietly, tidily. Paul was one of them. He didn't want a community. He didn't want a neighbourhood watch or residents' committee. They weren't needed. The children went to different schools around the area or in town. They would call into each other's houses and parents would say hello and wouldn't ask them anything about their own parents or their holidays in case they were told. The houses weren't big and they were semi-detached but really they were miles apart and that was how everyone along the road wanted it. You want a community? You want neighbours who are your friends? Go somewhere else because that is not what places like this are about. That's not for people like us.

Alan and Liam were kicking a ball back and forth. Robbie was sitting on the ground, leaning against the rock with Orla and Aoife. The two girls were talking and Robbie wasn't listening. The Aoife one was a pain in the arse, always there, always getting in the way. Always talking. Never saying anything worth hearing. Without her, he would have been in by now. He knew it. But every time he tried with Orla, Aoife was there. It was getting near the time that they would leave. They had to be back in by nine like kids. Seventeen years old. His parents didn't care. They let him do what he wanted, but because of Aoife he wasn't able to. He might as well be kicking the ball with the other two. He was about to stand up when he saw Joe Mitchell. He had come out of his next-door neighbours' house and was talking to them at the end of their drive, about to go back into his own place. Robbie watched them. The younger couple listening and nodding as Joe spoke. Another one, Robbie thought. Always getting in the way. Nothing better to be doing than causing trouble. Moaning, complaining, talking shit about Robbie and his friends.

'They're moving out,' Liam said.

'Who?' Robbie asked.

'Those two,' he said, pointing at the couple.

'They didn't stay long,' Alan said.

'Fuck them,' Robbie said. 'Never liked them.'

'Why?' Aoife asked. He looked at her.

'Have you seen them?' he said.

'No. What's wrong with them?'

Robbie shook his head. She was thick. When he looked over again at the three neighbours, thinking of something to say, he could see them staring at him. Joe and the other two. They turned away and started talking amongst themselves. Even from here, Robbie could see the expressions on their faces.

'That,' he said to Aoife. 'That there. Do you see?'

'I don't know,' she said. 'I don't know what you're on about. I'm going to go.'

Orla stood up.

'Me too,' Aoife said.

Robbie laughed.

'Bedtime,' he said. 'Fair enough.'

'Well, what's the point?' Orla said. 'We never do anything.'

'What can we do?' Alan said. 'Where can we go?'

'Don't know. See you,' Orla said and the two girls walked off.

'For fuck's sake,' Robbie said quietly when they were gone. 'It's a joke.'

Joe Mitchell was walking up the drive to his door. His neighbours had gone back inside.

'You wanker,' Robbie shouted and Joe checked his step for a second and then went on.

'What's the problem?' Liam asked.

'This place,' Robbie said. 'What a fucking shithole.'

That night Paul lifted his head off the pillow and looked at the clock radio glowing green beside the bed. It was four o'clock. He had gone to bed at twelve exhausted but still he was awake. He lay on his side, his back to Ruth, and listened to the pulse in his ears. He tried to count but couldn't concentrate. His mind was racing. He was worried. He tried to think.

When it had happened it was February and he was working in a hotel, saving money to go back to college and do a master's. They'd been going out for a year. It seemed like a long time. She rang him at work and asked could he come over when he finished.

It was after two when he got there. She opened the door and went and sat on the bed without looking back at him as he followed her in.

'What's wrong?' he asked.

'I'm fine,' she said, her face to the ground.

'What's going on? Why am I here?'

She looked at him and for a second he thought it was going to be all right. She smiled and he thought, it's a joke, she just wanted to get me over. But then her face cracked and she started crying. She hid her face in her hands and he watched her shoulders shake. He knelt in front of her and put his arms around her.

'Jesus. What is it? It's OK. Whatever it is. It's OK.'

She pushed him off. He sat waiting for her to speak, trying to work out what it could be. He was waiting and then she said, 'I can't believe I'm pregnant.'

His first feeling was relief and then cold. He saw himself as a guy who has heard that his girlfriend is pregnant and is failing to find in himself any natural reaction that isn't negative. In an instant he saw that everything would change. That he would have to provide. That he would have to do the right thing.

'OK,' he said. 'It's OK. It'll be fine.'

'How will it be fine?' she said. 'I don't see how it'll be fine. What am I going to do?'

'I'll look after it. I'll work. I'll do whatever I have to. Whatever you want. I love you so much and I'm happy and that has to count for something.'

She shook her head, still crying.

'It's very nice, Paul,' she said, 'but what are we going to do? What am I going to do?'

'You can do whatever you want. I'll be here. I can get money. I can work. I can do anything and I will.'

'I have to have it. I can't not have it. I can't do that.'

'OK. That's fine. I am happy. Do you understand?' He looked at her. She rubbed her nose and looked at him.

'I am happy,' he said again. 'This is what I wanted. This is good news.'

She smiled half-heartedly.

'It's not good news.'

'Yeah, well,' he said. 'It's all-right news.'

'It's not good news.'

'Worse things happen every day.'

'Not to me,' she said half laughing.

'It'll be all right,' he said again. It was like a mantra.

They got married in July. Her family paid. They were OK about it. Only his parents and his sister came and then his friends. To him looking back, the day was dominated by the bump in Ruth's stomach that showed through in the photos. The bump was why they were there. It was why the priest's sermon was short and cold and non-specific. Why when her father spoke after dinner and welcomed him into their family, his friends all made shotgun sounds. It was why they left the party while it was still going on and why the whole day lived in his memory tainted by sadness. There would not have been a wedding that day if there had been no bump.

They rented a flat and he used his savings for a deposit and getting the place ready for a child. He started work as a teacher that September. It was a good job. It was stable and secure, which was important for someone in his position. All the things that he didn't think about himself. Responsible and solid, with a secure pensionable job at twenty-three.

His friends joked about it. Going back into that world on the wrong side. They said they could smell the staffroom off him and put out their cigarettes when he arrived in the pub. They slagged him but they cared. When he sat among them as they talked about college and the dole, daytime TV and going to London or Boston, they'd put themselves down. They had the grace to feel self-conscious in front of him. They said they were all a pack of bums and he was the only worthwhile one out of them. He had stood by the girl. He had got the job. He was a man among boys and they told him that. You did the right thing. You can still have a few drinks. What are you missing out on? You've got the best life of all of us. Really.

They said all of this and he knew they meant it. He appreciated it. But he knew that when he left them in the pub to get the last bus home, when the door closed behind him and silence fell, that they would say to each other, with the best will in the world, the poor fucker.

It changed when Clare was born. He knew then that he could do it. It made sense. More than the pregnancy or the wedding. Seeing her answered the questions he had been asking of himself. He had a wife and a child and he would not let them down. He had a bond made of love and that would be enough. He went to work and came home and ate dinner and held his child and watched TV and it was real life and when he met his friends every couple of months, he got hammered after three drinks and they seemed different.

But as the years passed they all grew up. He worked and scraped to buy a house while they did MBAs and travelled the world. He lost touch with most of them but he knew how they were doing. They were doing well.

He should have done well. He could have. He didn't let himself think it during the day, on the train into work. It didn't occur to him at the dinner table in the evening or playing with Clare. But at night, when Ruth was asleep, it came and haunted him. A different reaction eighteen years ago, a couple of words and a different tone and he would not be lying here now wondering. If he'd just walked out the door saying nothing, what would have happened? What would she have done? Could he think what his reaction had cost him? That a desire to appear principled and no more than that had been where he'd gone wrong? With a master's in economics, ten years in London and if he'd come back here when it started to heat up where would he be now? Out with Jim and Brian drinking pints on Sunday mornings. Weekends away with some other girlfriend. Travelling on a whim, driving to the airport. Getting on a plane to anywhere.

He wouldn't be lying here worried about everything. He wouldn't be trying to calculate where they'd have to go to get a bigger house. He wouldn't be afraid that if they moved things might not improve. That the space that they gained would only prove that the problems in his family ran deeper than that.

He loved Ruth. He loved his family. When he thought of each of his children in turn, his fists clenched with the ferocity of his love. He hated the demons that haunted him. But at that moment when he tried to find a solution to the things that kept him awake, he could only find one in the past.

3

Robbie and Alan waited for the bus away from the Saturday afternoon crowd, sitting on the wall of a house, hoods up in the sun and smoking. When the bus came they waited until the queue had gone and the last person was standing in the door before walking over.

'Come on,' the driver said. 'Get fucking moving.'

Robbie dropped his fare in the slot. The guy waited before he gave him his ticket. Long enough to let him know that he was counting because he knew what they were like. Fuck him.

'I thought you were in a hurry,' Alan said.

'Yeah, but I'm not stupid,' the driver replied.

Upstairs. Down the back was still empty. Alan and Robbie spread out. Territory. The best place to be. Watch what was happening. See who came on. They watched old ones and young mothers and kids come to the top of the stairs. When they saw Alan and Robbie down the back they would turn away quickly. Looking at them like they were going to do something. Nervous. Robbie watched them sit and stared at them as they came. He wouldn't do anything. He didn't want to. But you had to give them something. With Alan he laughed at them, talking quickly between themselves, half-sentences and whispers and their own slang, which communicated nothing to anyone around them but it let them know. They knew the contempt that these people had for them and refused to accept it. Turned it back on this shower of fucking cunts on a bus. There was only so much that they could take.

Town on a Saturday was busy. They got off on the quays and walked through the side streets into the crowd on Henry Street. They went into sports shops and music shops and then into the department store to look at jeans. Check out the new stuff. At the entrance security goons in cheap jackets and stupid shoes talked into walkie-talkies and chewed gum. They were all fat, all thick, and Robbie hated them. They saw him when he walked in and he didn't look away. He wouldn't look at the ground and pretend to be somebody else. There were hundreds like him every second, dressed the same, walking in and out, and yet they always saw him. He'd never stolen from any of these places. Alan went off down the far end and Robbie found something he wanted. He took a pair of jeans to the fitting room and when he came out there was a guy waiting to go in. He had nothing in his hands. He stared at Robbie as he walked by. Plain clothes. Robbie laughed. Alan was somewhere else. He went to the till and stood in the queue. When he got to the counter and the girl took the jeans from him, he rang Alan.

'Are you right?' he said when Alan answered.

'Where are you?'

'I'm paying.'

'There's no tag on these,' the girl said.

'Where?' Alan asked him.

'Hang on,' Robbie said. 'What?'

'Where are you?' Alan said again.

'Shut up. No. What do you want?'

'There's no tag on these. I can't scan them.'

'They're ninety.'

'I need to scan them. You'll have to get me another pair.' Robbie ended the call. Behind him there was a line of people, watching him.

'You do it,' he said. 'I don't work here.'

'You see this queue?' she said.

'Not my problem.' He stood staring at her. She tried to smile and shook her head. Like she didn't care. Like she should have expected it. She picked up the phone and asked somebody to come over to her. Robbie was waiting. He knew not to lose it. He was right and she was wrong, and even though he wanted to punch her he had to just keep his mouth shut. Another girl arrived.

'What's the problem?'

'Can you get me another pair of these? I need a price.'

The second girl looked at Robbie and then at her colleague and they smiled at each other. She went off.

'Can you serve me?' Some old fellow standing behind him spoke up.

'Of course.'

'Here,' Robbie said. 'There's a queue.'

'I'm in a hurry,' the old guy said. He was a prick. Robbie could hear it.

'I don't give a bollocks. So am I. Talk to her about it.'

'You've no manners.'

Robbie said nothing. The girl stood frozen, waiting.

'Will you serve me, please?' the man said again and then the second girl arrived back.

'I'll get rid of him first,' the girl said. She took the label and scanned the jeans in. She turned to Robbie without looking at him. 'Ninety.'

He handed her two fifties. One after the other she held them up to the light deliberately.

'Are you joking?' Robbie asked.

'There's been a lot of forgeries,' she said. 'Do you want to see a manager?'

Robbie shook his head and tried to look like he found it funny. She put the receipt and the change on the counter in front of him.

'I'm very sorry for delaying you,' she said to the next guy.

Alan came up as Robbie was walking away.

'What did you get?'

'Jeans.'

'Let's see.'

'No, come on, let's go. I'll show you outside.'

As they walked towards the exit, Robbie saw the plain-clothes guy standing inside the door talking to one of the uniformed ones. They stopped and watched as Alan and he passed. Robbie went over.

'Do you want to see?' he said to them, holding the bag open in front of him. 'Do you want to search me?'

The two looked at him. Neither looked into the bag.

'No,' the plain-clothes guy said and the two of them started talking again. It should have felt good, Robbie thought, but instead he just felt stupid.

'What was that about?' Alan asked him. Robbie didn't say anything. Outside he turned towards O'Connell Street. Alan followed, trying to keep up. He knew from the way Robbie was walking that he shouldn't ask again.

Paul was standing in the kitchen of a house on the western edge of the city. He was at the window looking out across the lawn. At the back of the garden, beyond a wide lawn edged by flower beds, was a shed, rough overlapping stained planks and a tar-cloth roof with a small framed window. He had never thought that he would own a shed. He didn't care about gardening. Garden centres, pruning, weeding, raking, hoeing. Things they didn't do. When is it going to get us? they joked. When is it going to click and all make sense? When will middle age drive us to the earth on our knees, scrabbling and digging?

Ruth was somewhere upstairs. He had already been through the house. It was a Saturday afternoon and around him as he stood looking out on the garden people were passing through, tapping on walls, looking at the ceilings, stamping on floors and making notes. They were all couples, well dressed with nice hair and good skin. Expensive people. Younger people. When they passed each other in the doorways and halls of the house, they would look at the ground and smile and mumble sorry. Everybody smiling and apologizing. They talked between themselves in twos and threes, whispering, only speaking up to ask the estate agent about planning permission and rates and electrical certification. Intelligent questions. They had a shared interest. They must have similar tastes and desires and yet there was no crossover conversation. No banter about the carpets. No slagging the pictures on the walls. Paul could feel the competitive edge in the air. They were all just looking. It didn't mean anything now, but in two weeks some of them would be in a room together and they would square up to one another and then it would all be about money. In the end somebody was going to get it. Somebody was going to win.

Paul was hoping it wouldn't be him. They could afford the house and there was nothing wrong with it. It was in a cul-de-sac and there was a green space in front of it, a safe area for the children to play. It was big and full of light and open space and carpets. A blank space which told him nothing about the people who had lived there. Not the kind of place he'd ever imagined living. As he was standing, still looking out over the garden, he hoped that there would be something about it, some unquantifiable atmospheric problem that would put Ruth off. Something that he hadn't seen or felt that would dissuade her.

He couldn't tell her that it was too far from where he wanted to live. He couldn't say now that it was the wrong area and that he liked where they lived already, that the compromise in size was one he was prepared to make in order to stay. When Ruth had started making appointments with estate agents, he had been hoping that they would find nothing. Surely the explosion in the property market that everybody talked about all the bloody time would mean that they would have missed the boat and would have to stay where they were for a couple more years.

But when he had come home from work three weeks ago, she had been waiting in the living room to tell him that the estate agents had estimated the value of their house at some ridiculous sum. For a moment he had felt her joy, had felt a rush of excitement that they could go out and get anything. But as they spoke about what they would do next the doubts began to creep in. Because if this house was worth that much, then the kind of places that would suit them would be twice as much. He knew that they would have to move and that everything she said made sense, but he knew too that to get what they wanted they would have to move away. Out to the edges, where space and money were cheaper. He knew that when a compromise was made, it would be his.

'What do you think?' she asked as she came and stood beside him.

'Fine,' he said and then he said it again, more upbeat. 'Fine.'

'It's big. Big rooms.'

'Big price,' he said.

'I don't know. It's not so bad,' she said, looking away. He could see that his lack of enthusiasm was annoying her.

'There's a garden,' he said. 'And a shed.'

She nodded.

'For your dotage,' she said. 'Grandad's in the shed. Sharpening the shears.'

'Looking out the window. Cleaning the trimmer. Or the strimmer. Which is it?' he asked.

She smiled at him.

'Will we go?' she said.

'If you're finished.'

The estate agent took their number and they walked back to the car parked in between the driveways on the other side of the green.

'It's a nice estate,' she said as they drove away.

'It's a nice house,' he said.

'But?'

'No but.'

'There's a but, Paul. What?'

He knew what it was, but he waited and worked out how to say it.

'There's nothing wrong with the house itself. It's just miles out.'

'But that's what we're going to have to do. This is where we have to go. The whole point of moving is to get somewhere bigger and we're not going to get a nice five-bedroom on the sea for the money we have. I wish we could, Paul, but we can't.'

'You're right. I do know.'

'And it's not that bad. The kids could get one bus from here to school, you can drive to work. It's not perfect but it's better.'

'We can't afford perfect,' he said. His tone was too sharp.

'We can't,' she said, looking at him. 'But it doesn't matter,' she went on, trying to bring him back. 'Who can? Just imagine what the kids would say if they saw that place. They'd each have a room. They'd only see each other at meals. You could have a study. We could have our own bathroom. Think how much more we would be getting. And loads of people have had to do it.'

'Nobody I know,' he said.

She looked at him to see if he was joking. He smiled just in case.

'You sound like such a snob,' she said.

'It's not snobbery. It's just a fact.'

'Yeah, well, you're going to have to face it. We're going to have to go where we can afford and there's no point complaining about it. We're better off than most.'

'I know that. I know all that. But we don't have to move,' he said.

She turned and watched her reflection in the window. They stopped at lights.

'That was a joke,' he said. 'Ruth?' He reached up and touched the side of her face. 'Joke?' She turned and looked at him.

'I'm not doing this alone, Paul. I can't and I won't. I asked you and you said you were with me.'

'I am with you,' he said. 'I am, of course. I was joking. I'm sorry.' He stared at her, meaning it as he spoke the words and hoping that would be enough to convince her. She turned away again. A car beeped. Paul looked up and saw the green light. He waved to the driver in the car behind as he moved off.

It was a world he didn't want to be in. Surveyors and solicitors and bridging loans. An altered world where square footage and aspects and parking spaces were what mattered. Surface areas. It was all about facts and numbers and percentages. Newspaper supplements and agency brochures with dead language that tried to sound like it was all about passion and taste and lifestyle. Like it was about life and living, you and the person that you want to be. It was all about money. What costs more, price per square foot, how much will they take, how much will you give, how much do you have? The prices rising in tens and twenties and fifties and hundreds. The thousands weren't worth mentioning. A year's salary disappearing in the heat of a two-minute conversation. Everybody chasing the undiscovered gem. But there were no bargains. Nothing escaped. Nothing got through unnoticed or unseen.

It did not play to his strengths. Too many specifics and too much blind faith put in people he didn't know who seemed to know nothing for certain. An unsettling mix of vagueness and specificity, friendliness and formality, competence and blundering inefficiency, and all the time feeling that everything and everybody was conspiring to push him into doing what by now was the only acceptable thing to be done. He knew that the estate agents and bank managers could read him and Ruth as soon as they sat down. His silent nods of consent to everything Ruth told them made him a special target for their enthusiasm, like he was being wooed. It made him nervous. He couldn't say anything. He wanted to say something, but how could he when she was right?

Every justification and explanation that she gave him for moving was selflessly motivated. He knew that she had no interest in increased status. She wasn't doing it out of boredom or contrariness or to punish him for not having been able to provide a more adequate home. The family was their enterprise and between them they had to do their utmost to keep that enterprise working. She was right about the size of their existing home. She was looking in the right parts of town. She had gone through a friend to get the surveying done cheaply. It was all being done correctly and conscientiously but why then did he feel so disconnected from the process?

Because it was a change. Because he couldn't find his way around the area that would become their home with a map. He was worried about the impact on the children of taking them away from their home and their friends to a new place where they might not fit in. What would happen then? What would she say if they moved, sold their home and, six months after they got there, the children weren't happy? What if the issue hadn't been one of space at all but something darker and deeper that none of them could see now, but which would emerge when it was too late? What would that do to them? Would he blame her? Would she say that his lack of enthusiasm had doomed the whole project from the beginning? Would the children blame them both and drift away? Why was he so bloody worried?

He kept on asking himself this. Why was Ruth having to ask him every day if he was all right? Why he was so quiet? Had he got so boring that he couldn't deal with a change in their circumstances? Was he going to be static and unchanging, dragged along by Ruth? Could he not take a chance? Was this what middle age felt like? The conviction that he had felt eighteen years before when Ruth told him she was pregnant that things would be fine, that somehow he would strive and fight and struggle and beg to make sure that they would survive. Had that feeling gone?

It couldn't have. To even think of it made his heart pound. It was still there. All he had to do was to support her. The only thing that could make her wrong, that could mess up her assessment of the situation, was if he were to doubt her. Things could only fall apart if he was less than fully committed.

He didn't tell her about this revelation when it came to him.

'We should tell the kids,' he said when he got in from work one day. 'Give them something to look forward to for the summer.'

'Shouldn't we wait until it's definite? Until we get somewhere?'

'We'll get somewhere. We just will. We have the money. It's all there. We can get somewhere by the end of the week if we want it enough.'

She tried not to laugh. She had been waiting for this moment to come. This was him. This was what he was like. Resistant to change, cautious. But she knew what to do. He dealt with his doubts on his own. He didn't talk much when he was worried, but he would sort things out for himself. He always did. She didn't understand the process. She had asked him about it before and he hadn't understood. Hadn't been able to explain to her what it was that he was doing. There was no point in pushing him, she knew. He had always come through before, emerging before long smiling, convinced, solid, right. She never doubted his commitment or his love. It was a quirk. It brought her closer to him to feel that she understood that much.

'You're not worried any more?' she said to him.

'I was being stupid. It doesn't matter where we go or what we do. If we're together it will always be OK.'

She was half-smiling. 'That's nice. Very nice.'

'It's true. I'm serious. We have to move. We'll just do it. We'll get the right place and that's it. And it may be this place we looked at.'

'It may be. Depending on price.'

Paul shrugged. 'I don't know. If it's the right place, we'd be mad to let it go by.'

She laughed out loud.

'What?' he asked.

'Such a change in you.'

'Well, isn't this better?'

'Yes. Of course it is. And I'm glad you're enthusiastic but I don't understand what's prompted it.'

He wasn't looking at her when he spoke. 'I think that if we're working together, we can't go wrong. We will go to this auction and if you want it we will get it.'

'But what do you want? You can't just put it all on me. We're talking about our home. Our children. Do you think it's the right place?'

'I do. I honestly do. It's the right size. It's got a great garden. It's as good as we'll get. It's all good.'

'And you're not doing this to make me happy? You're not being all noble and selfless?'

'You know me better than that.'

She was sitting looking up at him.

'I'm serious,' he said. 'I go to the auction on Thursday and we'll get it.'

'You're sure.'

'I'm sure.'

'It may go too high for us.'

'It may but if it does we'll get somewhere else and it'll be fine. It'll all be fine.'

'OK,' she said, standing up and hugging him. 'But I don't know what goes on in your head.'

'I'm just repeating what you were saying last week. That's all. I've just caught up.' He could feel a lightness about her. He felt it. He felt his own belief and knew that they were doing the right thing.

It wasn't so clear two days later when he was standing at the back of the auction room waiting for the process to start, trying to breathe. Nothing was clear to him then. All he could do was repeat to himself the number, their number, which was as high as they had said they would go. It was the absolute. They had agreed on it. It played through his mind over and over. He thought of Ruth waiting at home with Lou, unaware of how her life could turn upside down on the basis of a roomful of people shouting numbers at each other. He was already moving away and he couldn't remember why. Yesterday he had thought he knew what it was about. He remembered understanding but the memory that he had understood was different from the actual knowledge. Where was his kitchen? Where was his house and where was this new house and where was Ruth, who could have dealt with this a lot better than he could? Big man with the big dramatic gesture. What had he been thinking? I'll take care of it. I'll look after it. I'll look after you because that's the kind of guy I am. Saying is the same as doing. I'm as good as my word. My word, my arse. What the hell? All he could feel was fear and all he could think was a number, three digits, the thousands dropped off because that was how it was done.

This was what he got for talking too much. None of it made sense. If he left now, just walked out the door onto the square, he could get into a taxi and go to the airport and fly anywhere and be halfway to a new life by the time Ruth knew anything. He felt it and called himself back. Stupid, treacherous him. His poor abandoned family. His life was not something that he wanted to escape from. He was here because this was what he had to do and he was strong enough to do it. His worry, the panic and the disconnection, were a part of the reason that they had to move. Ruth had seen in him what their life was doing to them and she had taken the steps to remedy it. To save him. She had the clarity and the strength to deal with it and he owed it to her to match her expectation. He had to be there. He would do it. He would get it.

He stood at the back. The room was full. There were guys around him whispering into mobiles. When it started Paul had no sense of being involved in something momentous. It was all raised fingers and nods. No one wanted to be seen trying or caring. The casual familiarity of the process seemed funny to him. When the time came for him to join, he lifted his hand and became a part of it. Then there were only three of them in it, then two. Paul felt a thrill when he saw this. Unexpected. He watched the other bidder from the side and could tell nothing. All about detail. Get it right.

'Too much,' he said when he rang her.

'Oh.'

'I did what I could,' he said.

'Yeah. OK.' He could hear her disappointment. He didn't want to drag it out.

'I thought we'd get it,' she said.

'Me too,' he said.

'Well, we keep looking, yeah?'

'Why?'

'Because we have to get somewhere, Paul. Jesus, I thought we'd agreed—' She was getting pissed off. He had to stop.

'OK, sorry. I got it.'

'What? You got what?'

'The house. I bought it.'

She screamed and then screamed again and then laughed.

'That's not funny.'

'Yeah. I thought it would be but it wasn't.'

'How much?'

'Oh, bollocks to that. I don't care. Do you?'

'Yes. Of course. Can we pay for it?'

'Probably. We can send Clare out to work or something.'

'The three of them. What have they ever contributed?' She sighed loudly and then said, 'Do we have it?'

'Yes,' he said. 'We have it.'

'What about our price?' she said again.

'I don't know. It just seemed stupid to let it go because of a couple of thousand. I knew you wanted it. I just knew that and I wanted it and it was the right place.'

'It was the right place. It is. I knew it the first time I saw it. When I walked in I wanted it but I didn't want to say anything because I wasn't sure if you'd like it but you do, don't you?'

'I love it. I love it.'

'How high would you have you gone?' she asked.

'You can't ask me that,' he said. 'There are still people around me. Somebody might hear.'

'How much? How much? Go on.'

'I don't know. We'll never know. You'll never know.'

'You're no fun. I can't believe it. What are you doing now?'

'I'm coming home.'

'Get a taxi,' she said. 'I want you here now.'

'It'll be the last taxi we'll be getting for a while,' he said.

The following morning, when Clare was about to go, Paul was still there.

'I'll bring you in,' he said.

'Why?'

'I don't have anything on until ten. I can go your way.'

'You never drive,' she said. 'What's going on? Mum? What's going on with the two of you? You're all smiley and laughing. It's not like you.'

'It is like us, Clare,' Ruth said. 'Take the lift your father is so kind as to offer you and stop your yapping.'

'What's going on?' Fin asked.

'Nothing.'

'Why are you being weird?'

'Come on,' Paul said. His eye caught Ruth's as he walked out. 'See you this evening,' he said.

'See you,' she said.

'I thought you said you didn't have to be in until ten,' Clare said as she followed him out.

'Oh shut up.'

It was stupid to think that they could have kept it from them.

'So what's the story?' Clare asked as he was reversing out of the drive.

'Will you hang on and let me do this?'

'I knew there was something. I knew it. The two of you couldn't contain yourselves. What is it?'

'It's nothing. Or it is something but it's nothing to worry about.'

'I'm not worried. Is Mum pregnant again?'

'What? No. No, she's not bloody pregnant. Jesus.'

'Well, I don't know. So what is it. Are you getting divorced?' She was joking.

'Not to my knowledge,' he said.

'So?'

'Will you just relax? I'm going to tell you now.'

'What is it?'

'Shut up. Just wait.'

She sat waiting, her eyes staring at the side of his face as he drove. The road ahead was clear. He had wanted to be looking at her when he told her.

'You know the way you're always fighting with the others?'

'I am not always fighting with them. And anyway you try sharing a room with Lou. She snores. She's bloody seven and she snores.'

'OK. We were talking about it and we saw this and we thought with her getting older and Fin getting more—' He'd lost himself for a second.

'Annoying?'

'Yeah. Or no. I don't know – bigger. Whatever. Anyway. It just felt like the house was getting too small for all of us and it's not been fair on you and next year you're going to have to be studying more so we thought we could think about moving.'

'House? Moving house?'

'Yeah. So we started looking at places that would be bigger for you and where you could have your own room.'

'You've bought somewhere?'

'Will you let me tell you—'

'Well, have you or haven't you?'

He nodded.

'It's not how I wanted to tell you but yes. Yes, we have bought somewhere.'

'Oh,' she said.

He waited. She didn't say anything. He let her think. After two minutes he said, 'So?'

'So why didn't you tell us before?'

'I don't know, we were just thinking about it and then it just – one came up that we liked and I went to the auction and that was it.'

'What do you mean? You bought a house by accident?'

She wasn't happy.

'No. Come on. Don't be difficult.'

'I'm not being difficult.' She spat the word out. 'I would have liked to have been asked. It's my house as well.'

'I know it is. I know it is, but it happened very quickly and it's a great house, the new one. You will love it. You can have friends over to stay. Whatever you want.'

'Where is it?'

He told her.

'I don't even know where that is. Is it in Dublin?'

'Yes, it's in Dublin.'

'I've never heard of it.'

'It's out west. There's a bus that goes from there to near your school. It's not that far.' She was looking out the window. Ruth did the same when she was annoyed with him.

'It's a nice area, Clare. You will like it.'

'How do you know?'

'Because there are loads of people out there your age. More than where we are now. You'll make friends.'

'I have friends. I don't need new friends from some place I don't know.'

'I know it's hard for you, but just wait and see the house, will you? Just give it a chance. It's so much bigger. You'll have your own space. The others won't be annoying you.'

'So what? If I see it and I don't like it and I want to stay where we are, will we stay?'

Paul breathed in to speak and then realized that he had no answer. No answer that he could tell her.

'Oh, come on, Clare. It will be fine. You'll get used to it in a couple of weeks. It will be so much better for you. You won't have to share a room—'

'I don't care. I don't want to move.'

'OK. Don't . . . I know you're upset, but you don't have to . . . I'm sorry, we should have told you but it wasn't like a big secret or anything.'

'You knew and you didn't tell me. What was it if it wasn't a secret?'

'I don't know,' he said.

They travelled the rest of the way in silence. He told himself that he was giving her space to get used to the idea, but afterwards, when she had gone, he realized that he just didn't know what to do. It hadn't occurred to either of them that they should tell her beforehand. She was just one of the kids. But when she was sitting beside him as the traffic crawled along and she stared blindly out the misted window beside him, sniffing every ten seconds, she was one of them and he knew they'd got it wrong. As they turned into the road where her school was, he said it.

'We should have told you, Clare. I'm sorry.'

She shook her head.

'You are old enough to understand,' he said, his voice as gentle as he could make it, 'that the reason that we wanted to move was to make your life easier and happier. More than for the others. More than for ourselves. It was for you.'

57

He pulled up outside her school and waited for her to respond. She didn't look at him as she unclipped the seat belt.

'That's such bollocks I don't think even you could believe it.'

She got out and slammed the door and walked up the driveway of the school, blending in among the other uniformed girls, so that when Paul looked up he couldn't see her. His hands were shaking as he put the car into gear and drove to work.

On the Saturday afternoon they were all in the car driving along the motorway. Ruth was trying to talk to the children and then gave up when the conversation drained away. They weren't here to talk. The worry on their faces as they confronted their new life made Paul feel sick. He could do nothing about it. They were heading towards it now and the sooner they got there the sooner he would know. He looked in the mirror and saw the three of them sitting in a line as though they were waiting for a dentist. They were in pain already. When they had told the two younger ones the previous day, they told them that it would be better. That they would be happier. But how could they know? They spent their lives telling the children that they had to do unpleasant painful things on the basis that it would be good for them. How were the children supposed to tell the difference?

They pulled up outside the house. The estate agent was waiting with the front door open.

'Thanks for meeting us,' Paul said as he shook her hand. 'We wanted to show them. Let them get used to the idea of moving here.' Ruth stood behind him with the two younger ones beside her. Clare was halfway down the drive facing out towards the green in the middle of the estate. They all looked depressed. The estate agent smiled.

'You'll love it here. There's loads of kids around and this house has a great garden to play in.' She was about twenty-five. Lou stood closer to Ruth. Fin sighed.

'I'll let you go on ahead. Would you like to see the brochure?' she said, bending to Lou. Lou shook her head and Ruth smiled and shrugged embarrassedly as they walked by her into the hall.

'Clare,' Paul said. 'Come in and have a look.' He waited on the doorstep as she walked slowly towards him.

'You might not hate it,' he said.

'It doesn't make any difference.'

'Oh, for Christ's sake, Clare. Worse things will happen to you in your life than moving house.' He felt the agent's gaze as he spoke. She was standing on the drive talking into a mobile. When he looked over she dropped her eyes to the ground. For the first time that day he thought he saw a smile on Clare's face.

He stood in the hall and waited. He tried to judge from the sound of the voices in the rooms above him how things were going. As the noise got louder, he could hear them running from one room to the next. He heard Fin calling him.

'What?' he shouted up.

Fin came onto the landing and spoke down the stairs.

'Who gets the big bedroom at the back? Can I have that one?'

'Ask Clare. She can choose first.'

'Oh.'

He couldn't wait any longer. He went up to them. They were all standing in the back bedroom, looking out over the garden.

'Well?' he asked no one in particular. 'Do you like it?'

'Yeah,' Fin said. 'It's great.'

Lou nodded.

'Do you like your room?' he asked her.

'Yep.'

'Clare? What do you think?'

'It's fine,' she said. She was trying not to smile.

'Look at you. You like it.'

'No, I don't.'

'It's not as bad as you thought it would be.'

'It's all right. It's just a pity it's on the moon.'

Paul laughed. 'It's not that far.'

'It's far enough.'

When they got outside, Ruth and the children went around the back to look at the garden. The agent locked the house after them and left. Paul got into his car and waited. As he sat there, he saw in the grey light of the April afternoon that there were three young guys standing around a huge granite block fifty yards away. They were staring at him. Paul waved at them. One of them raised a hand and then gave him the finger.

'Lovely,' Paul said to himself.

'Who's this prick?' Alan said to the others, his expression deadpan as he held eye contact with the fellow in the car.

'Is he the new guy?' Tim asked.

'Looks like it,' Robbie said.

'I'd say he's a gimp,' Tim said.

'Oh here. Look at this,' Alan said.

Ruth and the three children walked down the drive of the house and out to the car. The three boys watched them as they got in.

'Look at that,' Robbie said as Clare came around to the side of the car nearest them to get in the back door. The three of them watched her without speaking. She didn't look over and gave no sign that she'd even seen them, but if the light had been better the boys might have noticed that she was blushing. Paul started the car and drove around the green and out of the estate.

'Is she going to be living here?' Tim asked. 'Because if she is, I saw her first.'

'I saw her first,' Robbie said, not thinking, then annoyed as he realized what he'd said. 'Not that it makes any difference. Very nice. That's fucking all right.'

'She was lovely,' Alan agreed.

'Top-class bird,' Tim said. 'I hope she's stays.'

'Well, they looked like her parents, didn't they?' Alan said. 'What do you reckon, Robbie?'

'Don't know.' Robbie stood there thinking. The others waited. 'Who cares?' he said eventually.

'She was nice, though,' Tim said.

'She was all right,' Robbie said. 'So what?'

4

To be left alone. It could be the end of him. He couldn't think about it. Joe tried and when he tried, when he did things the way they were supposed to be done, there was no problem. He made the list and he knew it worked for him. When to get up. What to have for breakfast. Where to go and what to do. Start the day on time and keep it going. It was about timing and following the routine because without the routine he could fall into the gaps and he mightn't get out. Why would he bother? What was the point?

He persecuted himself. He knew it. Nobody to blame but him. It shouldn't matter, but when you're alone you need to be on the same side. You can't be falling out with yourself. There are the gaps. Don't look down. It wasn't like this always. He shouldn't think. He shouldn't but there was good there. Look but be quick.

He saw her first in a play. She was an angel in a play at the college drama society. A chorus of two and she was one of them. With wings on her back and a tutu. Beauty that he couldn't believe. He could never make people understand afterwards. Beauty devalued by everyone trying to find it where it wasn't. If they could have seen her then, they would have known what it was. But there were only forty people there that night. For him there was nothing else. He waited between scenes until she came out again, not listening, not seeing anything else. And there she was, looking straight at him. He was sure he was wrong. He couldn't believe. But when he smiled she smiled back, he knew she was there for him. His own angel. He wasn't good at this. He knew that the play would end and that he would have to do something. He tried to think but found nothing in himself. He had no answer. He would have to wait and see. It was the first night. There were drinks afterwards. He couldn't drink. They were all there, the director and all the crew and then the others. People who hadn't been at the play turned up for the party after. He stood at the back against the wall and then she came out. She was wearing jeans and he could feel his heart sink into his stomach and lie there aching. He could not let her go. He had to try and he didn't know how. He walked across the room to the table where she was pouring herself a drink. She looked up as he stood beside her and he had to speak.

'Hello,' he said. 'You were amazing.' She looked at him in the same way as she had from the stage.

'Thank you,' she said. 'It's not the hardest role, standing around in a tutu trying to be beautiful.'

'You were so beautiful I couldn't breathe.' He worried as he heard himself say it, but she smiled.

'I'm Maria,' she said.

'Joe,' he said. 'I'm Joe.' He held her hand and didn't want to let it go. She didn't seem to mind. How long could he look at her? How long would she look back?

'Will we go somewhere else?' she said and Joe laughed.

'I'm never going anywhere without you,' he said and she smiled.

He was a lecturer and she was a post-grad student in another department. If there had been a conflict, if anybody had said anything, he would have left. When he was away from her at night he would worry and wonder what he had done to deserve her and he could never understand it. He had never been good with women. Nervous and awkward. Conversation didn't come to him and that was what mattered with women. He would sit with his colleagues in a pub and keep an eye on the door and hope that nobody would ask his opinion.

He wasn't stupid. His work was respected and his students were involved and interested in his lectures. He loved his subject with its mix of rules and facts and emotion. To be able to communicate with the world of a thousand years ago. To smell and taste and feel their lives. How could anyone not love it? That enthusiasm lit him up and made him feel alive in a way that evaporated when he stepped off the podium. It left him sitting in a pub answering any question he was asked, before looking away and hoping that nobody had noticed.

But with her. She didn't care. She wasn't unsettled by his awkwardness. He did what he could. He tried with his second-hand, learnt version of romance and it didn't matter. She told him not to worry. He didn't understand the rules that applied and it meant that he could only be honest. She saw that in him. He didn't know himself. He didn't know what he should try to be. So when he told her that first night that he had never seen anyone like her, that he didn't know what he would do if he lost her, she believed him. And when they met the second time and then the third, she began to know him and understand that he was kind and generous and intelligent and not capable of cruelty. Too gentle for the world, but that was something to be cherished and protected and she could do that. She learnt these things and realized that everything he said was true. He would do anything for her. He loved her when he saw her. The love of his life. She was it and for her this was enough. She would have loved him anyway.

They lived in their own world. His family were distant and he wanted nothing from them. Her family were in Spain and when they decided to marry they went to tell them. Joe was lost. Her parents tried to like him. Tried to understand what it was that their daughter saw in him. They tried to encourage him but when he couldn't respond they assumed it was a language thing, so he sat silent among them. They went back to Dublin. She graduated and began working in another university as a tutor. They bought a house and settled into their own life.

It was that he felt he didn't deserve her. He couldn't make himself believe that he should know such happiness and so his happiness was compromised. Whatever she said it was there. She knelt in front of him as he sat at his desk looking out across the fields in silence. What can I do? she asked and he took her hand and told her: There is nothing. It's nothing to do with you. It's just me.

Happiness. It looked at him and asked him to believe and he tried. He had the only thing that he had ever wanted. What would it have been like without her? What would have happened to him if he had not been able to look at her every day and touch her and smell her and listen to her laughing at him? Would he have laughed himself? Would he have known what it was to hold someone and feel the touch of her skin on his? He couldn't believe it was true. And then she was gone. Taken away from him and he knew it was his fault because he hadn't had enough faith. Because he didn't believe. That was why it ended. He was right all along. He wasn't surprised. The roads are full of cars. Blocking the gateways, sitting together in lines at the gates of the college, not moving. People complained about it all the time. Traffic. For hours and hours. Going nowhere. Too slow. But they were moving fast enough to kill her when he didn't believe.

He was on his own for days on end and when he slept, when they stuck the needle into him, she told him it wasn't his fault but he knew. And when the fog cleared and she was gone, there were pills that could get him out of bed. When he felt his body coming back into itself, he knew what he would do until the end. This life on his own rattling around the house trying to get through the day came easily to him. Take the medicine, follow the plan and keep his head down. Nobody would see. Leave him to live with his pain and memory. Until they noticed him.

Clare went to school on the Monday morning. She met Caroline and Emma at the bus stop. They talked about how they had all met up in town on Saturday afternoon. Clare had meant to be there. She had sent them both a text to say she couldn't make it.

'What were you doing? Caroline asked her.

Clare shrugged.

'Nothing. I don't know.'

The two of them were looking at her now.

'No. My stupid parents. They told me last week that they were thinking about moving . . .'

'How come you didn't say anything?'

'I know – I wasn't sure. So anyway on Saturday they took us out to see this house.'

'What house?'

'The one they've bought.'

'What?'

'What?'

They were too loud. Clare saw people turning to look at them.

'I'm moving,' she said quietly. 'We're moving.'

'Oh my God,' Emma said. 'When?'

'Where?'

'I don't know when.'

'Where?' Caroline asked again.

Clare sighed. 'I don't know. Out west somewhere. Way out.'

'In the country?'

'Not the country. It's OK.'

Emma looked like she was about to cry. 'I can't believe you're leaving.'

'You're going to live in the country.'

'It's not the country.'

'So are you leaving our school?'

'No. We'll still see each other. It's going to be the same. It'll be OK.'

'But we're not going to be able to get the bus together any more. My God,' Emma said. She sniffed.

'This is terrible. I can't believe they're doing this to you. It's not fair. You poor thing.'

Clare began to think that it was true. She shouldn't be sitting on this bus having this conversation, people staring at her. She shouldn't be in a position where she had to console her friends because she was moving house. It wasn't her fault. She wished her father could be here to see what he had put her through. Then she began to feel ridiculous.

'I'm going to miss you,' Emma said.

'Really, it's OK,' Clare said. 'It's not that big a deal. I'm just moving house. There's no reason why I won't see you both all the time. You can come out and stay for weekends during the summer. It's a much bigger place. I'll have my own room.'

'We will,' Caroline said.

'Definitely,' Emma said. 'But I'm still going to miss you. Doing this. Getting the bus together.'

Clare rested her head against the steamed-up window. Drips of water rolled down to the rubber seal and gathered before spilling over and forming drops that fell on her leg. Caroline draped an arm over her, her head resting on Clare's shoulder. Emma sat sideways on the seat in front. The upstairs of the bus had returned to silence after the drama which had revolved around her. They were nice, Clare thought, and she meant it when she said that they would stay friends. But she wasn't going to miss this.

*

The following Friday Mark and Amelia came over for dinner. Mark had been at school with Paul and Amelia had known them both when they had been in college. Mark had spent most of his twenties drifting around before he came home and trained as a lawyer, taking over his father's practice. Their evenings together were spent catching up, before Mark got a second bottle of wine into him and spent the rest of the night reminiscing. Paul liked Amelia and Mark was still a nice guy, embarrassed by his success, moving the conversation from now to then as soon as possible. Back to when they had all been together.

They had all sat together in the living room when Mark and Amelia arrived. They made small talk, asking the kids about school and telling them how much they had grown.

'How's Max doing?' Paul asked. 'You remember Max, Fin, yeah?'

'Yes,' Fin said.

'He's signed up for sailing school for the summer,' Amelia said. 'Do you sail, Fin?'

'No,' Fin said.

They waited in silence but he didn't say anything else. Paul stared at him and Fin looked back and shrugged.

'Well, if you wanted to learn this course is supposed to be good,' Mark said. 'But I don't know. Maybe sailing's not your thing.'

'Not really,' Fin said.

'You could try it if you wanted,' Paul said. 'Give you something to do. Get you out of the house.' Fin looked at the ground and turned red. Amelia asked Clare was she going to stay in Dublin for the summer and the conversation moved on. After ten minutes Paul gave the nod and the children left. When he went into the kitchen later Fin was sitting at the counter drinking juice.

'I'm not going on a sailing course, Dad. Seriously.'

'It's OK. I was just being polite.'

'I can't swim. I really don't want to.'

'Relax. You don't have to. I was just making conversation.'

'Max is an idiot,' Fin said. Paul tried not to laugh.

'Yeah, well he's their son. Just don't say anything like that to them.'

'Yeah. I know. But he's just thick.'

Paul went back in. Ruth and Amelia were talking.

'So what's been going on with you?' Mark asked him as he sat down.

'Not much. God, I don't know. It's hard to remember the year.'

'They go quick. A year used to feel like ten. That summer in Martha's Vineyard felt like about two years but it was only a couple of months.'

'That's right. Long time ago.'

'Long time. Twenty years. More. Jesus. What have we been doing?' He laughed.

'I don't know,' Paul said.

'So no major news?' Mark asked.

Paul looked over at Ruth. She was deep in conversation with Amelia. He went for it. He didn't think she'd mind.

'Yeah, well. We're moving house.'

'Seriously.'

'Yeah.'

'Why didn't you tell us. Amelia, do you hear this?'

'What?'

They were all looking at Paul.

'We're moving house.'

'Wow,' Amelia said. 'Excellent.'

'Yeah,' said Ruth. 'It's very exciting.'

'I've always liked this house,' Mark said, 'but I suppose with the kids getting older and that it might be a bit, I don't know.' He looked at Paul, panicking, unable to find his way out of the sentence. 'What was it? Why are you moving? I just can't think.'

'It's too small,' Paul said.

'Well, I wouldn't say that,' Mark said. 'Or I tried not to say that, but anyway tell us.'

'Yeah. That was it. Clare and Lou are sharing a room and they're all getting older and it was just beginning to get on top of us.'

'They were fighting all the time. I mean all the time,' Ruth said. 'It would drive you mad but really it wasn't their fault.'

'So we had a look at it,' Paul said, 'and if we moved out a bit we were going to be able to get somewhere bigger and then we found a place and the auction went our way and that was it. We got it.'

'That's brilliant,' Amelia said.

'Fantastic. Where is it?' Mark asked.

Paul told him. Mark nodded.

'Fantastic.'

'Is that Northside?' Amelia asked.

'No, it's south,' Paul said. He smiled at Ruth.

'It's out west,' Mark said. 'Right near the mountains.'

'It's not the mountains,' Paul said. 'It's OK, Mark. You can say it.'

'Hey, come on. Some of those places have come up a lot,' Mark said. 'Apparently.'

Paul knew Mark well enough to know that he didn't mean to patronize him, that he was trying to be supportive. Despite the wife and kid and the practice, Paul could never think of Mark as an adult. He didn't understand how grown-up relationships worked. That you didn't have to say the right thing or make the big gestures. You just had to be there and be reliable, appropriate to your position in somebody's life. That trying to justify the area in which they had bought a house was pointless and patronizing. He didn't know these things. He couldn't understand it because he wasn't bright enough and Paul knew he shouldn't let himself get annoyed.

But when Mark returned to it later, when they were back in the living room after dinner, Paul couldn't stop himself.

'Seriously,' Mark said, leaning across the arm of his chair conspiratorially. 'Seriously. You've done well. To get anywhere at all now is doing well. It's doing great. I know it's not where you might have wanted. Ideally, like. Or maybe it is.'

'Maybe it is.'

'Fair play to you anyway. That's all.'

'Yeah. Well, I don't need you to tell me,' Paul said. He said it quietly, his voice showing none of the irritation that he felt. It felt good. No anger. The words were enough.

'What?'

'I don't need you to tell me,' Paul repeated. 'We're very happy. We know we've done well. We know what it's like at the moment. You don't need to tell me.'

'Oh fuck, Paul. I'm sorry.'

'Don't be. It's fine.'

'No, it's not. It's not. I shouldn't have said anything.' Paul felt crap. He wished he could rewind forty seconds.

'You OK, Mark?' Ruth asked.

'He's fine,' Paul said. 'Everything's fine.'

'I'm really sorry.'

'For what?' Amelia asked.

'He's nothing to be sorry for,' Paul said.

'I insulted Paul. I didn't mean to.'

'You didn't, Mark. Seriously.'

'I did.'

'Maybe we should get you home,' Amelia said. 'You're a bit the worse for wear.'

Mark nodded like a child.

'You really don't have to,' Paul said.

'No, we should,' she said. 'It's late anyway.'

They all stood up and Paul got the coats. They said goodbye in the hall. Mark was still apologizing. He hugged Paul.

'Are we all right?' he asked.

'I should be asking you,' Paul said.

'Are we all right?' Mark asked again.

'We're absolutely fine. I'll talk to you soon.'

'What was that about?' Ruth asked when they'd gone.

'It was nothing. He just kept on saying how well we'd done with the house. Over and over and I knew all he was thinking was that we're going to live in a slum and he feels sorry for us. Genuinely sorry for us.'

'Who cares?' she said.

'I know. You're right.'

'You know the truth of it. You know what's going on. You know how happy we are about it. You see him once a year. Why worry what he thinks?'

'I'm not worried.'

'OK. But you shouldn't let it get to you.'

'It doesn't. Really it doesn't. It was nothing. He's just pissed and making a fuss over nothing.'

'Exactly.'

Paul said it and tried his hardest to mean it. To forget and move on. He tried his hardest.

When Robbie left school that same evening, he did not go straight home. Instead he went alone down the next road to where the new development was being built. He walked carefully along the muddy verge as trucks full of earth moved out and diggers and tractors shifted rocks and pallets of blocks. The drivers ignored him. He turned left along the back wall of his own estate and when he got to the back of Liam's place he began counting. When he thought it was right, he put his bag against the wall and took a few steps back, then ran at the wall and jumped. He pulled himself up and looked across the back garden. It was the right house. He swung his legs over and jumped down. He ran along the back wall, then the side wall, staying low until he stood at the back door. He tried it but it was locked. He walked around to the narrow passage at the side of the house until he saw what he was looking for. The small upper window of the toilet was open. At the end of the passage behind the back door was a plastic bin. He turned it upside down and stood on it. He reached in and lifted the catch of the top window and pushed it open so that he was able to get the rest of his arm in. He waited for a second. There was no beeping or flashing, no alarm about to go off. He flicked the catch up and from the outside pulled the window open. He turned around and lowered himself in head first, putting his hands on the toilet to steady himself. When he was ready he somersaulted forward and ended up on the toilet floor. He waited there and listened. There was no sound. He walked out into the hall. The alarm box on the wall was dead. He was as quiet as he could be but every move he made echoed through the empty house. There was nothing left. Even the carpets were gone. He went back downstairs. The dining room at the back of the house was the biggest in the house with a fireplace and sliding glass doors onto the patio. There was a door to the front. Robbie opened it a crack and looked through the front window. He could see out across the green to his own house. He pulled the door closed. He walked through the dining room into the kitchen. The key to the back door was on the window ledge. He unlocked the door, replaced the key and closed the door behind him. He ran along the fence to the back wall. He jumped it, picked up his bag and went home.

*

'What are we doing tonight?' Alan asked at seven o'clock when they were standing around the rock.

'I've got something planned,' Robbie said. 'How much money have you got? All of you?'

The other three handed their money over. Robbie counted it.

'So I'm paying for half the drink,' he said.

'Are we drinking tonight?' Tim asked.

'Are you all right with that? Do you have a problem?'

'No. Yeah.'

'Do you have your ID, Liam?'

'Yeah.'

'So you go and get cans and smokes and skins.' Robbie handed Liam the money. 'Bring Tim with you. He can stay outside and help you carry the stuff. I'll see you at the back of Liam's in half an hour, all right?'

'We can't drink there, Robbie,' Liam said. 'I told you before.'

'What?'

'My ma will kill me if we're out there again. The last time she said she'd get the cops on us.'

'She's not going to get the cops on you. Will you relax, you sap?' Alan said.

'Yeah, well, we're not drinking there,' Robbie said. 'So shut the fuck up whingeing. Where's your scooter, Alan?'

'In my gaff.'

'We'll go and get it. See you after.' The two of them went off towards Alan's house.

'What? That's it?' Tim said. 'We're just the fucking booze donkeys?' He watched the other two go.

'Come on,' Liam said and they started walking out of the estate in the direction of the off-licence.

Alan and Robbie went on the scooter to the flats near the village.

Alan waited on the road while Robbie went in. After only three minutes he came back.

'Did you get it?' Alan asked.

'Yeah.'

'Will we go?'

'Hang on.' He had his phone in his hand.

There was a group of guys standing under one of the landings with their hoods up. They were beginning to look.

'Let's go, Robbie,' Alan said. 'I hate this fucking dump.'

'I'm just ringing someone. Just wait. Orla? What's the story? It's Robbie. All right?'

He seemed totally relaxed when Alan looked at him. Alan tried to hide his own nervousness. He started the scooter and revved the engine. Robbie took a few steps away from him. Alan looked across at the others. They seemed to be staring straight at him but he couldn't tell. He couldn't see their eyes. Robbie hung up.

'What's going on?' Alan said.

'She's bringing that fucking mate of hers. Pain in the arse.'

'Can we get out of here?' Alan asked.

When they got back to Liam's wall, the other two were waiting, drinking cans.

'How many of those have you had?' Robbie asked.

'This is the first,' Tim said. 'Where were you?'

'Getting gear. Did you get the papers?'

Liam handed them over.

When the girls arrived they all stood up.

'So where are we going?' Orla asked.

'Not far,' Robbie said. 'But we have to be quiet.'

They walked along the wall until Robbie stopped.

'Hop,' he said to Liam.

'Here?'

'Yeah.'

'But it's like five houses away from mine.'

'Six. Hop.'

Liam shrugged.

'OK.'

He jumped at the wall and pulled himself up. Tim passed up the two bags of cans.

'You're joking,' Orla said.

'No. Wait until you see. It's fine. It's nice. Give her a hand, Liam.'

Liam reached down and pulled her up. Robbie put a hand under her arse and pushed.

'Hey.'

'I'm just trying to help you.' He looked over at Alan and smiled. Alan laughed out loud.

'Now you,' Robbie said to the other girl. 'Come on.' She looked terrified.

'It's OK,' he said. 'We're just going into a friend's house. Give him a surprise coming in the back.'

When they were all over, Robbie led them to the back door.

'Are we going to break in?' Orla asked him.

'No. Not at all. I know the guy who owns it. He said he'd leave the door open for us.'

'Seriously?'

'Yeah.' He wondered if she was totally thick or just scared. If she wanted to believe him enough. He opened the door.

'You see?' he said. They went in. When they walked into the kitchen Tim turned on the light.

'Turn that off,' Robbie barked. 'You fucking plank.' The girls were looking at him.

'Better without,' he said.

He led them through to the dining room.

76

'So. Here we are.'

'Look at this,' Alan said.

'This is ours,' Robbie said. 'For a couple of weeks. Until my friend gets back.' The other three guys laughed.

They sat on the floor and drank. Orla and Aoife took cans and drank. Robbie sat with his back against the wall and put together a joint. He took the can that Tim handed him without speaking. He lit the joint, drew the smoke deep into his lungs and held it, then put his head back and blew into the air. The others watched him. His little show.

'Now we can relax,' he said and he passed the joint to Orla. She held it for a second, looked at it, doubting, and then held it to her lips and pulled.

'We could do with some music,' Tim said.

'No music. No lights. It's our own place. That's enough for fuck's sake. Enjoy it while you can.'

Aoife sat beside Alan, not looking at him. Robbie and Orla lay back and whispered to each other. Tim was lying on his back talking shit. The usual stuff but the others were laughing with him.

'So some poor gimp is going to turn up here in a couple of weeks and we'll have moved in. We'll have the locks changed, our own pictures on the wall and I'm going to go to the door and I'm going to tell him: You've got the wrong house, pal, this is my gaff, this is our abode. You are trespassing in our abode. Now fuck off. But you can leave your daughter. I'll look after her. I'll take care of her. Come in here, love. Do you like cider?'

Aoife laughed and she put her hand on Alan's knee and looked at him and he laughed too. Orla whispered something to Robbie. He nodded. After a minute or two when they settled down and Tim was starting again, he leant over and pulled Alan back. Aoife looked away.

'Make a move on her,' Robbie said quietly into his ear.

'Oh Jesus.'

'Come on, man. She's mad into you. Do me a favour?'

'You owe me if I do. OK?'

'OK. Just do it.'

Alan sat up. Robbie moved back over and lay down beside Orla. Tim was still talking. Alan leaned over to Aoife and pulled her face to him. Without speaking he kissed her and straight away she came back at him.

'Look,' Orla said to Robbie and he put his arm around her and kissed her.

'Come on,' he said and he stood up, holding her hand. The two of them left and went upstairs. Alan looked after them. He waited as Aoife kissed his neck and then he stood and she followed him through the kitchen into the converted garage. Tim stopped talking and sat up.

'Where's everybody?' he asked Liam.

'Shagging,' Liam said.

'So what are we supposed to do?'

'Don't get any ideas. Not my thing,' Liam said.

It was ten minutes later. Liam and Tim were still on the floor, not talking, stoned. A light crossed the ceiling of the room and flashed a reflection off the window.

'What's that?' Liam asked, sitting up. Tim was on his feet in a second. He walked over and opened the door. A squad car was parked at the bottom of the drive.

'Fucking coppers.'

'What? No way.' Liam said.

'I swear to Jesus.' The two of them ran into the kitchen. Liam looked out into the hall. He said Robbie's name. He was already halfway down the stairs with Orla behind him.

'Where's Aoife?' she said.

'With Alan,' Liam said.

'Where are they?' Robbie asked.

'I don't know.'

'You go out the back,' he said to Orla as they went through to the kitchen.

'I can't leave Aoife.'

'Just fucking go. Go on.' He opened the door to the garage.

'Alan?' he said into the darkness.

'What?' He was on the ground with Aoife under him.

'Cops. Got to go now.'

The two of them jumped up and then the three of them were outside running across the garden to the wall. They all got over. The others were waiting for them on the far side.

'You two go that way,' Robbie said to the girls. 'Go home. If anybody asks you you're just out for a walk. On your own.'

The two of them ran off round towards the main road. The boys ran and stood against the wall at the back of Liam's. Robbie and Alan picked up empty cans off the ground that they had thrown there earlier and held them.

'Been here all night,' Robbie said. 'That's it. OK?'

'OK.'

'Take this, Tim.' He handed the lump of hash to him.

'I'm not fucking taking that.'

'They're not going to search you,' Robbie said. 'Here we go.'

A torch shone over the wall of the empty house. Then a head appeared. The boys started walking.

'You stay there,' a voice called.

'Wait,' Robbie said. They stood in silence. A guard jumped down and started walking towards them, talking into a radio. They heard the squad car as it turned into the building-site entrance.

'Stay where you are.'

Two guards got out of the car.

'Against the wall.'

The boys stood there. They dropped the cans.

'Mr Whelan,' Quigley the guard said. Robbie didn't answer. 'What are you doing out here?'

'Nothing.'

'You're never doing anything, are you?'

Robbie shrugged.

'Were you in that house?'

'What house?'

'The empty one.'

'Don't know it. Which one?'

'I said it to the lads. I said this will be that fucking Whelan knacker again. I could smell you when we went in.'

Robbie said nothing. His cheeks were flushed.

'Have you been running?' the guard asked.

'No. We've been here all night.'

He walked over to him and put his hands in his jacket pockets. Robbie lifted his hands. Quigley took out a pack of cigarettes and threw it into a puddle.

'Watch them,' he said. He pushed Robbie away until they were separate from the the others and spoke so close to his face that Robbie could smell his breath.

'We're going to take prints from that house. From the cans, from the doors, from the windows, and they're going to be yours and you'll be back in court and I'll have you on a break-in charge. And we're going to get you on a possession charge as well.'

'I don't have anything,' Robbie said. 'You can look. Search them all. We don't have anything.'

'Look at the state of you. The eyes on you. You're off your head.'

'I've had two cans of beer. That's all I've had.'

'Empty your pockets.'

Robbie took out a lighter, some change and a pack of gum.

'I know it was you.'

'What was me?'

'We had a complaint.'

'Was it Joe?'

'It doesn't matter who it was. I know it was you.'

'Because he's a fucking weirdo. He's always complaining. Not right in the head. He's the one you want to watch. He's a dirty pervert. Scumbag. You know yourself.'

'Shut up. Stand there.' He walked back over to the other guards. The three of them stood together away from the boys.

'They say they've been out here since eight. One of them says he thinks he saw a couple of homeless guys hanging around just before we got here.'

Quigley smiled.

'What and the others didn't notice anything?'

'Apparently not.'

'What do we do?'

'What can we do? Is there damage?'

'No. Nothing.'

'Let them go. We'll take this clown back ourselves.'

The younger guard walked back to the others.

'Go home,' he said. The three of them started walking off. Robbie watched as they disappeared around the corner.

'Come on, you,' Quigley said.

They took him back to the squad car. He sat in the back beside the young guy. As the car drove out onto the main road, it slowed. The other three were waiting at the entrance to the estate. Quigley put the siren on once. 'Move on,' he said through the microphone. The three boys started walking again, heads down, not looking at Robbie as he passed. The car drove up the main road, past the entrance to the estate. At the lights at the end they stopped. Robbie watched the two girls walking back in the direction of their estate. They didn't see him. The guards didn't notice them. Robbie could feel his heart beating, could feel the words wanting to come out of him to talk to these people and tell them that he hadn't done anything. He wanted to say something in the car when he didn't know where they were going, but he knew he was just a bit stoned and he kept his mouth shut.

The light changed and the car moved on. At the roundabout it came all the way around and headed back down to the estate.

'Did you get lost?' he asked as the car pulled up outside his house. His father's car wasn't there.

'Get out,' Quigley said.

They stood on the doorstep. Robbie knew that behind him people would be looking. His mother opened the door. He knew the expression that crossed her face.

'Oh no. No. What now?' she said.

'Mrs Whelan,' Quigley said. They all went into the living room and he closed the door.

'What's this about?'

'We think he may have broken into a house. He may have been smoking drugs.'

'May have? What's may have?'

'He was there.'

'Was there anybody else there?'

'Yes, there was.'

'And where are they? Are you bringing them home to their parents? Why is it always him?'

'Because he's always there. Every time we get a complaint, every time we have to come into this area, he's there.'

'Well, where else would he be? Where can they go? They have to be somewhere.'

'Look, I don't want to be coming in here to you every couple of weeks. Don't complain to me. Talk to him. Tell him not to be breaking into houses.'

'But what? Can you prove it?'

'We could. Probably. But there was no damage done, so it's not worth it. I can't absolutely say that it was him—'

'Then don't,' she said.

Quigley sighed. He was tired.

'One way or another he was out behind the estate drinking and he shouldn't be doing even that. Can you just try and keep an eye on him?'

'How can I? He's seventeen. What can we do? Lock him up?'

'I don't know. But I tell you. If he's like this at seventeen he will be inside by twenty. I'm not trying to scare you. That's just how it is. I deal with this stuff every day. I know what I'm talking about. That's where these guys end up. Whatever you can do.'

They walked out into the hall. Robbie sat on the couch and waited.

'He's not that bad. I'm not saying he's a bad lad,' Quigley said. 'It's all small stupid stuff but there's too much of it and if he keeps it up, he will get into trouble. I mean serious trouble.'

'I'll talk to my husband.'

'Thanks. Goodnight to you.'

'Goodnight.'

She walked back into the living room. Robbie stood up.

'I swear to God it wasn't me. I didn't do anything. That Quigley pig has it in for me.'

'Pig? Pig is it?'

'Policeman. Guard. Whatever. But he is a pig.'

'I don't know, Robbie. All I know is he's coming in here with you every couple of days.'

'It's not. It's not. When was the last time? I can't remember.'

'The point is that I know his name. I'm seeing too much of him. If it's not him, it's Joe Mitchell.'

'There's nothing I can do about him. You know he's not—'

'What?'

'Normal. He's got his own problems. That's not my fault. And you know Quigley hates me. There were four of us out the back and I'm the only one he searches. I'm the only one he takes in the car. Why do you think that is?'

'I don't know. Because you're always there. Like he says.'

'Don't mind what he says. Me and the lads are always there. We weren't doing anything and he's just bored, so he comes around and gives us hassle and because I'm the biggest he picks on me.'

'What about this house? What about the drugs?'

'What drugs? He's just saying that to make you worry.'

'There's no drugs? You don't smoke hash?'

Robbie didn't want this conversation. It wasn't fair. They both knew it didn't matter.

'No. No. I don't.'

His mother stood up to go.

'I don't know, Robbie. Your father's not going to be happy.'

Robbie's felt the panic rise, cold up his back.

'Do we have to tell him?'

'Of course we have to tell him.'

'I promise you it's not going to happen again. I swear.'

'I've heard that before, Robbie.'

'Oh come on. I didn't do anything. Nothing happened.'

'Robbie,' she shouted. He was surprised. 'You came home in a squad car. That's not nothing.'

'It wasn't my fault.'

'Explain that to your father. I don't care.' She saw him in front of her. He looked about twelve. She went into the kitchen and put on the kettle.

The two of them sat in the living room watching TV for the rest of the evening. Neither of them spoke. Robbie sat staring at the screen, not hearing, not seeing anything. His father was working an evening shift and wouldn't be back for a couple of hours. He would be tired and stressed when he got in. It wasn't the right time to tell him, Robbie knew. But there was nothing he could do. He had to wait.

What was he supposed to do? They couldn't get into most of the pubs in town. The local places were full of old men. They went sometimes to the clubs but a night out cost fifty quid and he didn't have it, or when he did the others didn't and he couldn't go on his own. They could go to the cinema or the bowling alley and hang around with a bunch of kids. There was nothing to do. He wasn't doing anything wrong. He wasn't stealing cars or robbing houses or selling drugs. Just hanging around, trying to have a laugh. That was all it was and it was enough to make him into some sort of criminal. In the flats, on the corridors and at the corners there were guys dealing in everything. They could get you whatever you wanted. There were junkies getting the bus into town to put syringes to the throats of tourists. There were coppers who would put drunks in the back of a van on a Saturday night and beat them around when they got to the station because that's what they liked to do. What was a group of young fellows having a few drinks and chatting up a couple of girls in an empty house? What harm was in it for anybody? It had to be that Mitchell pervert that rang the guards. That fucking weirdo getting him into shit over nothing. When the time came Robbie would sort it out. He didn't know how but he would make it good.

And that fat bastard Quigley driving around just waiting for him to do something.

'He called me a knacker,' he said out loud. His mother looked over.

'Who did?'

'Quigley.'

'Did he?' She wasn't interested. Robbie was annoyed.

'That would make you a knacker as well. All of us. He shouldn't be able to get away with that.'

'I'm sure you've called him worse.'

'Not to his face.'

She smiled coldly. 'Is that better?'

'Yeah. Yeah, of course it is. He doesn't know.'

'I'm sure he does.'

At one o'clock, his father got back from work and they heard the car turn into the drive.

His mother stood up.

'Please, Ma. Please don't.'

'I have to Robbie. He'll find out anyway.'

'He won't. Please. Come on.' He was begging her.

'It's your own fault,' she said. She could have changed her mind. Might have, but he said the wrong thing.

'I didn't do anything.'

She shook her head and went into the hall. Robbie stood up and then sat down when he heard his father's key in the door.

'You're still up,' he heard his father say and then his mother closed the door and all he could hear was their blurred voices. He tried to gauge what was being said. His mother spoke quickly, then short bursts from his father as he asked questions and then in the middle of it, too early it seemed to him, the door opened and his father stood before him. He was wearing his work shirt and trousers, the collar open and his bowtie sticking out of his shirt pocket.

'So?' he asked Robbie.

'What?' Robbie said. He wasn't ready.

'What? What? You breaking into houses is what. That fucking Quigley bastard around here again. That's what.'

Robbie just looked at him. He didn't know whether he was supposed to speak.

'Huh?' his father shouted. 'What?'

'I don't know,' Robbie said. 'I didn't do anything.'

'That's fucking bollocks,' his father roared. Flecks of spit landed on Robbie's face. 'Bollocks.'

'I didn't.'

'So what happened?'

'I was out behind the wall with Alan and them and then Quigley comes up and starts hassling us for nothing.'

'What were you doing behind the wall?'

'Nothing. Just hanging around.'

'Drinking.'

'We had a couple of cans. That's all.'

'So when did you go into the house?'

'We didn't.'

'Who did?'

'I don't know.'

'You didn't see anyone?'

Robbie shook his head. He tried to judge which way his father was likely to go, knowing that the wrong answer, the wrong look or move could set him off.

'No.'

'No one?'

'Yeah.'

He didn't understand how his father could move so quickly. As soon as he had answered, Robbie found himself on the floor. The slap had come from nowhere, an open hand swung in an upward arc catching him across the jaw. His old man looked down on him, his breathing heavy.

'Quigley is an arsehole, but he's not stupid. You're the only fucking idiots around. You're standing around behind the house. Who else could it be? You've no brains.'

'I wasn't.'

His father stood above with a clenched fist.

'Just. Don't. Fucking say another word. The next time you get picked up, don't bother coming back here. I will give you a hiding you won't forget. Now get up to bed.'

Robbie stood up. He was taller than his father by a couple of inches. He walked by him on the way out without saying a word. Given the chance, he could probably do a bit better for himself. He hadn't seen it coming but there was only so much he would take. If there was a next time, he wouldn't go down so easy.

His father was like that, Robbie thought, as he lay in bed trying to ignore the pain. He didn't talk. He didn't think. He just reacted. Accusation. Judgement. Bang. All over nothing. Robbie would have to be careful. He would have to wait. He didn't mind that, but he would get Mitchell. Get him better than ever. Not the low-grade harassment and irritation that they'd pursued him with before. This time they would hurt him.

He got his phone out of his jeans pocket and texted Orla. Are you there? he asked and waited. After five minutes he sent another. What happened to you after? The reply came quickly. Don't ring me again. I don't want to see you. He felt a wrench of pain and disappointment as he read. Why? he wrote but she didn't reply. He dialled her number but it went straight to message. He hung up without speaking and turned the light off. Joe Mitchell was going to get it. That was what he was thinking as he went to sleep, his own pain adding an edge of viciousness to his plans of torture and humiliation.

5

Joe had never been like them. It was what his neighbours said. You know what young fellows are like. They're just bored. You must remember yourself. It was maddening because it wasn't true. Never. Not him. Never like them.

He was always different. He was happy in the national school. He did well, he was one of the best and it was a good thing. It wasn't embarrassing. He talked to the others and they liked him. He didn't notice anything strange. Nobody bothered him. At home it was even better. A long garden divided into sections where he could disappear. The summer before he went to secondary school was the best. He set up a tent out of view of the house, among apple trees, surrounded by nettles and long grass that had never been cut for as long as they had lived there. He lay there all summer reading, breathing in the smell of earth and apples rotting on the ground and smoke from early bonfires and when the books that he read described things so thrilling that they became real to him, that he had to do something, he would go out of the tent and, unseen by anyone, would become a part of the action. He lived them. There was no need to go anywhere else. He didn't care about what was happening in the world beyond their front door. Other places, other people. He wasn't interested. He didn't need to go beyond those trees, which were the boundary of his stage. This world, where everybody and everything lived up to his expectations, especially – always in the central heroic role – himself.

But then when he went back to school things had changed. The gap had begun to open. He didn't notice when the alliances started to form. It happened quickly in the intense environment of this new class. He should have chosen who he wanted to be for the next five years but he didn't and he was left on his own. He studied hard and kept quiet and bothered no one but that didn't matter. It wasn't that he was doing anything wrong. He was just alone and in that animal time it was enough to make him a target.

It was stupid. He didn't care when they beat him up or took things from him. It was just irritating. The noises they made when he read, his breaking voice turning the classroom into a farmyard of sheep and chicken imitations. How they laughed when he answered questions, the expressions that he used, the joy when he stumbled or got something wrong.

'With friends like these—' the teacher Mooney said to him one time in third year.

'They're not my friends,' Joe replied and there was a chorus of boo-hoos, but he felt it was a triumph. He knew what the story was and he didn't need sympathy or popularity. He was surviving on his own and none of them had to do it. None of them could.

The moment he realized that he was stronger than them, than they had to be, was the start of a change for him. He wasn't afraid of being alone. He took care over his work, presented everything perfectly. It became a statement of who he was and how he was different. When the others laughed at his margins and underlinings and colour codes and his neat, tight writing, he didn't care because he was right. They hated him more for it, but he knew that he was winning. As the exams got nearer, he could see that they were beginning to understand that getting kicked out of class and having to stay back every day and getting Fs wasn't so clever. The classes started getting quieter and Joe was left alone and he silently revelled as the others tried to catch up. The power switched. He was in front and the ones who had picked on him most, the loudest and meanest, were shown up as the idiots he had always known they were.

It was the same when he went to college. Wandering through the library during his first week, along the corridors, books from floor to ceiling, disappearing into the distance, the noise of the happy crowds gathered around the lake outside barely audible, he had found his place. He knew he would never be popular or smooth or comfortable in a group but he didn't have to be. He might sometimes want to be that person, but it didn't matter. He was happy on his own. A few friends, his family. All fine. Nothing to worry about. He could stay where he wanted to be, he could do what he enjoyed and that would be enough for him to get on in the world.

Because what Joe had was what mattered. The library was full of books written by people like him, for people like him. People who were trying to understand what the world was about and knew that it was something to be engaged with, thought about, analysed. So full of wonder and beauty, such an intoxicating mix of pattern and chance. The writers, critics, philosophers, lecturers and tutors were from his world. They weren't getting into fights outside the bar on a Friday night or hanging around the underground pool hall all day, bored, but at least certain that in their bunker they couldn't be contaminated by knowledge. They weren't sitting around the canteen making crap jokes and trying to impress a table of girls, like the meat-head from his tutorial, who the previous day had asked what the past tense of dog was. He was the big man now, all laughs and charm, but in six months it would be different. Popularity was something Joe mistrusted. He didn't understand how it worked, but he knew it didn't matter because when that guy was long forgotten by those girls, Joe's name would be on a page pinned to the board in the concourse with first-class honours beside it. He didn't want to be arrogant, but that was how it would be. The world rewarded people like him because he understood this. And those others, blind to it all, were going nowhere.

So when his neighbours said to him that these boys were just young and bored, he knew better. They were the same as the ones in his school who used to pick on him, the same as the ones in college who failed everything and dropped out. Thick, violent and frustrated. The world and its opportunities sailing away from them already and they could do nothing but watch it go. Left with no options, they would only get worse. Joe didn't want to admit it, but he was afraid of what they might do because he knew what they were like. And he had never, ever been like them.

Paul woke early the first morning. The light shone through the uncurtained window into his face, blinding him as he tried to remember where he was. He looked at the blank walls, the white carpet, and until he saw Ruth sleeping beside him he wondered was he in hospital, had he had an accident. Then he remembered and when it came back he didn't understand how he could forget. He got out of bed and went through into the bathroom and pissed. When he came back he stood in the window and looked out across the front garden. There was no one around. It was a Saturday. The estate looked orderly in the morning with nobody about. It looked safe. Happiness ran through him. Morning. No people. A new house. The space for all of them to do their own thing and not interfere with each other. Him and Ruth together again. From when they had met they had been getting things done. Getting to know each other, having sex, getting to know each other again, getting pregnant, getting married, getting a house, getting a job, having more kids, bringing them up. The spacing of the children had meant that they had always been busy. They had survived so long with so little time. But now they would get what they deserved, they would catch up with each other. In the space that they had bought for themselves he hoped that they could be selfish.

Paul was thinking this on his first morning. The sun was shining. A couple of days of moving had passed. What was supposed to be so hard about it? Paul wondered. Load the vans and say goodbye. Stop looking backwards and look instead to the potential and the hope and the certainty of the future. They had done it. They were in. The kids were happy. Ruth was happy and the summer holidays had just begun. He got back into bed. He spoke Ruth's name and watched as she began to move and opened her eyes. She blinked and shook her head.

'We're here,' he said.

'Where?'

'In.'

'Oh yeah. Yeah. We need curtains for that window.'

'Listen,' he said. 'Just listen.'

She lay there and after a couple of seconds she spoke.

'Nothing.'

'Nothing. This is what it's going to be like. It's like they're not there. Not a sound.'

'Maybe they've been abducted in the night. Maybe you didn't lock the door.'

'We can hope,' he said.

'Why would you say that?'

He climbed on top of her, holding his weight off her with his elbows.

'You and me in this big empty house. Think of all we could do.'

'We could decorate it ourselves.'

'That's not what I'm thinking of.'

'I know what you're thinking of. And it's not going to happen.'

'In this light you look about eighteen.'

'In this light? What do I normally look?' she asked.

'I don't know. Twenty-five? Maybe.'

She laughed.

'That's terrible. But it'll do,' she said.

It was the same bed that they had had for years but in a new room it was enough. The sun shone in on them as they kicked the duvet off the bed, making their skin look tanned, making Paul feel like they were on holiday and that it was something different. They each moved differently, more eager than usual, harder and younger and more animal, so much that Ruth wondered where his head was, but he was there. Right there living it and feeling it, engaged and thinking this is what it's going to be like.

In the shower later Paul checked to see if it showed. If the extra strength that he felt was something that had come about in his body unnoticed. He saw nothing. He looked the same as ever. Heavier than he had been at twenty-five when life was harder, but not as bad as others his age. His hair was still there. His face was the same he thought but then he knew that, when confronted with photos of himself, the person that looked back at him was not who he expected. He wasn't who he thought he was. He didn't look like himself. What did it matter now anyway? Ruth said the right things to him. He didn't have to worry. Who was he trying to impress? There was no one. No one ever looked at him. Not on the train. Not in school. Not in the shops. Not at home. He was just there. He was a middle-aged man and nobody saw middle-aged men. When he was younger, people saw him. Women noticed him. He remembered. His life then made him lean and energetic and driven, trying to keep it all going, and that showed in his movement as vitality. Edginess that gave him focus. Girls liked it and he enjoyed the attention. Then as he got older it went away. They stopped looking. He disappeared. But now in this new house, now when he felt some of that power again, he stood up straight and looked at himself. He held his breath and for a moment he thought maybe he could see something.

Paul wheeled the mower from the garage around the side of the house to the back lawn. The grass was long and covered in white daisies. It was an odd shape for a lawn, bordered by a curving flower bed on one side and a wall behind. He started the motor and pushed it onto the grass. Fin should have been doing it, but he was still unpacking and Paul had wanted to do it anyway. The sun was shining. He had a garden. He would cut the grass and smell the flower of the privet hedge and the faint traces of barbecue smoke, the damp earth of the flower beds. He shook the grass from the bag against the back wall. He saw Ruth with Clare and Lou in the kitchen washing the dishes as they unloaded them from cardboard boxes. They didn't notice him as he watched them. He looked at the upstairs of the house and over to the window of Fin's room. It was a big house he thought, the upper windows were high above him. The scale of it still took him by surprise. This house that they owned.

When he'd finished the back he went into the kitchen. He stood at the sink and ran the tap before taking a glass of water.

'That looks good,' Ruth said.

'It's not too bad.'

'Are you going to do the front?'

'Yeah, I'll do it now.'

Clare walked through from the living room, talking on the phone.

'Can Emily come over tonight?' she asked.

'What for?' Paul asked. Clare just looked at him.

'Yes, she can,' Ruth said.

'Yeah, it's fine,' Clare said into the phone, shaking her head at her father. She walked out into the garden.

'Well, I don't know,' Paul said to Ruth. 'What is she coming over for?'

'It doesn't matter,' Ruth said. 'It's good that she wants people to come over. It'll help her make it her own space. You should be glad.'

'I know. Fair enough, yeah. But Emily.'

'Stop,' she said, trying not to smile at him.

'Stupidity is catching, you know,' he said quietly. 'I see it in school all the time. Guys with great brains spend a summer hanging around with some moron and they come back thick. They think thick is cool.'

'It's not going to happen with Clare. Anyway, Emily's nice. That counts for something.'

'It does,' he said as she walked away from him. 'Nice and thick.'

When he was out mowing the grass in the front two older women came halfway up the drive and stood smiling politely until he looked up and noticed them. He smiled back and walked over. One of them started speaking but he couldn't hear her. He turned the mower off and as the sound died away he spoke.

'Sorry,' he said. 'What can I do for you?'

'We came to say hello,' the same one said. They both wore runners and jogging suits. 'You've just moved in.'

'That's right. That's very kind of you. I'm Paul.'

'I'm Sheila. And this is Joan.' He wiped his hand on his trouser leg and then shook hands with them. The second one still hadn't spoken.

'Have you been living here long?' he asked.

'Since it was built,' Sheila said. The other one nodded.

'Great,' he said. 'It's a nice estate.'

'It's a lovely neighbourhood,' Sheila said. Paul could think of nothing else. He wished Ruth would come out. She was better at this kind of thing.

'Do you live together?' he said. 'The two of you?'

They both laughed. Paul could feel himself blushing.

'No. I live at fifteen and Joan is—'

'I live at number nine.' She smiled at him. Her voice was lower than he had expected.

'That's great,' Paul said.

'We were just out for a walk and we saw you out here and we thought we'd welcome you,' Sheila said.

'That's lovely,' Ruth said behind them, emerging from the house. 'Will you come in for a minute?'

They went inside.

'I'm going to get on with this,' he said after them, pointing at the grass.

'OK, darling,' Ruth called back to him. Darling. He smiled at that. He started the mower up again.

Maybe it was because he worked in a school, Paul thought, that he found these small social occasions of adult interaction so difficult. Years spent supervising groups of young guys who had no sense that there was a right way of talking, of dealing with a two-minute conversation with a stranger had left him unsure of himself. It never came naturally to him, the right thing to say, the right gesture to make. The worry that he was going to get it wrong held him back from doing anything. And as the atmosphere stretched in the silence and he stood face to face with this other person he would feel that he had to do something, that he could hold back no longer and he would laugh out loud or pat them on the back and it would be wrong. Too many times. Ruth could do it. Always the right thing, the right question. If he looked back across his life and counted the years, then he understood that he was forty but it made no sense. He was a twenty-three-year-old who had been waking up older and older for seventeen years and the only thing that he had learnt en route was that the mere passage of time does nothing to inform or develop you if you're not looking. He watched his colleagues in work and how they established authority through sticking to their own rules. Whether they believed in what they did was irrelevant. Consistency was all. Was that what maturity meant? Choosing a position and sticking to it? Paul was sure that he was missing the point.

He was mowing the grass in his new house and the people from the neighbourhood were coming round to say hello. It was the start of summer. He thought about things too much. If this was where he had washed up, immature and unsure, then what did it matter? He waved to the two women as they left, smiling and shouting goodbye over the noise of the machine. They smiled and waved back. Everybody was happy. He'd done all right.

It was later that afternoon. Paul and Clare were going to pick up Emily. As they were pulling out of the drive, a car drove up to the house two down from theirs and stopped. The driver looked over and when he saw them leaving, he put the car into reverse and pulled back into the road in front of Paul's car, blocking him. The driver got out. He was a small man in his fifties. His expression said nothing. Paul felt adrenalin rush through him. He didn't know what was going on. He unbuckled his seat belt. By the time he had got out the man was standing beside him.

'Hello,' he said.

'Is everything OK?' Paul asked.

'You're new. I thought I should say hello to you when I saw you. I'm Joe Mitchell.'

Paul laughed.

'Jesus. OK. That's OK.'

'What?'

'It was just when you pulled up I wasn't sure . . . I didn't know—'

'Did I scare you? I backed out a bit quickly, did I?'

'No, not at all. Not at all. Sorry. I'm Paul. I'm glad to meet you.' They shook hands.

'Is that your daughter? Or your wife?' he said pointing in at Clare.

'My daughter. That's Clare.'

She waved at Mitchell. 'I'm his daughter.'

He smiled at her.

'You're married?' he asked Paul.

'Yes. We've three children. Clare's the eldest.'

'Very good. You're welcome anyway. If I can do anything for you just call in or whatever.'

'Thanks very much. It's kind of you. It's a lovely place. I think we'll be happy here. Everybody seems friendly.'

Mitchell shrugged.

'It's fine. Yeah. It's not the worst. Some people are very nice.' He shook his head.

Paul didn't know what to say. He wasn't sure if he was meant to ask the implied question. He smiled.

'Well, it's good of you to say hello. Maybe when we settle in, you could come over for a drink or something.'

'I don't really drink. But thanks.'

Paul opened the car door.

'Thanks again,' Joe said. 'Nice to meet you.'

'See you around.'

'Bye.'

Paul got into the car.

'Who's he?' Clare asked.

'Wait a second,' Paul said. They watched Mitchell start his engine and move forward enough to let them pass. As Paul drove by, Joe rolled down his window. Paul pulled up beside him.

'The bins go out on Monday,' he said. 'I just thought, if you're getting rid of anything. They'll take most things. Not garden stuff.'

'OK,' Paul said. 'Thanks a lot.'

'Who is that?' Clare asked as they drove out of the estate.

'Joe Mitchell.'

'Is he mad?'

Paul tried not to laugh.

'I don't know. Probably not. He was being nice.'

'He was being weird. Did he think we were married? And was he talking about the bins?'

'I'm glad he told us. It's good to know. We will be putting stuff out.'

'But not garden stuff.'

'No,' Paul said. 'Not garden stuff.'

When they got back with Emily, Ruth took the car and went shopping.

'Is there anything you want done?' Paul asked her before she left.

'Not really. You've done enough for the day. You just relax. I'll be back in a bit. I'm taking Lou with me.'

The two girls were up in Clare's room. He could hear the bass of her radio through the floor. He walked into the living room. Fin was lying on the couch watching a film.

'Hiya,' he said.

'Hi,' Paul said. 'It's a nice day outside. You wouldn't think about maybe going out?'

Fin looked up at him.

'What for?'

'Air? Sun? Exercise?'

'I'm watching this.'

'What is it?'

'I don't know.'

Paul laughed.

'Do I have to go outside?' Fin asked.

'No, you're all right. I'll go. I don't understand why you'd rather be in here.'

'I don't understand why you'd rather be outside. But go ahead. I'm not stopping you.'

'Because this is our first day here, I am indulging you and I know you know that. And I know that's why you're being a smart-arse. And I know that you know that tomorrow will be a very different story. Yeah?'

Fin spoke without looking at him. 'Tomorrow. Yes.'

Paul got a blanket and a book and went and lay on the lawn at the back of the house. The sun was starting to lower in the sky, but it was still warm. The trees along the back wall meant that the garden was sheltered from any wind or view. Paul felt the heat of the June sun soak into his skin. The smell of the cut grass was strong and he could hear the bees humming. His muscles ached from the work earlier. He closed his eyes and felt his body sink into the ground, as comfortable as a bed. His mind began to drift and he realized that very soon he would be asleep.

They were sitting out the back around a wooden table later that evening. Paul was pouring wine into glasses.

'Will you, Emily?' he asked. She blushed.

'Yes, please.'

'You don't have to. Only if you want,' Paul said.

'I do. I do.' She looked at Clare and the two of them started giggling.

'What?' Paul asked, looking at Ruth in desperation. 'What's funny about that?'

'It's nothing, Paul. Emily, take your drink.'

The two girls walked away, huddling together.

'Did I miss something?' he asked Ruth. 'Was there a joke I didn't get?'

'I don't know,' Ruth said. 'It could be anything. Don't worry about it.'

'I swear to God I had my fill of teenage girls laughing at me at sixteen. I didn't expect to have to still be dealing with it at forty.'

'They're not laughing at you,' she said. 'Or they might be. Who knows? That's what they do.'

'It pisses me off,' he said.

She smiled at him.

'Does it? Really?'

'Yes. Well. I don't know. Maybe not.'

They sat at the table away from the children and watched Fin cook.

'What do I do with these?' he called over to Ruth, holding up a packet.

'Do them the same as hamburgers. Just the same,' she said.

'What are they?' Paul asked.

'Veggie burgers. Emily's a vegetarian.'

Paul smirked.

'Since when?' he asked Ruth.

'I don't know.'

'She better not start—'

'Be quiet.'

'She better not—' Paul began again, quieter.

'Enough. Leave her alone.'

'I haven't said anything to her.'

'Seriously, Paul. Stop. She is a guest here. Be nice to her.'

'Only if she's nice to me.'

Ruth laughed at that. She tried not to but she did.

Fin called them to eat. They sat at the table.

'Emily's a vegetarian,' Clare told him, when he gave her a plate.

'So? What does that mean?'

'She won't eat that or that or that.'

'She won't have much else then.'

'Those veggie burgers are for her, Fin,' Ruth said.

'Which? These grey things?'

'Yes.'

'OK.'

'What made you become vegetarian, Emily?' Paul asked. Ruth flashed a look at him.

'When I heard that pigs are more intelligent than dogs.'

'OK,' Paul said. 'Fair enough. Yeah.'

'What about chickens?' Fin asked. 'They're thick, aren't they?'

'And also because there's plenty of other things that you can eat without hurting anything,' Emily went on, ignoring him. 'We don't have to eat animals, so if we do we're making a conscious decision. I don't want to make that choice. That's all.'

Paul saw Ruth trying not to laugh at the surprise obvious on his face. He'd never heard Emily speak before. Not a full sentence. She was Clare's whispering, giggling friend, who wore nice clothes and blushed when she talked. He felt bad about trying to expose her stupidity, even as a joke. Ruth was right. He should leave her alone. It wasn't fair. He was sobering up.

Fin sat down beside him.

'Here's what I think. Chickens first, then sheep, then cows and then pigs. Pigs brainiest, chickens stupidest.'

'What about ducks?' Clare asked.

'Between chickens and sheep,' Paul said. 'I think.'

'What are you talking about?' Lou asked.

'Animals,' Ruth said.

'I like bears best,' Lou said.

'I wouldn't eat a bear,' Emily said.

'For intellectual reasons?' Paul asked.

'No. I just think they'd taste like shit,' she said. They all laughed. Paul felt happier then.

Paul and Ruth were still out the back after dinner. Lou was on a bike on the grass. The two girls came out.

'We're going out for a walk,' Clare said.

'Where?' Ruth asked.

'Just around the estate.'

'There's people out on the green,' Ruth said. 'Young people. You could say hello. Introduce yourselves. I'm sure they're very nice.'

'Are you joking?' Clare said.

'Or we could come with you,' Ruth went on. 'And introduce you. See what they're all like. See if they'd like to come over and play Trivial Pursuit.' Paul smiled. As he watched, Emily blushed.

'You're very funny,' Clare said. 'We'll be back later.'

'Hang on,' Paul said. 'When's later?'

'I don't know.'

'Will I come out and get you when I think you should come in?' Paul asked. 'Or do you want to give me a time?'

'Jesus. I don't know. We might go and get a video. I don't know.'

'I don't mind,' Paul said. 'Really. It's all the same to me.'

Clare looked at Emily, who just shrugged.

'Half-ten?' Clare asked. Emily nodded. 'Half-ten,' Clare said to Paul.

'OK. But if you're not back, I will be out. Shouting.'

'You're a pain,' she said. 'See you later.'

'Bye,' Emily said.

'Have a lovely time,' Ruth said.

'What do we do now?' he asked Ruth after they'd gone.

'Will we go to bed?' she said.

'Lou. Time for bed,' he said standing up.

'It's not. It's not late,' she said.

'Yeah, well you're going.'

Clare and Emily walked down the drive.

'What were your parents talking about?' Emily asked. 'Were they going to come out or what? I didn't get it.'

'They were joking. They think it's funny to try and embarrass me.'

'What's funny about that?'

'Nothing. They're just being stupid.'

'They're all right.'

'They're very annoying.'

'Will we get a video first?'

'OK.'

As they passed the rock, they looked over at the group standing around. There were four guys, probably about the same age as them. The noise of the conversation faded away as they walked by until only one voice could be heard. It was the smallest guy, who seemed to be talking about cars. Together Clare and Emily picked up their pace.

'They're still watching us,' Emily said after a moment, looking over her shoulder.

'Don't look back.'

'Why?'

'It's not cool.'

Emily laughed.

'I think we're OK. They didn't look too hot to me.'

As they turned out of the estate onto the main road, Clare took out a packet of cigarettes. She passed one to Emily. The two of them stopped as Clare lit them, Emily holding her hands around the lighter.

'Oh Jesus,' Emily said as she exhaled.

'I needed this,' Clare said. 'I've been in the house or out with Mum for two days. I've been freaking out.'

'Moving house is one of the most stressful things you can do, after murder or something. Apparently.'

Clare looked at her.

'What are you talking about?'

'Your dad was telling me earlier in the car.'

'Where was I?'

'When you went in to pay for the petrol.'

'And he told you this?'

'Yeah. I don't know why,' Emily said. 'It's not like I'm going to move house.'

'Maybe he just wanted to say something. Break the silence.'

'Maybe.'

'He's pretty smooth, my dad, when he gets going,' Clare said.

'Yeah, right,' Emily said. 'Real master of conversation.'

When they got back to the estate, the group were still there.

'Will we go over?' Emily asked.

'Do you want to?'

'Maybe just for a second. See what they're like.'

'I don't know. You go home tomorrow. I have to stay here. What do I do if they're all dopes?'

'They can't all be dopes.'

'Yeah, they could,' Clare said, but Emily had started crossing the road onto the green. Clare caught up and they arrived together.

'All right?' one of the boys said.

'Did you just move in?' one of the others asked.

'I did,' Clare said.

'I didn't,' Emily said. 'I'm just visiting.'

'What do you think?' the first guy asked her.

'It's nice. Very nice.'

'Try living here,' one of the others said.

'What's wrong with it?' Clare asked.

'It's boring.'

'Where did you come from?' one of them asked.

Clare told him.

'Very nice,' the small one said. 'So what happened? Did your da go to jail or something?'

'Shut up, Tim,' said the one guy who hadn't spoken.

'I don't know,' Clare said.

'Is there anything to do around here?' Emily asked. 'Anywhere to go or do you go into town to drink?'

'Usually we drink in fields,' one of them said. 'Maybe you don't do that where you're from.'

'Yeah, we do,' Emily said. 'Or in parks. Knacker drinking.'

'Is that what you call it?' the boy said.

An hour later, Paul stood looking out the window of their bedroom, waiting for Ruth to get out of the bathroom. He could see a group of kids standing around the rock. Even at this distance, he could see that the boys were doing most of the talking, swaying and rocking and gesturing as they spoke to Clare and Emily, who stood around, not moving, watching, at the edge of the group. He watched one of the guys who was talking, animated and involved, when suddenly, mid-story it seemed to Paul, the two girls said something and started walking back towards the house. He watched the boys' movements slow and stop as they looked after them. Paul sat down to make himself less visible in the window. He looked at his watch and saw that it was a quarter past ten. He didn't know anything about the boys outside. They were probably fine. But still he could not help himself feeling a peculiar happiness, something like pride, as he heard Clare open the front door.

6

The boys were sitting on the grass at the rock. It was late afternoon and the air was warm. There was nothing to do. They were trying to fill the hour until they would be called in for dinner. Tim was talking the way he did when there was nothing to say. He wanted to be at home on the Playstation, but his mother had sent him out. There was no escape. He had to be with them. He had to be there but he wanted to be comfortable and he knew he never would be. He knew he came last in the order, but without them what would he do? What would he be? When Joe Mitchell came out of his house and started his car he was glad of the distraction.

'Look at him,' he said. 'The dirty bastard.'

Joe slowed down as he drove by them. He looked over and when he saw Robbie he smiled, then changed gear and sped off.

'What's he smiling about?' Alan asked. 'What's the story?'

'Do you know what I think?' Tim said. 'Do you know what I reckon?'

Robbie spat. Tim looked over at him and then waited.

'That guy,' Robbie said. 'That guy is going to—' He stopped and shook his head. He was staring at the ground, his face hidden by the peak of his cap. The others watched him and when he looked up, he was smiling.

'Alan,' he said, 'let's go.' He stood up and walked off. Alan followed him. The other two got to their feet.

'You stay there,' Robbie said.

'Why?' Liam asked. 'Where are you going?'

'I don't know. Do what you want, I don't care.'

'Why can't we come?' Tim said.

Robbie turned around and stopped.

'You just fucking can't. Don't ask me anything. I'll see you later.' The two of them walked away.

'I'm getting sick of this,' Liam said to Tim. 'Him treating us like we're pricks.'

Tim started to say something and then he stopped. He didn't really like Liam. He didn't know if he trusted him.

'I don't know,' he said. 'I'm going home.'

Robbie and Alan walked up the main road towards the shops. Robbie was talking. He was animated, moving his hands as he spoke and laughing. Alan's hands were in his pockets and he was looking at Robbie sideways. Occasionally he smiled, but the smile faded quickly. At the traffic lights beside the garage they stopped and as they waited Robbie pulled at Alan's arm and said something straight into his face. Alan looked at the ground and didn't speak. Robbie pushed him on the shoulder. Alan looked up and nodded. Robbie laughed and as the lights changed they crossed the road.

Later that evening Robbie sat in his living room having dinner with his parents. They sat in front of the television. His father was on good form. He'd picked up a video and some cans on the way home from an early shift and when they finished eating, Robbie made tea and brought it through.

'Are you going out?' his mother asked him.

'Not tonight.'

'Are you sick?' his father asked him.

'No. I just can't be bothered.'

'Well, get back into the kitchen and grab a couple of cans.'

The three of them sat and watched the film. Robbie had seen it before but he didn't care. It was a shit comedy but his parents laughed at every stupid joke and for once Robbie laughed along with them.

Alan rode his scooter into town along the quays. Occasionally he stopped at a set of lights and waited in the bus lane, then moved back out into the traffic. He stayed behind, watching all the time, speeding up, slowing down but always there. There was enough traffic around that he didn't have to worry. He drove up onto a square on the Northside. He slowed and watched a car swing into an empty space and park, then he drove on slowly, once around the square, until he came back to the same spot and saw that the car was still there. He went straight on and parked the scooter on a side street. He took off his helmet. There was sweat on his forehead. It was a warm still evening, nine o'clock and the sky was beginning to darken. He locked the helmet to the front wheel of the scooter and walked quickly back into the square. There was no one around. The occasional car drove by but nobody would have noticed him as he walked. When he came to the spot, he stopped. He looked around and then cursed to himself and kept walking. Fucking Robbie. After a minute he lit a cigarette, then turned. He listened and heard nothing. Just the distant sound of traffic. He walked back to the car and stopped beside it. He stood at the driver's door, keys in his hand and checked one more time. Then he ran the key in a circle around the lock and dragged it along the side of the door, feeling the metallic scratch vibrate in his fingers, hearing the low crackle as the paint broke and fell in tiny flakes. He walked back onto the pavement and looked around again. A bus passed, empty and dark. It was out of sight in seconds. He approached the car again on the other side and walked along, his hand moving in loops from the front wing to the petrol cap, the grey swirling line that he marked visible in the half-light. He crossed the road and put his keys back in his pocket. He went back to the scooter, unlocked it, pulled on his helmet and drove off back down to the river and got out of town as fast as he could. He had felt sick. He hadn't wanted to think about it, but it was there. Now he was happy and the nausea was gone, replaced by hunger. He stopped at a chipper and then drove up to the canal and sat on a bench and ate. There were ducks standing around the bank underneath the bridge. He threw the bag among them when he had finished and watched as they surrounded it. He laughed as they tore at the greasy, salty paper and tried to eat it. Stupid ducks.

It was ten o'clock when the film ended. Robbie sat and watched the news with his parents. He had been waiting all night and had heard nothing.

'I'm going to bed,' he said. 'I'm knackered.'

'A couple of cans and you're falling asleep. I don't know,' his father said. 'You're no son of mine.'

Robbie laughed.

'I'm a lightweight,' he said. 'Goodnight.'

He went upstairs and got ready for bed. When he was lying down, he checked his phone and read the message from Alan. He turned off the light and tried to sleep.

He was still awake when the doorbell rang. He got up and walked to his door. He opened it silently and listened to the conversation coming up from the doorstep below.

'He's upstairs,' his father was saying. 'What's the problem?'

'Was he out? Why am I even asking? He's always out, isn't he? When did he get back?' Joe's voice was high-pitched. He sounded like an old woman.

'What are you talking about? It's half-eleven. Why are you knocking on my door?'

'Because your son did my car over.'

'When?'

'Tonight.'

'He's been here all night. He couldn't have gone near your car.'

'He must have got out. Where is he now?'

'He's in bed. He's been there for the past hour and a half. You'd want to be very careful making accusations. I don't know what your problem is but Robert's been here all night.'

His mother spoke then.

'He was with us all evening. He didn't leave the house.'

'What's the problem?' his father asked. 'What happened to your car?'

'It's destroyed. It's been keyed all over. It'll cost thousands to put it right.'

'Thousands? I don't know about that. And I don't care either. It's nothing to do with us. It could be anyone. But it wasn't him. I'm telling you that.'

'He's been operating a vendetta against me. Him and his gang.'

'He doesn't have a gang,' his mother said. 'They're just a group of young lads and you can't be blaming them for everything.' She was trying to calm him.

'I saw him today looking at me when I was driving out and then tonight I come back to my car and it's ruined. I know what it's all about. It's because I called the guards on him when they broke into that house a couple of weeks back. I'll call them again. I'm telling you. You may think he's some sort of angel but they've got his number. They'll know what to do with him.'

Robbie could hear the threat in his father's voice when he spoke.

'Look, I know perfectly well what my son is like. I know what he gets up to and it's just a group of bored young lads hanging around messing. That's all. I was the same. Most people were the same. Maybe not you. But you're talking shite. Robert was here all night. He did nothing to your car and I don't like you coming round here making accusations in the middle of the night and threatening us with the guards. You can do what you want, but they're not going to believe you and all your mad talk of vendettas and gangs. Where was your car?'

'In town.'

'Oh goodnight. Do you think you're the first had a car interfered with in town? Go to the guards. Tell them. They'll laugh at you. You'd want to cop onto yourself. Go to a doctor. But don't come back here ever again or we're going to have a serious problem. All right?'

Robbie listened to the silence. He could picture his father and the expression on his face. He could picture Joe in front of him, terrified.

'All right?' his father shouted. 'Now piss off and leave us alone.' He slammed the front door.

Robbie walked away from the door and got back into bed. He rolled over facing the wall. He could hear his parents talking in the hall downstairs. He waited, holding his breath. Their conversation was quick and low. He heard one of them coming up the stairs, then his door opened.

'Robbie?' his father said.

'What's going on?' he asked. 'Was someone at the door?'

'Joe Mitchell.'

'What did he want?'

'Christ knows. He's lost the plot.'

'He's a weirdo. Lunatic.'

'Yeah, well listen. You are not to go near him. I don't want you talking to him, looking at him, nothing. He's got it in for you. He's looking for trouble and you are not to give it to him. All right?'

'OK. What was he saying?'

'It doesn't matter what he said. Just stay away from him. The lot of you.'

'All right.'

His father stood outlined in the doorway, the light streaming in around him. Robbie couldn't see his face.

'You've got to watch yourself. You can't be hanging around acting the prick. I know there's no badness in it, but if you're not careful you could mess things up for yourself.'

'I didn't do anything,' Robbie said. 'What did he say?'

'Nothing. Don't worry about him. I'm just telling you to mind yourself.'

Robbie waited.

'OK. Fair enough.'

'Goodnight. Good man.'

'Goodnight,' Robbie said.

His father closed the door. Robbie lay there in the darkness on his back. He curled up in a ball and laughed silently, his whole body shaking, with the thrill and the fun of it all.

Paul got up early before any of the others. He left Ruth asleep in bed and went up the road to get the paper. The sun was out and the sky was blue. It hadn't rained in two weeks and Paul was beginning to hope that it would be a good summer. Hope but not believe. The traffic on the road was heavy, with commuters making their way towards town. Paul walked by them, free of it all. He could have been working in a grind institute teaching grumpy, unhappy, lazy kids whose parents made sure that their summers would be compromised by their sins of omission through the year. He could not put his own kids through it. Summer was about freedom. He could remember the thrill of those months when he was a kid, twelve weeks of nothing to do. He had never been bored, never looked for distraction, the distance from school enough in itself. He was still enjoying the same feeling that moment as he walked by the traffic clogged up at the lights.

It wasn't even a village, just a bunch of shops at a crossroads. It didn't have a name yet. They called it the shops or the cross. On one side there was a row of houses, old houses for the old people who had been there since this was still the country. Grey houses with dirty windows and net curtains and no light, as if they didn't want to see what had happened to the world outside. Opposite was a series of low, modern, custom-built units, with eaves and arches and new red brick with graffitied steel shutters. Low walls in front of the shops for kids to sit on, people waiting for the bus, people standing around smoking, queuing at the post office. There was a small supermarket, a Chinese takeaway, a bookie's, an off licence, a butcher, a video shop, another bookie's and a florist. Every time Paul went up he was struck by how chaotic it was. Kids on bikes and groups of young people and women with prams and shopping trolleys, all shouting and laughing but not happy. Everybody was too young. The girl in the shop, who had to get a manager to sell him wine because she was under age, the mothers with buggies, the security guards, the guy in the Chinese handing orders through a hatch. The ground was sticky outside the shops, splash stains and black chewing gum everywhere and Coke bottles and cigarette packets. There was nothing growing, nothing green, not one attempt at decoration or embellishment, as if the shops and their customers were engaged in a battle of mutual contempt. Fuck you, the shops said, you can't afford aesthetics. And the people responded by treating it like the shit-hole it was. All the young guys sitting along the wall, spitting on the ground. Fuck you too.

Paul tried not to hate it. He knew the reasons it was the way it was. It wasn't built for people like him. This was how other people had to live, forced into it with no option. They were stuck out here, going nowhere. He could go back to the house and drive in half an hour to their old area. He could get the same half-familiar treatment in the shops. He could get the things that he wanted and not have to make do. He could feel like he belonged. It was easy for him.

Not for this lot. The ones who went up to the council estate while Paul went down to their estate with trees and driveways and front gardens. It felt like home then. In contrast to the world that was five minutes up the road, this was where he wanted to be. It was almost as good as where they came from. Or it would be in twenty years.

It was when he was going back home, as he walked through the estate, that he met Joe Mitchell. Joe was wearing a Walkman and seemed to be talking to himself. When he saw Paul he took the headphones off and stopped.

'Lovely morning,' Paul said.

'You'd want to watch out,' Joe said.

Paul stopped, confused.

'Why? What's the problem?'

'I'm sorry. Yes, it is a nice day. It's warm. I'm distracted. I don't know what to do.'

Paul waited. Joe was looking around, anywhere it seemed but at him.

'There's people here are no good,' he said at last.

'Where?' Paul asked.

'Here. In that house there,' he said pointing. 'And that one. And there. Boys.'

'I don't know what you mean,' Paul said.

'Start again,' Joe said. 'These boys. You must have seen them. Standing around over there. Up to no good. Spitting and shouting and throwing things.'

'I know them,' Paul said. 'Are they really that bad? They're just bored. They've nothing better to be doing.'

'Everybody says that. Everybody makes excuses as if it's not their fault, the things they do. As if boredom let's them do anything.'

'Not at all,' Paul said. 'Just I've never seen them do anything wrong.'

'But they do. I see it. They throw things at me and they tell stories about me. Have you heard?'

'I've heard nothing. I wouldn't know.' Paul wanted to go. He wanted to be back with Ruth and the kids. But he waited. He could wait. He felt sorry for him.

'Well, it's all rubbish and lies but people will believe them. And I know it's because they've nothing better to do. I know that. But what good is that to me when it's my reputation they're destroying? When people look away and avoid me?'

He was staring at Paul, his eyes searching for recognition, for an answer.

'I don't know,' Paul said.

'They broke into your house, you know. Before you moved in. And last night they destroyed my car in town. Scratched all the paint. I went to the father of the main one and told him.'

'Did you?'

'I did. Whelan. Over there. He told me to . . . He told me . . . I won't say what he told me, but he threatened me. Covered for the boy and told me I was mad. Is it any wonder they're the way they are?'

'I don't know,' Paul said. 'I suppose so.'

'And people don't believe me. That's the thing. They think I'm making it up. Why would I? I just want to go about my business and be left alone. Why would I bring all this on myself?'

'OK,' Paul said. 'It's a problem.'

'You don't know me. I understand that. I'm sure you're wondering what sort of a fellow I am to be telling you this.'

'Not at all.' Paul's head was beginning to hurt.

'You're polite and I appreciate it. But the reason I'm telling you is because you have children. You have a girl and she's the same age as this lot and you should be careful because they're no bloody good. Watch them. That's all. I'm sorry. I don't want to worry you but you should know.'

'OK,' Paul said. 'Thanks very much. I'll bear it in mind.'

'Goodbye.'

'Goodbye. I'll see you.'

Paul walked back up to the house. He didn't know what to think. He wished now that he had stayed in bed. He knew that the complexion of the day had been changed. Cloudy now.

The others were up when he went in. They were in the kitchen sitting around the table.

'Where were you?' Ruth asked. 'There's coffee.'

'I was getting the paper. Thanks.'

'What kept you?'

'Joe Mitchell wanted to talk and I couldn't get away.'

Clare made a noise. Fin laughed.

'What?' Paul asked.

'Mad Joe Mitchell,' Clare said.

'Don't,' Paul said. 'It's sad. I don't know what's wrong with him but he's not happy. You shouldn't laugh.'

'He's a pervert. Apparently,' Clare said.

'A what?' Paul said.

'What?' Louise said. 'What is he?'

'Enough,' Ruth said. 'Clare, shut up.'

'Where did you get this?' Paul asked.

'Everybody says it. Everybody around here.'

'Paul,' Ruth said.

'OK. But you,' he said to Clare, 'I'll talk to you later.'

'What did Clare say?' Louise asked Ruth.

'Nothing,' Ruth replied.

'What are people doing today?' Paul said and that was it.

Later that morning, when Ruth went into town with Fin and Lou, Paul went out in the garden where Clare was lying on a blanket on the grass reading.

'Hiya,' she said.

'Listen.'

'Are we going to have a serious conversation?' she asked, smirking.

'I don't know.' He didn't know how to start. 'Listen,' he said again. 'Why did you say that earlier?'

'What? About mad Joe?'

'Clare. Don't talk about him like that. It's not fair.'

'He is mad.'

'He's not. Or I don't know. But you don't know either. And you can't just dismiss somebody that way. I would have thought you'd know better than that.'

She didn't react, just looked up at him.

'And a pervert? What the hell is that?' Paul went on.

'Do you need me to tell you what it means?'

'I know what it means. I know it's a stupid nasty word that stupid nasty people use and you're not like that. Where did you pick it up?'

'That's what the others were saying. They told me the story and apparently it's true. He's sick in the head.'

'What others? Who?'

'The guys. The ones who've been here for years. They all say it's true.'

'You should know better, Clare. You should know not to listen to stupid stories from a bunch of guys with nothing better to do.'

'Well, what do you know? We've been here like five minutes and you know it's not true? Do you even know what it is? Do you know what they told me?'

'I don't want to know. I don't want to listen to gossip.'

'Even if it's true?'

Paul had to think without being seen to.

'I don't know what's true and what's not. But I do know what he was telling me about those guys and there's obviously two sides to it.'

'Like what? What was he saying?'

'It doesn't matter. The point is that there's some problem between Joe and these guys and you can't assume that their story is right. He tells it his way and it's naive to just believe them.'

She laughed at him.

'How come I'm being naive but you're being sensible? How's that?'

Paul could feel the argument slipping away from him.

'Because he told me himself. He said that they had spread rumours about him. He asked me had I heard them. He told me that they were driving him mad and hassling him. He was really upset.'

'He could be pretending. Maybe he wants you to believe him.'

'But I do believe him, Clare. That's the point. And I know he's not normal and the way he talks and carries himself might make you believe any crap that people tell you, but I don't. I think he's a bit odd and maybe damaged and I hate the idea that you'd call anybody a pervert or mad or anything like that. I thought you were better than that. I thought we'd brought you up better.'

'Well, maybe you didn't,' she said. 'But remember that first day in the car. You and me, when we met him. You were laughing. Weren't you? The two of us were laughing at him then.' She spoke with a certainty that scared Paul.

'I shouldn't have. That was wrong. But it was different.'

'How?'

'Because it wasn't cruel. We laughed because it was funny and we didn't go around telling people about it.'

'You told Mum.'

'Yes, but—' Paul hated the fact that he was struggling. 'That's her.

That's completely different from a whole load of people spreading rumours and hassling him because he's different.'

'I don't know,' she said. 'I don't know how you can be so sure that what I heard isn't true. I don't know why you'd believe one person's word against ten people's.'

'Because of who they are,' Paul said. He was getting angry now. 'A whole load of young lads hanging around together all day. He probably told them to pick up their rubbish or something stupid and that would be enough to get it started. Get them talking and speculating and plotting. Do you know how easy it is to start a rumour? I know what young lads are like, Clare. Don't forget it. I work with them all the time and they can be hard and cruel and unfair and, whatever they tell you, you should remember that. These guys will do anything if they're bored. The truth doesn't matter. They're probably laughing at you to think that you'd believe whatever ridiculous lies they told you. They're picking on this guy because he's different. There's not a single thing that makes me think it's anything other than that.'

'He had a fourteen-year-old rent boy living with him for two months. Did you know that?'

Paul laughed.

'That's it? That's the story?'

'He did. They all said it. They even told me what he looked like.' She blushed as she said it.

'Clare, don't be an idiot. I've had enough now. I never want to hear you use that word again. I don't want you talking with anyone about Joe and if those guys start telling you stories about anyone else, whether they're believable or utterly stupid and ridiculous, you'd be a lot better off not listening. I know it's summer and you don't have a lot to be doing but, seriously, hanging around with this lot is doing you no good. I'm surprised at you.'

He went inside. He had been worried when they started talking but then he ended stronger. It wasn't the time to gloat, point made, just move on. He got juice out of the fridge and took a glass down from the cupboard.

'Do you want a drink?' he called out to her. She didn't answer. He walked to the back door and looked out. She was sitting up, faced away from the house.

'Clare?' he said.

'What?' she said without turning.

'Do you want a drink?'

'What?'

'Do you want some juice? Or anything?'

'No.'

He stood looking at her, waiting to see would she turn to look back at him but she stayed completely still.

'Are you OK?' he asked.

'I'm fine.'

'I'll be inside.'

'OK.'

He went in and sat on the couch in the living room reading the paper. The window was open and from outside he heard the sound of kids playing football on the green.

In the kitchen later on Paul and Ruth were finishing a bottle of wine. The dinner plates were still on the table. It was the first time they had been alone together that day. Ruth was doing the crossword and Paul sat across from her looking out the window at the back garden. The sky beyond the trees at the back wall was glowing red.

'It won't rain tomorrow,' he said. 'Apparently.' Ruth looked up and nodded before returning to the paper.

'It's great to have the garden to be able to enjoy it,' he said. The wine was having an impact.

'What?' Ruth said.

'The sun. The summer. We have the space to enjoy it now,' he said. 'I don't think the kids are going to miss going away. When the weather's like this, why would you go anywhere.'

'Are you all right?' she asked.

'Fine,' he said, glad to have her attention. 'Why?'

'You seem a bit morose.'

'No, I'm OK. Not used to drinking. I'm perfectly happy. Ask me something?'

'What?'

'From that,' he said, pointing.

'It's nearly done,' she said.

Clare came in.

'I'm going out.'

'OK,' Ruth said.

'Where?' Paul asked.

'Down the road. Is that all right?'

'What for?'

'Nothing. Just to see the others.'

'What are you going to do?' Paul said.

'Nothing. Jesus, if you're worried you can look out the window and watch,' she said.

'Go on,' Ruth said. 'Have fun.'

'OK. Bye.'

'What was that about?' Ruth asked Paul when they heard the front door close.

'"I'm going out," she says. We should ask surely?'

'But you know where she's going,' she said. 'Where else would it be? Isn't it good that she's making friends?'

Paul shrugged.

'Yeah. I suppose so. I don't know.'

She was looking at him.

'What?'

'Do you remember what she said this morning? That pervert thing?'

'Yeah. What was that about?'

'Apparently there's some stupid story going around about Joe Mitchell. He told me himself that those young guys had been spreading rumours about him. He was saying that they're waging some sort of campaign against him, hassling him and damaging his car. He was saying that they broke in here before we moved in. You wouldn't know what's going on, but there's some problem between them.'

'There's always somebody at war with the local kids in places like this.'

'I know but it's sad. You should have seen him this morning. He was nearly in tears.'

'But that's what he's like, isn't it? He's a delicate character. He's not happy.'

'I know, but Clare believed this stupid story that those guys told her about him. Totally stupid. I mean it was just obviously rubbish.'

'Well, she's only young. You know what it's like. They want to believe anything. It's not about the story. It's about the group of them together.'

'Yeah, but she should know better. A bunch of young lads talking crap.'

'She's just trying to fit in. What can she do?'

'I don't know. I don't know if that lot are good for her. I don't know if they're suitable. I mean who are they? I haven't met any of them.'

'They're the children of our neighbours.'

'So what?'

'So I'm sure they're fine.'

'They could be up to anything. They could be druggies or criminals or anything.'

'Ah Jesus, Paul. Look out the window at them. They don't do anything.'

'That's not what Joe was saying.'

'So are you going to believe him? He's hardly the most reliable witness. You have to trust Clare. She's bright enough. She's able to make her own judgements.'

'That's what I would have thought,' Paul said, exasperated. 'I would never have doubted her, but she sat on the grass out there and told me this ridiculous story.'

'What was it?'

Paul smiled. 'That Joe had a rent boy living with him for a couple of weeks. A young guy.'

Ruth laughed.

'I know,' Paul said. 'Exactly. She sat there and told me this. And she believed it. And calling him a pervert. It's dreadful. It's so bloody . . . I don't know. Tabloid.'

'It's ridiculous,' Ruth said, 'but wait and see. If that's the kind of conversation they're having, she'll see it for what it is and she'll get bored. She won't be bothered with them. She's new to the area and she's making an effort and that's good. Don't forget what she was like when we told her we were moving. And now, a couple of months later, she's happy and she's settling in. We should be glad.'

Paul sat back in his chair.

'You're right,' he said. 'You're probably right.'

'And the other two. Where are they? I can't hear them and how often could we say that before? Have you seen them? They're getting up early, they're out and about and doing things and I haven't heard any of them say once yet this summer that they're bored. Not once. They're meeting people, they're playing and we can see them the whole time. We don't need to worry. Or you don't need to worry. Because I'm not.'

'I know. You're right. But I do think we should check these guys out because we don't know who they are. We don't know what they're like and we should.'

'So talk to their parents. Go around and introduce yourself. Talk to them.'

'Maybe. Yeah.'

He stood up and started putting the plates in the dishwasher. Ruth sat watching him.

'She's old enough to make her own decisions,' she said. 'She'll be going off to college in a year and we won't have any control over who she meets or what she does. You know what she's like. She won't put up with any crap. She's not an idiot.'

'But she's so young.'

'She's five years younger than you were getting married.'

He smiled. She touched his hand as he passed her. He looked down at her.

'Everything is fine,' she said. 'Just relax.'

Out on the green Clare was with the others. Robbie was different tonight. He was leading the conversation. When he spoke the others guys listened in silence, waiting for the end, for the punchline, when they would dissolve and laugh and punch each other and spit. As Clare watched she realized that she had not seen Robbie laughing before, his face lit up and innocent. He looked younger. She smiled and he caught her eye. As he looked at her, he straightened up and she thought in the warm orange light of the evening that she could see him blush. She looked away.

He was talking about what they could do the following night.

'Let's go into town,' he said. 'Go to a club and get locked.'

'Let's get locked,' Tim said. Clare couldn't imagine him getting in anywhere.

'Why are we going into town?' one of the boys asked.

'Celebrating,' Robbie said. He looked at Alan and the two of them laughed. Tim and Liam smiled to themselves but they didn't mean it. They were lost.

'Celebrating what?' Clare asked.

'Summer,' Robbie said. 'It's a Saturday. Does there have to be a reason?'

Clare shrugged.

'Will you come?' he asked her. His gaze was so direct that Clare didn't speak for a moment. She realized then that they were all looking at her. Waiting for her response.

'Yeah, maybe. OK,' she said.

'Bring your friend,' he said. 'What's her name?'

Clare tasted the disappointment. Bitter.

'Emily,' she said. 'Sure. I'll see if she's free.'

'Got to keep Alan happy,' he said.

'What? Shut up, you,' Alan said. He punched Robbie on the arm and the two of them started fighting, messing around, slapping at each other. Clare smiled.

'There he is now,' Tim said. 'Scumbag.'

They turned and watched as Joe drove past on the way home.

'Leave it out, Tim,' Robbie said.

'What? Are you joking me?'

'Enough. Just fucking stop.'

Joe got out of his car and walked down to the end of the drive towards them.

'He's coming over,' Liam said. 'Robbie, look.'

'He won't come,' Robbie said without turning. As he spoke, Joe stopped and stood staring across at them.

'Is that true?' Clare asked. 'What you were saying the other day?'

'I swear to Jesus Christ,' Tim said. 'I saw him myself.'

Robbie nodded. 'It's true.'

'He's going in now,' Liam said.

'I told you,' Robbie said.

'How did you know?' Alan asked.

'My old man,' Robbie said. 'There's no way.'

Clare didn't understand. It was getting late.

'I'm going to go. I'll see you all tomorrow, yeah?'

'Yeah, we'll sort something out,' Alan said. 'We'll call up to you.'

'OK. See you.'

She walked away.

'Don't forget your mate,' Robbie called after her and when she looked back Alan was kicking him. She walked up to the house, her phone in her hand already texting Emily.

7

Clare waited in her bedroom for Emily to call over. She was getting ready to go out. She sat in front of the mirror thinking about how to broach the subject with her father. She knew what she was going to do and it worried her. She couldn't tell him what she was going to do. She knew what he would say if she told him and she couldn't do it. Emily was on her way. Everything that he thought about these guys was wrong. They were fine. They weren't idiots and neither was she. He should have trusted her to make her own decisions. She had never done anything to make them doubt her. She looked at herself and smiled slyly, realizing that she was conning herself. She had no option. They didn't trust her. Everything would be fine. They should let her make up her own mind. She was old enough. It was their own stupid fault. She would have to lie.

When Emily arrived she told her what the plan was. She told Emily to keep her mouth shut. She texted Robbie to arrange a place to meet them in town.

'It's better anyway,' she said. 'What were we going to do? Get the bus with them?'

'Yeah,' said Emily. 'Not likely.'

'We can be late. It's better.'

They went downstairs. Paul and Ruth sat in the living room watching TV, the two young ones in front of them on the floor.

'Don't you look lovely,' Ruth said when she saw them.

'Thanks,' Clare said. 'Listen.'

'Oh no,' Paul said.

'What?'

'You're going to say something that's going to upset me.'

'Why would you think that?' Clare said, smiling.

'Am I right?'

'You're not really doing anything, are you?' she said. 'I mean you're not even watching this. And the car outside. I can hear it. It's cold and lonely. It wants to be driven.'

'Where does it want to go?' Paul asked.

'I don't know,' Clare said, looking at Emily. 'What do you reckon? Into town?'

'That should do it,' Emily said. 'Keep it happy.'

'What's the occasion?' Ruth asked.

'Nothing. Just some people meeting up in town.'

'In a pub,' Fin said. 'They're going to get mouldy.'

'Shut up, you,' Clare said. Paul was looking at her. 'When have I ever?' she asked him.

'I said nothing,' he said. 'Who's going to be there?'

'Just some of the crowd from school. Caroline and those.'

'When will you be back?'

'I don't know.'

'Come on. How are you going to get home?'

'Taxi.'

'At what time?'

'Two?'

'How about twelve?' Paul said.

'Oh, come on. It's a Saturday. Things will only be getting going.'

'One,' Ruth said. 'OK?'

'OK,' the two girls said.

'So what? Do you want to go now?'

'If you're ready.'

'I'm ready,' Paul said. 'What else would I be doing?'

They walked out to the car. Clare sat in the front, Emily in the back behind Paul. As they drove by the green, the guys standing there waved to them.

'Dopes,' Clare said as she lifted her hand. In the back Paul heard Emily laugh.

When they arrived in the centre of town Paul stopped.

'Have you money?' he asked Clare. She smiled at him.

'I've some,' she said.

'Have you enough?'

'How much is enough?'

'I don't know,' he said. He took his wallet out and held a twenty in front of her.

'This is for your taxi and whatever else you need. Don't spend it all on drink. OK? I'll be waiting for you when you get back and I'm going to check you. I'll know if you're drunk.'

'Relax,' she said. 'Jesus, you're embarrassing.' She reached out and he pulled the note back.

'I'm paying you enough for it. Sorry, Emily, for delaying you. You're not embarrassed, are you?'

'I am a bit, yeah.'

'Well, watch out for each other and be careful.'

'We will,' Clare said. He gave her the note and the two of them were out in a second.

'Hang on,' he called after them. Clare stuck her head around the door.

'What's up?'

'You have your phone?'

'Yeah.'

'Well, ring if there's any problem. OK?'

'OK,' she said. 'Stop worrying.'

'I can't help it,' he said and she smiled at him. It was enough to break his heart.

He didn't know that he'd have to do this. It had never occurred to him that he would be delivering his seventeen-year-old into the centre of town so that she could drink with her friends. She was sensible and smarter than the others but still he had to worry. Everything that everybody said about the city, the violence and drunkenness, made him wonder was he doing the right thing. The streets were packed with people heading out for the night, all young. Guys and girls in groups all laughing and pushing. When he stopped at traffic lights he could feel the bass pounding out of the bar beside him, the noise of music and people shouting, the bouncers in black standing on the door, pent up with rage, waiting for one of these fuckers to put a foot wrong, say something smart that would let them unleash their energy. It was a hard cruel ugly world and he'd left her in it. For a moment he wanted to pick up his phone and ring her. Turn around and get her and bring her back to the house. They could watch a video, all of them together. Anything. As long as he could see her and know that everything was all right. But as he drove on he got himself together. He was getting old. He couldn't see the fun of it. He had forgotten what it was like to be that age, the thrill of the world outside, the joy that could be found, the friendship and love and excitement. She would be all right. Ruth would tell him when he got back. You have to let them live. Make their own worlds. It would be easier with the others when the time came. But she was the first. And she was a girl. Such risk. So close to danger. Her life could be ruined by being in the wrong place, making the wrong decision. Anything could happen and they were risking it all. That was a fact. He knew it had to be this way but he didn't have to like it and he didn't. Bite his lip. Smile. Nod. Watch her grow up. Let it happen. He was an observer now. That was all. He stopped at a garage and bought himself an ice cream and then when he was walking out he turned around and bought three more for the others at home.

Clare and Emily stood at the statue waiting for the others. They were late.

'Let's go,' Clare said. 'Walk around the block. I don't want to be here when they arrive.'

'Yeah, but what if we miss them? What if they don't wait?'

'They'll wait,' Clare said.

'They might not.'

'They will,' Clare said. 'Trust me, I know.'

'How do you know?' Emily asked, laughing.

'You weren't there when they invited us. If you'd seen them, you'd be sure.'

By the time they got back, the others were there.

'Sorry we're late,' Clare said.

'No problem. We were late anyway,' Alan said. 'Bleeding buses.'

'No buses for you,' Liam said. 'Travelling in style. What way did your old fellow come that you're only getting in now?'

'He had to stop,' Clare said. She didn't look at him and he didn't say anything else. Robbie was standing at the back. He was wearing a shirt and jeans. He looked better dressed up. He hadn't spoken yet. As they walked down towards Temple Bar, she slowed her pace until she was walking beside him.

'How are you?' she asked.

'All right,' he said. He seemed nervous. She'd never seen it in him before.

'Did you do anything today?' he asked after a minute.

'Not really. Hung around the house. Lay in the sun for a bit.'

'It was hot today,' he said.

'Yeah.'

He laughed to himself. 'I need a drink. Here, where are we going?' and he walked ahead among the other guys. Emily and Clare stood at the back.

'What's going on?' Emily asked her.

'I don't know,' Clare said.

'What were you talking about?'

'The weather.'

'That's great,' Emily said. 'Alan hasn't said one word to me. You're doing well.'

'I don't know if I can be bothered with this,' Clare said. 'We'll go along and see what happens, but if it stays like this will we just go?'

'Sure,' Emily said but Clare knew she wasn't.

They got into the pub. The bouncers checked them for ID. He took Clare's student card, looked at it front and back, then waved them through. The bouncer put his hand in front of Tim and took his card. He asked him his date of birth and Tim told him. It made him nineteen.

'I'll be watching you,' the bouncer said as he handed it back.

'What's the story?' Tim said. 'It's not my fault I look young.'

It was a dark basement. The ceiling was low and the air was heavy, the smell of cigarettes and sugary fruit hanging. Robbie stood at the packed bar and bought a round for everyone. They sat on couches at a round table set into the wall beside the tiny dance floor. The table was covered in bottles, all the same drinks, cigarettes, mobiles. They all smoked. Clare sat beside Robbie on one side, Emily on the other, then Alan. The other two sat on the ends. It was hard to hear with the music pounding from a speaker above them. Clare and Emily talked to each other. Alan watched them, waiting for an opportunity to get into the conversation. Robbie spoke to Liam. Clare saw Tim on the end, looking around the room. He looked so young compared to the others, out of place.

'Is Tim OK?' she asked Robbie.

'I don't know. Tim,' he called over. 'Tim.'

'What?' They saw his lips move.

'Are you OK?'

'What?'

Robbie smiled at him. Tim shrugged and looked away.

'He'll be all right in a bit,' Robbie said to Clare, leaning in close, speaking into her ear. She could feel the warmth of his body beside her, could smell aftershave and chewing gum and the sweet smell of the drink on his breath. 'He'll go off now and find himself some young one.'

Clare laughed. She looked at him, his face only inches from hers.

'Really? Him?'

'Another couple of drinks and he'll be off. Watch him.'

Alan went to get another drink for them.

'I can give you money,' Clare said.

'Not at all. You're grand,' he said.

She smiled at him.

'I don't know a lot but I know that much,' he said.

'Very nice,' Clare said to Emily when he was gone. 'You're doing well there.'

'I like him,' Emily said.

'So you don't want to go.' She tried not to laugh when she saw the expression on Emily's face.

'Do you?' Emily said, her voice full of concern. 'Because we can if you want.'

Clare laughed.

'I'm only messing with you,' she said.

'How are you getting on?'

'Fine. I think.'

'He definitely likes you.'

'I don't know.'

'He does.'

'Did Alan say something?'

'No. But I can see.'

'Me too,' Clare said and the two of them laughed because it was funny. Clare looked at her watch. It was nine o'clock. There was plenty of time.

When Alan came back, Tim stood up and let him sit beside Emily. They passed the bottles around and drank, clinking bottles together.

'So where do you want to go later on?' Robbie asked Clare. She watched as Tim stood up and came over and said something to Liam. The two of them wandered off, bottles in hand. They disappeared into darkness and noise.

'I don't know,' Clare said. When she looked over she saw that Emily and Alan were kissing, his hand behind her head, leant back on the couch.

'That didn't take long,' she said to Robbie. He smiled. When she thought about it a second later she couldn't remember who had moved first, but all she knew was that she was kissing him. Her eyes closed, the sound of the pub around them faded away and all she could feel was his mouth on hers, her tongue in his mouth and it was good.

'I fancied you the first time I saw you,' he said. 'That day you came in the car with your parents. You didn't see me, but I saw you and I couldn't believe that you were going to live across the road.'

She smiled at him.

'Shut up,' she said and they kissed again.

They spent the rest of the evening on the couch. The boys bought drinks and they stopped occasionally to smoke cigarettes and drink.

'What's he like?' Emily asked her when Robbie had gone to the bar.

'All right,' Clare said. 'What about your one?'

'Not bad,' Emily said.

'What are we going to do after?' Alan asked. 'Go to a club or something?'

'I don't know,' Clare said. 'We should probably go home after this.'

'Ah, come on,' he said. 'It's Saturday.'

'We could go somewhere,' Emily said, 'just for a bit.' She was looking at Clare. Clare could feel the worry start to grow again.

'Maybe for a bit.' Emily smiled and turned back to Alan. Clare looked at her watch. It was half-eleven.

They got their stuff together, the four of them. They found Tim with some girl at the bar. He was standing with his arm around her. She was taller than him. She looked about twenty-five.

'We're going,' Robbie said.

'Where?'

'I don't know. Club. Are you coming?'

Tim looked at the girl and she nodded. 'All right.'

They found Liam and left. Out on the street they walked down towards the river in twos, Liam in front of them on his own. They came to a door down a lane. The queue disappeared around the corner.

'I don't know,' Clare said to Emily. 'This is going to take ages.'

'Five minutes,' Emily said. 'I swear that's all. Can we just go in and have a look? Five minutes. One minute even.'

She was drunk, Clare could see now. But what could she do? They were all there.

Clare paid for Emily and herself. She handed over the twenty that Paul had given her and waited for change until the girl in the cubicle shouted next. She took the tickets and they went in.

She stood with Robbie on a balcony overlooking the dance floor.

The crowd moved in unison, bouncing up and down, facing the DJ. Robbie's arm was around her waist as they stood. She was trying to think how she could do this. Could she go out and phone home and tell them some lie? Could she say that there were no taxis and her phone had died? Was there any way she could just relax and enjoy this and stay until the end? She thought about it but could find nothing.

'I have to go,' she said to Robbie.

'Why? Do you not like it?'

'No. It's not that. I have to get home.'

He looked at her and saw that she was embarrassed.

'You stay,' she said. 'I'm sorry. I don't want to go, but I have to.'

'Is it your parents?' he asked her.

'Yeah,' she said, looking away.

'I'll come with you,' he said.

'You don't have to.'

'I will.'

They went and found Emily and Alan.

'We've got to go,' Clare said.

'What?' Alan said. 'Already?'

'We have to,' she repeated.

Alan looked at Robbie, who just nodded.

'Can you not stay?' Alan said to Emily. Emily looked at Clare hopefully.

'You can do what you want,' she said.

'I better go,' Emily said. 'We can't stay a bit?' she asked Clare. Clare sighed. Drunk people were a pain in the ass.

'I'm going,' she said. She turned and walked off. When she got to the door Robbie was right behind her.

'Where is she?' Clare asked.

'She's coming now.'

Emily arrived and they walked outside into the cool air. Alan and the others stayed behind. They walked up to the Green and queued for a taxi. Clare had an arm around Emily, who was getting depressed. She was going to start crying. Robbie stood away from them, watching the queue. When their car came he got in the back and told the driver where they were going. Emily got in the front.

'Oh here,' the driver said. 'If this bird pukes, my night's ruined.'

'She's grand,' Robbie said. 'Aren't you?' He put a hand on Emily's shoulder. She looked up.

'I'm fine.'

'You're not going to puke?'

'No. I am not going to puke,' she said.

Clare sat in the back holding hands with Robbie. None of them spoke. The red light of the clock on the dashboard said two twenty-five. Clare rested her head on Robbie's shoulder and thought about her story.

When they pulled into the estate, Robbie directed him to go up the back towards Clare's house. He paid the driver and they got out.

'OK,' Clare said. 'Thanks for everything.'

'No problem.'

'I have to get her in, you know. I'm sorry.'

'I know.'

'I'll see you tomorrow or whatever.'

'OK,' he said. He stood two feet away from her. Clare was standing with her back to the house, wondering what was happening. Her father could be on the doorstep or standing in the window looking out. She could feel the presence of the house towering above her, bearing down behind her. Then as she was about to turn away, leave Robbie standing there on his own, she changed her mind and stepped forward and kissed him. She was as quick as she could be.

'I've got to go,' she said again. 'I'm sorry.'

'You're all right. I'll see you later.'

'I'll talk to you tomorrow, OK?'

'OK. See you.'

Clare took Emily by the hand and led her up to the house. As she was opening the door, she looked back down the drive out to the road. Robbie waved once before turning away and walking across the green to his own house.

Paul woke with a start from a dreamless sleep. He thought backwards, trying to hear the echo of what had woken him. Then he heard the noise from the hallway, his daughter whispering.

'They're back,' Ruth said.

'What time is it?'

She sat up and looked at the clock beside the bed.

'A quarter to three. Can that be right?'

'No way.'

Paul got out of bed and put on trousers and a T-shirt. He went downstairs. In the kitchen Clare was standing at the sink, the cold tap running. Emily was sitting at the table, her head resting in her hands. Clare looked around as he walked in. She looked scared.

'So?' he said.

'I know. I know. I'm sorry.'

'You're two hours late. Where the hell were you? What happened?'

'I'm so sorry.'

'Did something happen? Are you OK?'

'We're fine. It just took ages to get a taxi.'

'How long were you waiting? Two hours?'

'Something like.'

'Why didn't you ring?'

'My phone died. Emily didn't have hers.'

'Oh, for Christ's sake, Clare. There's a payphone on every corner.'

'I know. I didn't think. We didn't want to lose our place in the queue.'

'Well, which was it?'

She looked at him. He could see her trying to figure out what she should say. Whatever it was, he knew he couldn't believe her. She turned away and said nothing.

'Are you all right, Emily?' he asked, looking at her. She lifted her head and he saw that she was drunk.

'I'm fine. I'm sorry too.'

'Did you have a bit to drink?' he asked her.

'No. We only had a couple of bottles. I'm OK.'

'You don't feel sick or anything.'

'No. Why does everybody keep asking me that? I'm fine. I'm not going to puke.'

'Well, go to bed the two of you. Clare, come in here for a sec.'

He walked with her into the living room and closed the door behind them.

'I'm not even going to ask you again what happened. We'll talk in the morning. You know this is not acceptable. Is Emily all right?'

'She'll be fine.'

'She's totally pissed. You're going to have to keep an eye on her.'

'I will. I don't know what happened to her.'

'Don't be stupid, Clare. Don't insult me. Just make sure she's OK.'

He was about to leave and then stopped, unable to hold back.

'Whatever about anything else. I just cannot believe you let her get into that condition. Do you understand that we're responsible for her? If she gets sick and chokes in the night, it's our fault. Her parents will blame us and what are we supposed to say? That we trusted you? That we believed you when you said you'd be careful? I don't think they're going to be too impressed with that. Because what they'll see is that we took a chance with their daughter's safety because we decided to believe you. They'd say that we should have taken our responsibility more seriously and they'd be right.'

She was crying silently.

'Go to bed,' he said and went back upstairs.

'What happened?' Ruth asked as he walked into the bedroom.

'I don't know. Some story about taxis. They weren't able to phone because . . . I don't know. I didn't even bother trying to find out. Emily is drunk and Clare is crying. I said we'd deal with it in the morning. I told her to keep an eye on Emily, but I'll go in myself later on. I don't know. What do you think?'

'I think you're right. We'll leave it until the morning. We'll find out what happened then. Will they be OK tonight?'

'I don't know. Probably.' He stood at the side of the bed getting undressed. 'We have to do something about it.'

'We'll deal with it. We'll sort it out in the morning.'

'I was right to leave it, wasn't I? Not to push it now.'

'You were absolutely right.'

He got into bed beside her. He set the alarm for an hour later and turned out the light. He lay there on his back, listening to the cistern in the attic refilling.

'What were they doing?' he said into the darkness. 'And why were we asleep? We should have been up. We should have known they were so late. We should have done something.'

'They're home now. They're OK. We couldn't have done anything anyway.'

'I don't know.'

'And maybe she's telling the truth. Maybe it did take them that long to get a cab. Everybody's always going on about it. You know that.'

'I suppose so.'

He was beginning to drift, his mind just starting to race when the alarm rang. He went into the landing and pushed open the door to Clare's room. The light streamed in, picking out the two shapes. Emily was in the bed and Clare on a mattress on the ground. He stood in the doorway and held his breath to hear theirs. He stepped forward and looked down on them, both asleep. They were fine. They were different people from the two who had left the house earlier. He thought of how he would look in on Clare when they first put her in a room on her own, before the others were born, woken by the fear that someone so new to the world might have forgotten how to keep herself alive. He remembered the same relief. The same tenderness. The wonder that she could be taken from him in an instant without reason or fault. He pulled the door shut and went back to bed.

Clare was not asleep. She heard Paul come in. She felt his gaze as it fell on her. She had not wanted to let him down. She didn't want this distance between them. She had had no choice. It was the conflict between her world and theirs. If they had seen her when she tried to leave. If they had seen Emily and how she had pushed her. If they had known that she met this boy. They could have understood. They must remember what it was like. How could they forget? When you're out and everything is there, everything that you want is in front of you, promised and available. She was supposed to walk away from it then. Who could do that? She knew the reasons that they would be angry and disappointed and worried. She understood them. But she knew too that she would not be able to explain that it was all innocent and fun. They thought she was too young for this but she could handle it. Emily couldn't, but that wasn't Clare's fault. None of it was her fault. As Paul closed the door she wanted to sit up and call him back and hold him and tell her she was sorry and that he shouldn't worry. But what was the point?

In the morning Fin was out the back mowing the lawn. He had

moaned when Paul told him to do it but now it was great. The machine was better than their old one. It was about twice as big and it started first time and it had a handle on it that when you pushed it up made it go. It just took off and he had to run after it. It was brilliant. It ate everything in front of it, a shorn yellow path left behind him. The grass was long and lazy. It was full of dirty daisies and he was sorting it out, killing them in straight lines, mowing them down. He didn't even have to steer it. He could take his hands away and run behind it as the animal machine did its work. Up and down. Into the edges of the flower beds, the crackling growling as it sucked up soil and stones. When it began to chug, he turned it off and emptied the bag on top of the pile his father had started a week before. It was hot when you put your hand into the middle of the rotting grass. Hot enough to burn you. He made Lou put her hand in and when she'd pulled it out and burst out crying, he'd had to pay her off not to tell. It smelt weird. Sweet and a bit like shit. It was almost nice. Then back to the machine, his machine, and off again. He was doing it. Getting it done. If he could do this, did it mean that he could drive? It seemed to be the same. His father had said that with the weather they should be cutting the grass twice a week. If he could get ten quid out of him every time he'd be doing all right. In his head he tried to count the number of weeks left in the summer and multiplied it out and added to what he already had he could maybe save something. All for doing nothing because this wasn't work.

When he had finished he cleaned off the mower and put it back in the garage. He went around the back and looked at the lawn. He'd done a good job. He had to show them. He went into the kitchen. His mother and father and Clare were sitting around the table. Emily must have gone home when he was working.

'Come and see,' he said. 'It's all done and I only took twenty minutes. Come and see.'

His father looked up. For a second Fin thought he'd done something seriously badly wrong.

'What is it?' he asked.

'I'll be out to you in a bit, Fin. Go on ahead.'

Fin looked at Ruth but she was staring down at the table and then he saw that Clare was crying or had been, her face red and puffy.

'What did you do?' he said, teasing. 'Did you get drunk?'

'Out, Fin. Go on,' Ruth said.

'I want you to see this, though.'

'Get out,' his father shouted. Fin walked backwards out the door and closed it. He stood beside it for five minutes not moving, listening, trying to hear what was going on. There was nothing. Maybe the door was too thick, but then he heard a chair being pushed back and somebody stood up and he ran as fast as he could around the side of the house out to the front garden, where he sat on the grass and tried to look like he'd been there for ages.

It wasn't until that evening when they were standing at the rock that Robbie saw Clare for the first time that day. She walked out of the house with her parents and then the two young ones. They all got in the car and backed out of the drive.

'There's your mot,' Tim said as they drove by. Robbie looked over but he couldn't see her. Her mother was in the front passenger seat and the young fellow in the back window. They didn't look too happy. For a second he could see her, see the side of her face. She didn't look over. Robbie felt the wrench as he watched the car pull out onto the main road.

'Don't think much of that,' Alan said. 'Did she just blank you?'

'She didn't see me,' Robbie said without thinking. The other three laughed.

'Yeah, right.'

'She fucking blanked you.'

'She must have been locked last night.'

'I know I was.'

Rage hit Robbie hard, slapped him across the face and asked him what was he going to do. They couldn't talk like that. In front of him. What the fuck? He punched the rock and didn't feel the pain. They shut up quick enough. Pricks. He grabbed Tim by the back of the neck because he was closest. When he looked at him, he saw that blood was running down his knuckles, staining the back of Tim's jacket.

'Don't think that I—' He trailed off. He knew what he wanted to say but he didn't know if he should. He had done enough. He let Tim go.

'What's wrong with you?' Liam asked.

'Nothing,' Robbie said. 'Let's do something. This is a fucking waste of time.'

8

Paul spent the rest of the weekend trying to avoid Clare around the house. She wandered from room to room seeking him out so that she could flop onto a chair across from him, turned away from him, subjecting him to her silence until he ended up lying on the bed in their room reading the paper.

'Does she even know she's doing it?' he asked Ruth when she found him.

'Ask her.'

'I can't. How can I? That's what she wants. She's just waiting for the opportunity to ignore me. She's following me around like a sick cat to show me that she's not speaking to me. If I ask her she'll just do that shut-down thing she does.'

'Well, tell her not to, Paul. She's in the wrong. We shouldn't let her sulk.'

'Yeah, but if I start talking to her I'll just get annoyed. I'll start shouting and then I'll be in the wrong. I'm just trying to preserve the moral high ground here. If I talk to her I'll lose it.' She was looking at him.

'You sort it out,' he said to her. His tone was pleading. More than he had realized.

'I can't, Paul. You've got to tell her. You can't be afraid of her.'

'I'm not afraid of her. It's me.'

'Well, that's no good either. What's the problem?'

'I'm just sick of how she treats me.'

'She's upset and annoyed at the moment. But it's not your fault. She knows that.'

'But it's not just now. Not just this. It's all the time. Like I'm an idiot.'

'She's a teenager, Paul. You know what they're like better than me.'

'Yeah, but I can't remember the last normal conversation I had with her.'

'Do you really need me to tell you? She's upset because she has to live with her parents and her stupid brother and sister. She's upset because she doesn't have the money to do what she wants. And because we think we know what's best for her but she believes that the only one who can decide that is her. That's it. That's all it is. You can't let it get to you.'

He lay back on the bed and looked at the ceiling.

'It's more than that. I'm telling you there's something wrong there. There's something not right with her.'

'Well, I don't know. I don't know what you're talking about. Try and work it out one way or another. You can't hide away up here. You're worse than her. Seriously. Her sulking. You hiding. I've got four kids.'

She left. He got up to follow her and then sat back down and waited.

It wasn't just the row with Clare. They'd been fair with her. She had broken the rule after she'd agreed to it so she shouldn't complain. She'd known she would be punished for it. She could have done something to avoid it if she'd tried a bit harder at the time. No point sulking now. But why wouldn't she? She couldn't go out. She was stuck there in the house so why should she try to be nice? Why would she bother?

Because she should. She should know. She was old enough. There was something more. There was something and he could feel its disruption in the air in the house. Here we all are and we are happy. But it didn't feel right.

He tried to think but nothing came to him through the fog of seventeen years of inaction. Having children had made him stupid. He couldn't read these situations any more. He didn't deal with people. He didn't have instincts. He used to have a brain to parse, read, interpret, analyse. Now he just had children. He stood up and walked out of the room. Let Ruth worry about it. Her instincts were still good.

Clare lay on the bed in her room. The window was open and the sound of the young kids playing football on the green came in to her. Shouting and cursing and arguing and cheering. It never stopped. Stupid boys. Stupid kids. Fighting and shouting.

She was annoyed with her father. She had to remind herself of it when she woke in the morning. She didn't know how long it would last but she knew that he didn't know how to deal with her. She wanted to keep it going out of interest. As an experiment. For research. What would he do when he didn't know? When he wasn't sure? It wasn't that he was in the wrong. She knew that she had to take some punishment for it. It wasn't her fault but there was no point in telling them that. What she told them the morning after was exactly how she felt. That she knew that she had made a mistake and shouldn't have let Emily get so pissed and that she should have rung. But she had been in control at all stages. They needn't have worried. She knew that it was too late to tell them this now, but there had never been a problem. She told them this because she didn't want the same bollocking that her father gave Fin when he got mouthy or broke a window. She was beyond that now and she thought they would be capable of understanding that.

But no. She sat and watched as Paul talked himself into a fury.

Talking about drowning and rape and spiked drinks and all the evils of a night in town. Could have. Should have. Might have. Anything. How worried they had been.

'When you woke up,' she said when it got too much, breaking into his flow. He didn't hear her at first. He wasn't listening but then it registered.

'What?'

'You can't have been that worried,' she said. 'You were asleep when we got in. That's all I'm saying.'

'It's not the point. It's not the point at all. I can't believe you.'

'You can't have been that worried if you were asleep. I can't sleep if I'm worried.' She kept her face straight but she was enjoying how lost he seemed, buying time while he thought.

'I was tired,' he said. 'Tired of you and your stupid bloody friends. Driving you around like a chauffeur and handing out cash like some ... money machine. I don't know. I don't know how you can sit there—'

And on he went. She wanted to laugh. But why bother? Sit there and let him finish. It was too much. She looked at Ruth and could see that even she was getting bored. When he told her she couldn't go out for the rest of the summer, she knew that he was just charged up and there was no point objecting. She could change it later. If she said anything now he'd stick to it.

So what else could she do? He wasn't prepared to have a normal conversation. He wasn't going to treat her as she deserved to be treated, as an equal. So she was going to be a sulky little girl and not talk to him because she knew it drove him mad. It was a cold war that caused him discomfort and made her want to laugh. She wasn't being cruel. Just showing him. Making him think because sometimes he needed to think. As soon as Ruth said the word she'd call it all off and feel him relax again. She hoped it would be soon for his sake, but she wouldn't make the first move because she had to make him see. If he wanted to keep her around the house all the time, all summer long, he was going to have to put up with her silent presence.

She didn't mind not going out. Emily could come over and she could talk on the phone. Nothing was happening anyway. Most people were away or working or doing grinds. She could lie around the back garden and get a tan because the sun was there every day. She had seen Robbie the previous week. She was going to a film with all of them, all her family. She knew he would be there when she walked out of the house to the car and as she got in she was still trying to decide what to do. Look up. Wave. Nod. No. Do nothing. Send no signal for him to misinterpret. Don't have him talking in front of his friends. She kept her head down as they went by and then she wished she'd looked up to see him. Just to see him.

Because he was nice the previous night. He was a good-looking boy when he looked up and spoke. He was a good-looking boy when he looked at the ground and didn't say anything. Maybe he was brighter than the others. They shut up when he spoke. And when he talked to her he looked her in the eye and his voice was different, like the two of them were on a different level. He smiled a lot that night and he bought drinks and he kissed her more slowly and gently than she had thought he would. She had been ready to kiss him hard. To bite and push but then he was softer and it was better. He held her while they were waiting for the taxi and it was normal. She was comfortable then and if she hadn't had to go she wouldn't have. She would have stayed out with him and gone wherever they were going. He didn't talk too much and he was cool without trying. She wanted to see him again.

She knew afterwards that not looking up was better. It made her seem stronger and not some pathetic little girl going to a film with her parents and her kid brother and sister. She thought that maybe he'd be pissed off, that he'd think she was ignoring him and that he would go off and head out with Alan to find other girls. Lots of other girls. But he liked her. He couldn't hide it from her. He didn't try to. Nobody ever talked to her like that. Even the guys before. They didn't look at her. She was in charge. But maybe this guy was more. Maybe there was something more. She wanted to find out.

She was lying on the bed. She was thinking about stupid boys outside and the nice boy. Her nice boy. Nice – what a shit word. Because he wasn't really nice. And she didn't want to be nice to him. She wanted to have space and time to see what happened and let it happen because he seemed all right. She wasn't thinking about Paul when he came in.

'We're going to go to the beach,' he said. 'We're going down to Brittas. Do you want to come?'

She shrugged. She had to say something. He hadn't spoken to her in days.

'Do I have to?' she asked. 'I mean—' She stopped when she heard the stupid clichéd teenage phrase come out and couldn't think of anything else. 'Yeah. Do I have to?' She stretched and yawned like it didn't matter.

'I don't care,' he said.

'Well, then I won't.'

She didn't enjoy the pain that was in his face when he nodded and tried to smile.

'Thanks,' she said to his back as he was going. He didn't turn around. She felt bad. She thought about how he had pissed her off and about the lesson that he had to learn. How life would be better for them both if she held firm. It started to depress her so she picked up a book from under her bed and read the last page.

She came down when she heard the front door opening and the

noise of them loading the car. In and out with bags and food and drinks and Fin and Lou shouting at each other. Ruth looked at her as she came down the stairs.

'You're not coming,' she said.

'No.'

'Why?'

'I'll stay here. I'll be fine.'

'Yeah, but it's a lovely day. You could swim. You can lie on a beach instead of hanging around here on your own.'

'I don't mind being on my own.'

'OK,' Ruth said and again Clare felt a pull. She could be a part of this happy family. She could drop the silence and start talking to Paul, say one small thing to him and she knew he would melt. It would be over and they'd all go to the beach and she could play with Lou in front of a whole load of other happy families and make Lou laugh and talk to her and have a nice time. Enjoy herself instead of always being on the edge, not one thing or another. She could have that day and probably go out tomorrow night with Emily if she wanted. If she could make Paul laugh enough. She could do all that. But she wouldn't and when she wondered why she knew the answer but she didn't let herself think about it in case it would show. She felt herself blush. Sitting on the bottom step of the stairs as they moved around her, she looked at the floor until it passed but no one was looking.

'Why aren't you coming?' Lou asked.

'Cos she's not allowed. Because she got drunk as a skunk,' Fin said.

'Shut up, Fin,' her father said. 'She can come if she wants but she doesn't want to.'

'Why?' Lou asked her again, standing in front of her, a hand pulling at Clare's jeans.

'I'm lazy,' Clare said. 'I can't be bothered.'

'It'll be fun.'

'You'll have fun.'

'I won't,' Lou said. 'Make her come,' she said to Ruth who was passing.

'I won't make her do anything,' Ruth said. 'Come on. Get in the car, Lou.'

Lou went out. Paul and Fin were outside messing around arranging stuff in the boot.

'See you later,' Ruth said.

'Yeah, OK.'

'I don't know why you're not coming. It's silly.'

'I'm just not into it.'

'Yeah, well,' Ruth said. 'That's been going on long enough. OK?'

'OK.'

'I'm serious. Enough of the moody thing. It's not fair.'

'OK. OK.'

Ruth smiled at her.

'And don't go out. You're not allowed to go out.'

'I'm not going to go out.'

'I know,' Ruth said. 'Ring if there's a problem.'

'OK. But there won't be.'

'See you later.'

Afterwards Clare was glad that she hadn't asked when they'd be back. She wanted to know, but it would have been wrong to ask because it might have made Ruth think. And if Ruth had thought about it, she might have worked it out and then they would have turned around and come straight back. But she hadn't asked. Because she knew that they would be gone for the day.

She went into the kitchen and looked at the phone and pretended that she wasn't going to pick it up. She looked at it, turned away, sat down, stood up and then lifted it and she dialled. She rang Emily first. They talked for half an hour and then she rang him.

She couldn't remember the conversation afterwards. She sat down when she spoke to him. She knew that because she felt dizzy when she was talking to him. Nothing to do with him, but because of the risk she was taking. It was a simple conversation. All she knew was that she had asked him did he want to come up and he had said yes. He would be there in less than five minutes. Maybe she should have done something. Gone to put on make-up or made her bed or stood and looked at herself in the mirror and seen what he would see, but she didn't. She sat at the kitchen table and waited. She wasn't sure what she would do. What she was doing. She didn't have time to think. As the car pulled out of the drive, she had walked to the phone. Don't think. Just do. Because she knew what it was. She knew what she wanted. Too late now to change it. Then he was at the door and she had to go.

He was nervous. She could see it when she opened the door. He saw her and said hi and looked down. He walked by her into the hall. When she closed the door and turned around he was waiting behind her, standing rigid. She could feel herself relax as she walked by him into the kitchen and then on out into the back garden.

'Come on,' she said when she saw him hesitate.

They sat opposite each other on the grass in the sun. The sun was behind her and when he spoke, he had to shield his eyes with his hand.

'Where are your parents?'

'Out.'

'And the others?'

'All out.'

'So we're alone.'

'Yeah. Do you want a drink or something?'

'Do you have a Coke?'

'We'll have something.'

She stood up and went inside. From the fridge she took a bottle. As she poured out two glasses she looked at him sitting with his back to her. As she watched he took off his top and then sat on it. He was wearing a T-shirt underneath. His arms were nice, thin and toned. She brought the drinks out and sat again. He smiled as she handed the glass to him. She thought about what she would say and then stopped.

'I'm sorry about the other day,' she said. 'In the car.'

'When was that?'

She felt panic. She kept it cool.

'My parents were going out. I was in the car with them.'

'Oh yeah. I saw them. Were you there as well?'

'Yeah.'

'Didn't see you.'

'No, I was in the back. I thought you were there but I was pissed off with my parents and I didn't want to do anything.'

'Ah yeah. I know.'

She was not enjoying this conversation. She had wanted to be relaxed and open and he was being cagey. She knew he'd seen her. She knew that he was trying to be cool, but still she wondered and when she wondered she started to doubt and then she didn't know what to do. She looked up at him and he smiled shyly before turning away. She was beginning to get annoyed. Try for fuck's sake she said to herself and to him. Just try.

'So why were you pissed off with your parents?' he asked then.

'I got home later than they wanted that Saturday and they started giving me shit. It was nothing but it pissed me off.'

'We weren't that late.'

'I know,' she said. 'But Emily was with me and they wanted us back early and then Emily ended up pissed and it was all a load of hassle and stuff. But it's fine. They're gone now.'

'When are they coming back?' he asked.

'This evening.'

'So there's no one here all day?'

'No.'

As soon as she said it, the fear flashed by of what he might drive into that space. A day on the piss. Get all the boys over. It could be anything. But then he reached over to her and held her hand.

'I missed you,' he said and it was lame but when she looked at him he might have meant it. She moved over and kissed him.

'That's a crap line,' she said after.

'Well, I did,' he said, smiling, 'and I had to say something.'

'You could have done better than that,' she said, relaxing again.

'Well, you weren't saying much yourself. Before you start accusing me.'

It should have been easy. She thought that later. They wanted the same things. She wanted to kiss him and take him upstairs to her room and he should have wanted the same. She should have been able to say what she wanted and so should he, but there was too much getting in the way. What he might really think. What he might really be after. What did he want? Maybe it would get easier later. No more of these stupid cringing conversations, sniffing around each other like dogs. When she took him inside, he didn't seem surprised. When she took him upstairs, she thought maybe his hands were shaking as they went into her room but maybe it was her.

They were lying on the grass out the back later on. She wanted him to go now. It had been fun, but her parents might come back any time and she really didn't need it. His eyes were closed and there was a small smile on his face. It was the same smile that she had liked a few days before, but it annoyed her now. She knew it was because the pressure was rising. She wanted to shake him and tell him to fuck off home but she couldn't.

'How many blokes have you been with?' he asked her when she thought he had fallen asleep.

'I'm not telling you that.'

'Why?'

She laughed.

'Because I'm not stupid. You tell me. Girls.'

He sat up.

'Ten,' he said.

'Really?'

'Yeah. And you?'

'I'm not telling you.'

'But you said if I told you—'

'I didn't say that. I didn't say anything like that. I'm not telling you anyway. It's not a good thing for you to know.'

'Why?'

'Because it's a mystery,' she said. It was so easy. He was fun but she wasn't sure if he was up to it.

'And here's a thing,' she said then. 'If you tell any of your friends, if you say one word about anything that we did, one word, I'll know and we'll never do any of it again. Ever.'

'Are you serious?'

She laughed.

'I'm totally serious. And I will know.'

'How?'

'I just will.'

He looked at her. He was trying very hard to look cool but he didn't know what to say. Then he smiled.

'You can't tell me what to do. I'll do what I want.'

'You can do what you want,' she said, 'but not with me.'

He laughed.

'Unbelievable.'

'I know,' she said.

'OK. OK. I won't tell anyone. But you have to promise too.'

'Why?'

'Because I say so.'

'OK. I promise.' She said it like it was nothing. 'But you won't know if I tell people.'

'Yeah I will.'

'No you won't.'

'Yeah I will.' Then he thought. 'Why won't I?'

'Because you just won't. Because you're a silly boy.'

She knew she was pushing it with him. She watched him for the reaction but he was smiling. There was something else there beneath it but he was keeping it down. He was liking it and that was good.

'Now you've got to go,' she said.

'Why?'

'In case my parents come home.'

He stood up and stretched. They went through the house and she let him out the front door. They stood on the doorstep.

'Will I give you a ring later?' he asked.

'I'll ring you,' she said.

'OK.' She knew he was trying not to make a fuss. Then when she was thinking this, he kissed her.

'I'll see you later,' he said.

'OK,' she said. She went back into the house and closed the door. If he had come back right then, if he had come and knocked on the door she would have let him in and she didn't know what would have happened after that. She looked out through the window, standing back away from it, but he wasn't there. He was gone.

Robbie walked across the green. He saw Joe Mitchell at the bottom of his drive, sweeping up garden rubbish. Joe was watching him, but

Robbie didn't care. He wasn't thinking about sad old Joe. How could he be?

He had got her wrong. Totally wrong. He'd have liked to think that the reason he'd been drawn to her in the first place was because he'd seen something in her, but he knew he was lying to himself. He just thought she looked good. He'd seen her looking at him and when he'd talked to her, he had known she was interested. When they'd gone out he knew it would happen and he was glad when it did. She wasn't like her friend who was all posh and fluffy. But this one. This Clare one was more like him. She watched what was going on. She saw things.

When she drove by in the car with Mummy and Daddy and the kids, he was ready to give up on her. He wouldn't have minded. He would have forgotten about it and maybe tried to fuck her friend. But he didn't. Because he liked Clare. He didn't want that one night to be the end of it. Last night when he was in bed he had thought of her and it pained him to think that she had blanked him. Not just because of the others. Because he wanted her.

Nothing like that had ever happened to him before. With girls he always had to push and cajole and argue and bide his time and negotiate, even with the ones who were keen. He knew what they would do. But it all took so long and he wasn't sure if it was worth it. It was something to do because that's what you did. Arguing with some tight, terrified sixteen-year-old wasn't fun. It was afterwards, thinking about it and talking. But this one. No problems. No messing around. Better. More mature. Made him feel older, even though she had to be younger than he was. What did all her games mean? What was that about? Do what you want but tell no one. He must tell no one. But it was what they did. Him and Alan. They told each other everything. Why couldn't he this time, when he really had something to say? And why had he told her that he'd been with ten girls? What did she think of that? Was ten a lot or a little for her? He thought it was a lot when he said it but he'd never met anyone like her. If he'd been thinking about something else he might have missed her and she could have ended up with Alan or one of the others.

But then he thought that she wouldn't have. She wouldn't have gone with any of the others because when he saw her he knew that there was something. Right from the first moment. He knew then that he would tell no one. That he wouldn't say a word because, whether it was true or not that she would know, it was too much to risk. The only thing that he wanted was another afternoon like this one. That was all and if he had to do what she wanted to get it, then he could keep his mouth shut.

When he got back to the house, his mother was in the kitchen standing at the sink. Her back was to him and the radio was on. He walked in quietly and stood behind her. He leant in and kissed her on the back of her neck. She nearly fell over.

'Jesus Christ.' She turned and saw him. 'Robbie.'

'Hello,' he said.

'Are you trying to bloody scare me to death? I could have stabbed you. Jesus.'

'Just saying hello.'

'Well, just say it.' She stopped and looked at him. 'What have you been at?'

'Nothing,' he said. 'Why?'

'Have you been tormenting some poor neighbour. I don't like that smile.'

'No,' he said. 'I've been good.'

'I need to sit down,' she said. 'You can make me a cup of tea.'

'OK.'

'I swear, Robbie, if someone turns up here tonight complaining about you I'm going to be pissed off.'

'They won't,' he said. 'I promise you.'

When Clare heard the car pulling into the drive that evening, she opened the front door and stood waiting. The kids ran past her first and then Paul came, carrying bags.

'Hi,' she said.

'Hello,' he replied, not looking at her.

'Have a nice time?'

'Yeah.'

'I'm sorry,' she said before she could think.

'Why? What happened?'

'Nothing. I'm just sorry for having been such a pain.'

He put the bags down and hugged her before she could see it coming. He held her tight and she could smell the sea off his skin.

'I'm sorry too,' he said.

'It was me,' she said.

'I don't care,' he said.

They stood on the step holding onto each other for a minute.

'Are we back to normal?' Ruth asked as she passed them.

'I hope so,' Paul said.

'We are,' Clare said. 'I'm sorry.'

9

Three days later Joe saw Robbie leaving the house for the third time. He saw that Robbie only visited Clare when her parents were out. He didn't have to try but he could see. He wasn't watching. Nothing else to do and big windows in these houses. So he saw when Robbie went over and how he always left before the others got back. He wondered what they were doing. He'd seen the two of them kissing on the doorstep but nothing else. She was so young it seemed to him. But then she was maybe seventeen and what did that mean now? He didn't want to scare Paul. But the third time he knew he had to do something. He was doing them a favour. If it was his daughter he would want to know. If it was his daughter he would lock her up or send her away or do whatever it took to keep her away from a boy like that. He wasn't bored. He wasn't poor or lacking facilities or options or a future. He wasn't damaged or dyslexic or traumatized. He was bad. Joe could see it in him. The violence in his gestures. The facility of the lie in his mouth. The outrage at the accusation as he began to believe his own lie. The persistence that would never let Joe win. If he got him this time, Robbie would take what was coming with bad grace and protestation but he would already be plotting his comeback and Joe knew that he could never let his guard down because this guy was evil. An animal whose survival depended on his ability to destroy everything and everyone that got in his way. It was time that Paul knew because his daughter would be damaged by her contact with him.

He had to contrive the meeting. He knew that if he turned up on their doorstep – ding-dong, I've news for you – Paul wouldn't believe him. He wouldn't want to. But if they met and Joe was as casual as he could be, then it would have an impact. He wondered what Paul might do. What he would do to Robbie. He was big enough, serious enough and he would be defending his family. Animal versus animal and that skinny little prick would lose. Joe let himself smile. To see the boy getting beaten. Physically beaten. His stupid mouth split and his teeth loosened, his nose flattened and his body on the ground being kicked. In the back, in the ribs, in the shins, maximizing pain and humiliation. If Joe could be there he would spit on him and tell him that he had brought it about. He let these feelings come and then was surprised by their viciousness. He was a civilized, intelligent man but he knew that for too long he had lived too close to this force that dominated his life. He had been made sick and had to change medication. He had been ostracized by his neighbours. He was a laughing stock with the guards and all because of this boy. He was powerless. But now. Let it flow. He let the fantasy run wild because now it was going to happen.

He knelt in his front garden that afternoon weeding a flower bed. He watched Paul's house. He could see the son out in the front kicking a ball against the garage door. The front door was open and Joe waited for Paul to come out. He could stay there all day if he had to. He would find a way to start a conversation, some stupid premise. It didn't matter. In his head he mapped the path that the conversation would take.

When Paul came out and spoke to the son Joe stood up and looked over. Seeing him, Paul waved.

'Hello,' Joe shouted over. There was a question in the way he said it. Not a greeting but an opening.

'Hi,' Paul called back. Joe took a couple of steps down his drive.

Paul watched him and then started walking over to meet him. Joe picked up his pace in his eagerness and then slowed down and let Paul come to him.

'Some day,' Paul said.

'Beautiful. I'm taking advantage. Just getting out to do a bit of weeding. The flower beds. They come up very quick in the summer, don't they?'

'They do.'

'How are you?' Joe said.

'Fine. We're fine. Settling in nicely.'

Joe thought.

'Is your—' and then he stopped because it couldn't be the first thing. 'Is your wife happy here?'

'She's delighted with it. All the space. It's great.'

'And the children?' Joe asked.

'Yes, absolutely. It's great for them.'

'What are the names? The three?'

'Clare and Fin and Louise,' Paul said.

'Finbar, is it.'

'Yes.'

'And which is the oldest one? The nice girl?'

'That's Clare.'

'She's settling in well, I see.' Paul had been looking over Joe's shoulder as he talked to him. Joe was used to it. It was what people did when they were afraid of being bored, afraid of where Joe's conversation might go if they encouraged him by looking. But now Paul's head turned and faced him.

'Yes,' he said shortly. Space. Silence. Joe had to move.

'She's friendly with some of the local fellows, I see. Or one in particular.'

'Is she? I don't know. I wouldn't know. She wouldn't tell me. How do you know this?'

'I'm guessing,' Joe said.

'Oh, right,' Paul's eyes moved off again. Poor mad Joe.

'That young Whelan fellow is up in your place the whole time, I see,' Joe said. 'Maybe he's not as bad as I made him out.'

'Who?'

'Whelan. The young fellow. Robert.'

'I don't think so,' Paul said. 'I've never seen him around the house.'

'Ah no. I don't know. He's been up and down a lot over the past week or so. Maybe you're out when he's there. It's great that you're fitting in anyway.'

'Yeah,' Paul said but he wasn't listening now. Stuck on the previous sentence.

'Nice to talk to you,' Joe said.

'I'm sorry,' Paul said. 'Hang on. You're sure you've seen him going into our house?'

'Yes. Absolutely. Absolutely. I noticed because the first time he went up I thought there was no one home and I was watching because, you know, just in case. But then your daughter opened the door so I knew everything was OK. And then another couple of times. I'm here all day, you know, and I'm in the garden a lot so I see what's going on.'

'Right,' Paul said. 'Anybody else?'

'No,' Joe said happily. 'Just him.'

Paul shook his head.

'Right.'

'I should get back to the weeds,' Joe said. 'They'll have started growing back already. It's amazing how quickly they take over.'

'OK,' Paul said.

'I'll see you again. Say hello to your wife.'

'I will,' Paul said and he wandered off.

Paul was having trouble breathing. His head was foggy. He lost himself in it as he tried to replay the conversation in his head, stumbling into patches of clarity and then disappearing again as he tried to piece together the most likely version of the truth. Joe was mad and would say anything. Joe was mad but could be a reliable witness. Joe was trying to worry him about the local young fellows. Joe was waging a one-sided vendetta. Clare was a lying brat who'd been letting some gangster into their house when they were out. None of it was true. None of it could be. But what should he do and why would Joe care enough to invent something so ridiculous? Ask Ruth first because Ruth would know. Or maybe not. Maybe it was better to go to Clare and ask her quietly what was going on. Level with her. Tell her that Joe said something strange just now and see what happened. It was only a week ago that they had made up over her staying out and he didn't want any more drama. It would be easier just to forget it. Maybe he should say nothing. It would be easier if he knew for sure that Joe wasn't delusional. But the last time they had spoken Paul believed him. This time Joe was more normal than he had been then. What if it was true? He had to know. He had to ask her.

He didn't know the guy. He knew nothing about him. Clare never mentioned him by name. The thought of her going out with any of those guys upset him. They all looked the same, all tracksuits and runners and caps and gold chains. All standing around and shouting and talking bollocks. Acting tough at a rock in the middle of a housing estate. Nobodies. Clare was in a different league. He couldn't see anything that she would find attractive or appealing about a crowd like that. She couldn't be impressed by their posturing. A bunch of tracksuits at a rock. Say hello and have a chat. Yeah, sure. But get involved with one of them? Surely not. She was in a different class. Neighbours or not.

When he got back to the house he found her out in the back on the grass.

'Hi,' he said.

'How are you?'

'I'm fine.' He sat beside her. He couldn't wait. He had to ask. He had to know.

'Has one of the boys from the estate been calling up here when we're out?' he asked. The sentence hung in front of him accusing him. He didn't know how to do this. Always wrong. But it was out there. Said. If she had not been so surprised Clare would have heard the hope in his voice, the undertone that begged her to give him the answer he wanted.

'What?' she said, squeaking to show surprise.

'Has some young fellow been coming up to see you this past week? Whelan. Whatever his name is?'

Clare laughed. Less than a second to choose her path and then she had to stick with it.

'No,' she said. 'Why? Where did this come from?'

'I met Joe just now and he was saying that he'd seen your man coming up here a couple of times.'

'Him? You know what he's like.'

'He seemed pretty definite.'

'He's mad, Dad. Seriously. He sees all sorts of things. You said it yourself. He's sad or depressed or whatever. He's got nothing better to be doing than making up stories about everyone.'

'So that's it. No secret assignations with boys.'

'No.'

She looked him in the eye and watched as the tension melted and drained away. She could see that his desire to believe her outweighed any doubts he might have. He wanted the world to be like this. She wanted to cry right then. She wanted to be able to tell him everything because really it didn't matter any more. She wanted him to be able to take it. But he wasn't and so she had to do this. She didn't like it. It came easily to her and she was good at it, but she didn't like it.

She was right about Paul. He wanted to believe and so he switched off his judgement. He watched her tell him that none of it was true and he heard only the words. He didn't see the colour that came into her face or the higher pitch that she spoke with or her eyes that dropped and then looked up at him, begging him to believe. She needn't have bothered. All he heard were the words and he realized then how afraid he had been that Joe might have been telling the truth.

Because this was not where they were supposed to be living. The house was fine. The neighbours were OK. The facilities were perfect. But it was not home for them, not for him. He could never feel comfortable here. Too far. Built too late. Away from their old area that belonged to the city. This was a suburb and he wasn't suburban. Estate living. Young people gathering. Old people waiting to die. Crappy cars that people lavished attention on. The graffiti and empty cans and broken glass that surrounded them. Young fellows waiting for him to turn his back. Waiting to get at Clare. But the time to say something was back then. Not now when it was too late. It was too late. They were in the wrong house and it wasn't going to work and the world that surrounded them was not their world. It was another harder world, which would seep in under the doors and down the chimney and through the windows that they left open at night.

He'd failed them and before long his children would be marked by it and he would have lost them. With Clare it was OK this time. But he knew that it wouldn't be long before it would rise up again and the next time he would have to confront it and what would happen then? Maybe Ruth could tell him because he didn't know.

These thoughts were in Paul. He would have put them down to the heaviness of the weather that day or the slump that hit him in the middle of summer. Boredom. A bad mood. Anything. What are the thoughts that we do not allow ourselves? What are the voices that we silence? For Paul they guided him as though he were hypnotized. As though he were unknowingly being dragged along by a ghost that Ruth and the children could only occasionally see a shimmer of and, when they did, they didn't mention it. They didn't say anything because the glimpse they caught was so fleeting.

Clare went into the living room where Fin was watching TV. She sat on the couch beside him.

'Hi,' he said.

'What?'

He looked at her.

'What's wrong with you?' he asked.

'What's wrong with me? What's wrong with me?' She shook her head and sneered and then felt bad as Fin looked back at the television, his face red. He didn't know what he'd done wrong. He didn't know that there was nothing. She watched him try to remember what he had done to offend her, trying to sort it out in his head. In a couple of years he would be able to tell her to fuck herself, which was what she deserved. She saw that it wasn't fair and she reached over and held his hand.

'Sorry,' she said.

'What's wrong?' he asked.

'Nothing. It's nothing. I'm just—' She let it fade away and after a minute he relaxed. Back to the telly. He was funny. Ten-second moods. Pure reaction. No thought. But he was nice. He could drive her mad but then she was old enough not to let him. What was it? Why was she at him? And then she thought. Then she remembered.

Because she didn't want to lie. She wanted to be straight with her parents because she liked them. Why couldn't they have a normal relationship where she didn't have to filter everything? Take the sting out of it all, tidy it up, censor it and give them a version that wouldn't worry them. It was stupid. They asked her to behave like an adult so that they could trust her. But if they trusted her in the first place she wouldn't have to lie. The truth was that she could look after herself. She could have a drink and get around town at night and decide if she liked someone and she could spot an idiot or a sleaze or a weirdo and stay away from them. Not like Emily, who would talk to whatever madman sat beside her on the bus. Not like Emily, who got too drunk and would let anybody do anything if they smiled and bought her a drink. She wasn't like that. Because she knew what it was to lose control and she'd nearly done it once and she had seen where it was going and she didn't like it. She had learnt her lessons on her own. She had to lie to them the whole time because they didn't know what she was like. Every time, going out, it was the same list of warnings, horror stories, cautionary tales and all the time she would be there going: I know, I know, I know, and they didn't believe her.

She knew why they were worried. She understood it. She knew about love and fear and saw the stories on the news and tried to tell them that she was all right and that the people who got caught out, the girls who ended up mugged or raped or attacked were the ones who were stupid. Went the wrong way on their own, got too drunk, couldn't read the guy, got in the wrong car, forgot their friends. Because there were always signs and you had to be able to see them. It wasn't hard. Walk away. That's what she did and it worked out fine. There would always be the times where nobody could be blamed.

Where no one would have known. Nobody could have seen what was coming, but that was bad luck. That was all and what can you do about bad luck? Stay in bed with the curtains drawn and hope the ceiling didn't fall on top of you? You couldn't live thinking that luck would go against you.

She didn't want to be lying to her father about some boy coming over like she was thirteen. Stupid bloody Joe Mitchell rattling around the house on his own with nothing keeping him alive but hatred and suspicion. Easier to tell. Should be. Wasn't. Couldn't be. Not yet.

There was nothing to tell. Because Robbie wasn't who she thought he was. The hard guy who stood at the back of the crowd running the show saying not very much didn't have hidden depths. The moodiness wasn't a burning intelligence stifled by his surroundings. He might just be thick. He was shy. He seemed angry and damaged but he couldn't do anything about it. He couldn't talk to her, open up and show her where he came from. Silence was only interesting if turned into something. If it was going somewhere. On either side of something happening silence had a meaning, but on its own it was a vacuum and nothing happens in a vacuum. What did he feel? What did he want? Where was he going? Nothing. Awkward and silent and nervous. When he was with the lads, that gang of little guys trying to be big, he seemed older than the rest of them. When he was here with her he seemed younger and that didn't work for her. What was the point in putting herself through all this hassle for a guy who wouldn't talk? He couldn't talk. It was disappointing, but she decided then that she would have to end it. Get him over and tell him. Go to her parents and say to them, now that there was nothing in the way, that they had to let her do what she wanted, they had to trust her because she knew what she was doing and she didn't want to lie any more. An easier life. She was still holding Fin's hand. She raised it to her mouth and kissed it. He drew it back in horror.

'What are you doing?'

'I'm just happy,' she said. She was messing.

'Get lost, you.'

Clare laughed and stood up. She went into the kitchen and took the phone up to her bedroom to call Emily.

Joe's wife's family kept in contact with him after she died. He knew it had nothing to do with him. He was her husband and it meant that they would try, even though they didn't know or like him very much. So Joe found himself trying to deal with the letters they sent and the impossible phone calls, limited by their English to simple, childish phrases that might have conveyed how much they all missed her, but never did. There was nothing to say. It was too much effort for so little return.

When her sister wrote after a year, asking could her son stay with him for a term while he studied English, Joe said yes. He didn't want to at first. Didn't know if he would be capable. But they made the effort and so he felt he should. It could be a new start for him, maybe. Somebody else around the house. It would give him a focus. He wrote back the same day and two months later he was at the airport waiting for this boy whom he had met once before, apparently.

'It was very sad when my aunt died,' Jorge said as they shook hands in the arrivals hall. He didn't look anything like her.

'Thanks,' Joe said. 'It was. For us all.' They both stood nodding gently into the distance.

'Will we make a move?' Joe asked.

'Hmm?'

'Will we go?'

'Yes. Let's go.'

He was sixteen. He didn't know much English. Joe tried in the car on the way home but it was embarrassing for them both. By the time they got back the silence was becoming normal. Joe showed him his room and where things were. He went downstairs and sat in the living room, trying to remember what he had been doing before.

He tried to make Jorge welcome. He gave him a set of keys and told him to come and go as he pleased. Kids were older in Spain, he knew. More mature. Jorge wouldn't be going out and getting stupidly drunk. His mother had sent money, which he gave Joe the first morning, embarrassed, not knowing how to say what it was for or maybe just not knowing. It would be better, Joe thought. He could manage. The noise that another person brought into the house, coughing and talking on the phone and banging around in the kitchen, the colours that he wore, confident Spanish colours that crashed into Joe's fuzzy black-and-white world and woke him up.

The first week Jorge went to school in the morning and came home at five. Joe cooked meals and they ate together in front of the television. Jorge ate everything. He said nice things. It was fine. School was good. There were people in his class who were OK, some from near his part of Madrid. They didn't talk much but Joe thought he was happy.

Then he came home late one evening on the last bus and Joe was waiting, not knowing what to say. He couldn't deal with a row. He didn't know what was reasonable but he tried.

'If you're going to be late, you have to tell me,' Joe said. 'I need to know if you want dinner.'

'OK,' Jorge said. 'I am sorry.'

'It's not a problem,' Joe said. 'I just need to know.'

So the next day, Jorge told him he would be late. And the day after that.

'Where are you going?' Joe asked.

'A friend's house. To study.'

'You can bring your friend back here,' Joe said. 'I wouldn't mind.'

'No,' Jorge said. 'This is better.'

It worried him. When the mother rang, Joe asked her about it. Said he was coming back late after studying.

'If he's studying, it's OK. Is it not?'

'I don't know,' Joe said. 'I thought I should check.'

'What time does he come back?'

'Eleven maybe.'

'That's not so late. Is it a problem for you?'

'No. If you're happy, that's fine.'

But it wasn't fine. Every night Joe waited and at six o'clock started to worry that this would be the night. He was responsible for this kid and he felt he wasn't doing enough. His mother might think it was OK, but she didn't know Dublin and what it was like. She didn't know the kind of people who were out there. Drunks and drug addicts and violent bastards, just waiting for someone like Jorge. But what could Joe do about it? Nothing. Just wait and try not to worry and pretend when Jorge came in, relaxed and breezy, that he didn't care.

That was the start. It didn't take long. The powerlessness of it was what damaged Joe. He should have done something but he didn't and that became a reason to torment himself. All the concern and doing nothing about it. It demonstrated for him what his problems were. Too indecisive. Afraid of conflict. Afraid of showing that he didn't know what to do. He thought by doing anything he might make it worse. And yet paradoxically, by doing nothing, he knew that the situation was deteriorating. He talked to himself sitting in the chair in the afternoons. You should just stand up and call his mother. You should talk to him. Explain. He's only a boy. What is the problem? Stand up. What are you afraid of?

But as soon as the question was asked, the answer grew so big that Joe could do nothing. He sat there trying not to think. The world outside got worse and inside in his head he was falling apart. It was too much. It was too soon. He wasn't ready. Responsibility. The word alone made him shake his head. Not for him. Somebody else's child. What had he been thinking? It was too late now. He'd thought he was up to it and he'd pay for that now.

It was Jorge who dealt with it in the end. Joe didn't know what it was that he saw, but he must have realized that something was wrong. He asked Joe was he all right and Joe said he was fine.

'Are you sure?' Jorge asked. 'Because I don't think you are.'

Joe looked at him and saw the concern and for the first time, in that expression, he saw something of her. It was there. It wasn't fair on the kid. It couldn't go on.

'Maybe not,' Joe said.

He made the phone calls that he had to. Everybody was fine. Jorge was able to move in with with a family nearer to the school and his mother understood when the situation was explained to her. Joe saw the doctor and went in for a couple of weeks. When he came out he was feeling OK. He settled down again. And then they started.

He couldn't understand it. He never did anything to them. He hadn't even noticed them before. He had been passing through life unhindered by anyone. What was it that they saw? His weakness? His unhappiness? An easy target? They were like dogs, the way they surrounded him, nipping at him, worrying him. He went to their parents. He went to the police. He went to the residents' committee. They all said the same thing. They'd nothing to do, there was no malice. No malice? Where were they when he was face to face with the main one? Let them look him in the eye then. See what was in him and tell him after that that there was no malice. These were not bored children. These were apprentices honing their skills for their future lives of crime. Such cruelty. What could he do? People knew about him. They knew where he'd been and that made everything he said subject to the eye-rolling that Joe could see in front of him, to the patronizing tones that they used. What could he do when he knew he was right but he couldn't make anyone believe him? The new guy today. His daughter, so young and innocent, would be corrupted and spoilt by these animals. He told Paul that and watched as he turned away. Fighting the yawn, wanting to be at home with his wife and lovely kids away from this madman. He wasn't bad, Paul. He was polite and he had the grace to listen and Joe could see that he was sympathetic, which was nice and all very well. But he was not hearing the warning. It infuriated him. Grab him by the hair and shout it into his ear. They will ruin you. They will destroy your life like they have mine. Look at me and see what I am reduced to. Whispering warnings that will never be heeded, never be believed and when it's too late, when it's all gone bad, you'll see then that I was right.

Paul thought he was doing the right thing. His decision to ask Clare without involving Ruth was a vote of confidence in her. It was a bonding moment between them at a time when he felt it was needed. He wanted to trust her. Clare would know that he hadn't told Ruth and she would understand his reasons. She would feel them. It would be strong enough to have an impact, to mean something in a way that neither of them would have to talk about. It wasn't a secret but it was stronger for Ruth not knowing. It said to Clare: I trust you. I trust you enough not to make a fuss. I believe what you tell me. I don't care what anybody says. I am with you on your side believing you and please see it and understand it because I don't know how to say it without spoiling it.

Some men could say everything. They would know how to tell Clare what they wanted and felt. They could do it without blushing. But that wasn't him. Clare was old enough to read the signals that he sent her. Even if she wasn't, she would get it later. When she was older, looking back, she would remember that when their neighbour told lies about her Paul made no fuss. He didn't tell her mother. He just asked her and took her word. She would remember.

But over the next couple of days Paul began to wonder. He questioned his own abilities to read Clare, to interpret what Joe had said and how Clare had reacted, to watch how she behaved after their conversation, and doubt grew in him. He tried to remember the expression on her face, her reaction and the words she had used when he had asked her about it. It was no good. There was nothing there. If he hadn't seen it at the time he wasn't going to be able to find it now in his two-dimensional memory. He drove in and out of the estate and tried not to look at the skinny tall kid who was causing this unrest in his mind. He tried not to turn at the bedroom window and see the crowd of them standing there for hours doing nothing, just shouting and barking and laughing with a cruelty that he could hear even at this distance. He could go out there and stop them laughing. He could make them react, make them look at him and think, but it wasn't right. What had they done to him? What had they done wrong?

In the end it was straightforward. After two days of thinking, ignoring, trying to forget, confronting himself with all that was in his head, he saw what he would do to answer the questions that worried him. He found the answer and he knew that by two o'clock that afternoon it would be clear and he would live with it. It was not even that he had to do anything. Straight circumstance would give him an answer and that would do.

It was a Wednesday at eleven o'clock. Clare was still in bed. The others were around. Lou was out the back somewhere and Fin was watching telly.

'If we do the shopping early today, we could go to the beach in the afternoon,' he said to Ruth.

'Get it out of the way now.'

'Is that OK?'

'It's fine with me,' she said.

'Now?'

'OK. Now.'

He went and called the other two and told them to get in the car. He went up to Clare's room and knocked on the door. She called him in. She was sitting up reading.

'We're going shopping,' he said.

'Now?'

'Yeah. Are you going to stay or what?'

'I don't know. I suppose so. Yeah. I'll stay.'

'OK. We'll see you later.'

'OK.'

He went downstairs. Ruth was putting the breakfast stuff in the dishwasher.

'Is she coming?' she asked.

'No. Are the others in the car?'

It could have happened. That was what Paul was telling himself as he was driving along the canal. The two young ones were in the back, whining at each other, and Ruth was telling them to shut up. It wasn't lying because it might have happened. It had happened before. With everything going on, with all the noise and distraction.

When they got to the shopping centre, when they had parked the car and were walking in he went to put his ticket into his wallet. The tiny charade, the little moment of untruth. He said it. It sounded right.

'I'm an idiot.'

'What?' Ruth turned to him.

'My wallet. Do you have cash on you?'

She never would. Not when she was with him.

'No. Where is it?'

'At home.'

'Ah, Jesus, Paul.'

'I'll go back,' he said. 'You go on ahead and get started. I'll meet you in there in forty minutes.'

She shook her head at him.

'You're a dope,' she said.

'I know,' he said and he smiled at her. There was such warmth when she smiled back at him that he felt bad. But what could he do? He had to go back now. There was nothing to worry about, he thought. Everything would be fine. Clare would still be in bed, yawning and reading and thinking about getting up and using their absence to get on the phone for a couple of hours to Emily or one of the others. That would be all.

He was sure when he parked on the drive. He was completely relaxed, the nervousness that he had felt on the trip to the supermarket dissolved when he had seen Ruth's reaction. When he realized that this was not a big elaborate deception that he had created. It was a silly mistake. That was all. Her belief changed it for him. There was no drama. There was no horror waiting for him on the other side of the door. This was what he was thinking when he put his key in the lock and turned it.

The door opened and he stepped into the hall. The air told him nothing. Everything was as it should be. He dropped his keys on the table and called upstairs.

'Clare?'

And in that moment it all changed. He knew then that things were going to be different. He tried to hope that the scramble that he heard and the whispered, panicked voice that met him as he pounded upstairs could be something else. That Clare might have gone out and burglars could have come in and if that was it they were in trouble because the rage that was rising in him now was going to make him do something and he wasn't going to try and stop it. He heard the voices again and opened the door into Clare's room. She stood in the middle of the floor and beside her looking terrified was the boy. It was him. Paul stopped and stood in the doorway.

'You told me,' he said to Clare.

'Wait a second.'

'I asked you and you told me,' Paul said. He didn't know what he was saying, trying to process what this meant.

'We're not doing anything,' she said. 'It's all right.'

'No. No, it's not all right,' Paul said. Then, pointing at Robbie, he said, 'You get out.'

Robbie looked at Clare and was going to say something.

'I don't want to hear anything you're going to say,' Paul said. 'There's nothing.'

Robbie faced Paul and his expression made Paul want to hit him. He raised his hand and clenched it into a fist and held it in Robbie's face.

'I don't want to see you again. Anywhere, anytime. You understand? You hear me?'

Robbie said nothing. He walked out without looking up and Clare and Paul listened as he left, the familiar creaking of the stairs incongruous in the heightened strained moment between them. Paul waited until they heard the door close before speaking again.

10

Robbie walked down the driveway. He could feel his face burning but there was no one around to see him. That fucker. That fucking prick. Walked in on them in the middle of something that they had to sort out. It was something that he could have sorted out right then, right there, if this guy hadn't turned up out of nowhere. What business was it of his? His daughter too good for him? She was too young maybe? Didn't want a guy like him in his house? Snobby fuck. It was there. The way he looked at him. The tone in his voice. Did he think he was so stupid that he couldn't hear the way Paul talked to him? Like dirt. Put a fist in his face? Like to try? A grown man like him. An old fucker like him. Not as fast as he would think. Robbie would have him on the ground in two seconds and then there'd be some fun. Sort him out. Threaten him. You don't do that. Sad old cunt.

But her. What was she doing? What had she been saying? There was no time to think between her saying it and Paul walking in. She was dumping him. She was saying that there was no point and Robbie didn't know what to say back, to let her know. He shouted at her to stop and listen to him. But as she stood waiting for him to say something, watching and listening, he knew it was no good because he didn't know what to tell her. The fear, the darkness that came over him when she spoke, he could feel these as real as pain. But he couldn't tell her. And then Paul came in and it was over.

What had she said? No point any more. It had been a bit of fun but she didn't want it now because she didn't think they got on that well. She didn't want him. She was saying no. He could have thrown it back at her and told her she was a stupid bitch and she didn't know what she was doing. She was a slut and he'd let the world know. She could go back to going out with fucking kids from her old area who would puke after two pints and knew fuck all about anything. Posh pricks who he'd sort out one-handed. Batter the head off them. Easy. Who was she to do this? Who was she to say what he could and could not do? He wouldn't be told.

But what good would it have done him, getting angry? He knew that she would laugh at him because she thought he didn't have the language for anything else. He could feel it in himself. He saw the gap that there was between them. He could understand why she was saying what she was saying but he couldn't do anything about it. He couldn't open his mouth and say the words that would make her think.

He was at home now. His mother was in the kitchen when he went in. She said something to him but he didn't hear her. She watched him as he went upstairs. She thought about going after him. He looked upset. But she knew what he would be like if she went to him and she didn't need it. He'd sort himself out. He'd have to.

When he was upstairs in his room he sat on the bed and tried to think. He rolled over and punched the pillow. Because it was no good. There was nothing he could do and he knew it. Nothing that he could do. He lay there on his side and felt his eyes burn and he swallowed hard to keep it down, to keep it in, because he didn't know what would happen to him if he didn't. The words would come to him now when it was too late, away from her, and the moment was gone. If she had been there with him now he could have told her what it was that he felt. He could have explained now and told her that she was wrong about him. That he wanted to say more when he was with her but couldn't. It wasn't his fault. It was because he wasn't used to being around a girl long enough to talk to her. He knew what to say at first and what to do to keep things moving but then afterwards he didn't have it. School was with boys and men. No girls. No sisters. A mother, but what was that? Everybody has a mother and what do you learn about women from your mother? He was used to girls who pretended not to like him, pretended not to notice and then when he pushed, when he tried, they fell apart in front of him offering themselves. All grabby and needy and a pain in the arse.

But it was hard for him because this was the first time he had cared. The first time that he didn't know what was happening. He couldn't tell her what was going on because he didn't know. He couldn't talk to her because he never talked to anyone. He didn't know what she would think. He didn't know what she wanted him to be. And what he wanted was to be able to relax with her, to hang around and get to know her. He wanted to be able to tell her that he thought about her all the time and she wasn't like every other stupid girl he'd been with. She made everybody else seem like a kid. He wanted to forget his home and the others and school and his stupid life on this estate. He wanted to go away with her. Do something else. He didn't know if that was what she wanted so he kept his mouth shut rather than scare her. And for that she'd dumped him. That was the end of it and it wasn't fair. She had to give him a chance. She had to let him explain and tell her this because she couldn't know it. She could have been pushing him to find out. She might have wanted to see if, when confronted by the alternative, he would tell her what he thought and how he felt and what he wanted. He would have. He could see it now. He wouldn't have kept standing there in silence. He wouldn't have gone ballistic and told her she was a stupid bitch. He would have waited and thought and then it would have come to him. He would have told her everything and then it would have been different. If she had heard him, she would have seen that it was all true. That he meant it, that he wasn't who she thought he was, and she would have stopped and changed her mind and it would have been all right. They could go on and nothing else would matter. Nothing in his life and nothing in hers. Just them. Him and her. It was the only way that he could imagine being happy. If her father hadn't turned up in the middle of it, they would have sorted it out. Now he had to start again to try and convince her. He knew now what it was that he had to say. He would tell her when he saw her next and he would sort it out.

'I asked you,' Paul said again, when Robbie was gone. It seemed an odd thing to pick on, Clare thought.

'I know you did. And I lied.'

'Why? Why couldn't you tell me?'

'Are you joking? Are you serious? What could I say to you? What was I supposed to do? Tell you the truth? You would have gone mad.'

'No, I wouldn't.'

'Of course you would. Look at you now. You can't deal with something like this.'

'Watch what you say, you. You're in trouble here. Don't make it worse.'

'How could it be worse?'

Paul stopped. He didn't think about it. He couldn't.

'So what's the story with this guy?'

'I don't know.'

'You don't know.'

She looked at him defiantly.

'No.'

'Is he your boyfriend?' She laughed. Paul couldn't tell if she was laughing at him or at the idea of it.

'Boyfriend? No. Not a boyfriend.'

'Well what then? Clare, you have to talk to me. You have to tell me what's going on. Why was he here?'

Paul could hear how stupid he sounded. There was no answer he could imagine that would make him happy, that would satisfy him, that would not send him running from the room in a rage across the green to kick the door in of that house and grab the boy and beat him. There was no answer. Clare knew it too. She said nothing.

'So he's been here a few times,' Paul said. 'Joe Mitchell was right then, was he?'

'Good old Joe. Silly prick.'

'Oh, shut up. He told me because he knew what you were at. Sneaking him in here when we were out. He knew we didn't know about it. I'm glad he told me.'

'Why?'

'What?'

'Why are you glad? What good has it done you? Or me or anyone? How has you knowing improved anything? It makes no difference to what's already happened. It just makes the future less comfortable for us all. I'm a liar and a slut and you've at last got an excuse not to trust me.'

'I don't want an excuse. Why would I? But how can I trust you now?'

'You didn't anyway.'

'Yeah, we did. Of course we did. And you abused that trust.'

'You didn't. You didn't. Mum maybe, but not you. I don't know why.'

'Look at what happened when I did. When I asked you and believed your lies. Look what happens a couple of days later.'

'This is you trusting me? Why are you here? What did you come back for? It didn't take you too long to get up the stairs when you came in. This is your trust? Why are you here?'

'Because I forgot my wallet.'

She laughed.

'Good one. Right.'

'I did.'

She turned away.

'What are you talking about anyway?' he asked. He heard his voice. He sounded defiant now. She was cooler. 'It's not about me. It's about you. Why are you inviting some boy up to your room when we're out? Are you totally stupid?'

'No.' Her denial was so absolute, so quiet and calm and true that Paul had to stop and think before speaking again.

'Well, you're acting like you are.'

'No, I'm not. I'm not doing anything wrong and if you just relaxed for a second you could understand that. If you let me explain.'

'So explain. Explain.'

'Are you sure you wouldn't prefer to let Mum deal with this? She's better at it, isn't she? More her thing. You're out of your depth.' She could see his doubt. It maddened him.

'Stop it,' he shouted. 'Shut up. Shut fucking up.'

They stood face to face. She flinched when he shouted. He saw it and thought he should wait. It was hard. She was a kid. She was his kid and she couldn't talk to him like this. She shouldn't know how to talk to him like this.

From the hall they heard the phone ring. Neither of them moved. It rang four times, then silence, then the beep and Ruth's voice could be heard coming up saying Paul's name. Paul lifted a finger and this time when he spoke his voice was as he wanted it to be.

'I have to go and get them. You stay . . . No. You come with me. You don't say another word and when we get back we will continue this conversation.'

He turned and heard her follow him downstairs. He picked up the phone and called Ruth back. He told her he would be there in ten minutes. When he hung up he turned to Clare.

'Whatever else. Whatever the excuses or arguments. Whatever happens, you should know that you cannot talk to me the way you just did upstairs. That's it.'

He opened the front door and when she had gone out he pulled it behind him. As he was locking it, he thought he heard her say something.

'What?' he asked without turning.

'Do you have your wallet?'

He unlocked the door and went back inside. When he was in the kitchen, he kicked a skirting board. His shoe left a mark.

They drove to the shopping centre in silence. Paul tried to read Clare's mood without being noticed. Was she upset, angry, defiant, embarrassed? She stared out the window for the whole trip. She had been right. He needed Ruth to deal with this. The certainty that she would bring to the situation. If she was relaxed he would be ready to go along with her. He wanted this drama gone as much as Clare did. When that idea came to him he almost said it to her because he thought she should know. He couldn't wait for normality to return, for them all to be happy again. The house to be quiet and relaxed and no more drama. If he could undo the events of the previous forty minutes without consequence he would. But he couldn't and because of that the two of them would have to wait and see. They were in it together and he shouldn't be angry. He only wanted to protect her. He only wanted to stop her from making stupid mistakes with an ignorant no-hope waste of space who would hold her back from the things that she wanted out of life. The guy could barely speak. Why would she bring into her life all the potential that this guy presented? Violence, ignorance, drugs, criminality, depressing sex, teenage pregnancy, compromised hopes. Everything turned to nightmare. What could he give her? He was seventeen and his life was over. Already doomed. This was as good as it would get for him. Living with his parents and hanging around a rock with a bunch of idiots braying and plotting how to antagonize their mentally disturbed neighbour would be the high point. Paul knew that these guys were biding their time before boredom and frustration and stupid bravado drove them on to the next level. Clare would have boyfriends. She would go out with boys and get drunk and be stupid and take chances and risks and he could do nothing about it. He couldn't keep her in a bubble before letting her out into the world at eighteen. He wasn't naive. He knew what the world was like. He knew what he had been like when he was her age. It was different for girls, but not that different. He had known what he wanted. There would be boys. And he wouldn't like them. He knew that what she would want from a boy and what Paul would like would be very different. An asexual intellectual who would treat her well. It wouldn't work. He couldn't choose. But there had to be some space for him. For what he thought and felt and what he knew. He had to able to say no. Not this guy.

Could he hear it then? Could he hear the voice? Did he feel the finger of blame turn and point at him? Could he see it? From Ruth and Clare and from himself? Because it was all his fault. Should have tried harder, done more, pushed longer, suffered for his family to get them as far away from this life as he could have. He could have packed it in and started again and driven himself and watched his children grow up in safety away from this kind of place. Away from these people who would drag them all down. Clare finished as she was getting started. Fin and Lou going the same direction. Just wait and watch and see what happens and know that all this could have been avoided if he'd tried harder. Go forward ten years and watch his own parents look at his family and they would know, it would confirm what they had always suspected. They had predicted this eighteen years ago when he came home and told them that his girlfriend who they'd never even met was pregnant. The pause waiting for the word to come out and when it came it was as ugly as that. Not expecting, not going to have a baby. No hiding the nasty fact with a pretty euphemism. As ugly as the situation which meant that their son was not going to be what they had hoped for. It was all there in the look that went between them, before his father started telling them both that everything would be fine, everything would work out, because what else could he do? Face the reality? Tell Paul that he'd fucked his life up? Smile and hope for the best and ignore the fears that were as good as knowledge. It all came true. Out on the edges. His daughter paired up with the local scum hooligan. It was going to get worse and now, at this stage, at this age, it was too late to do anything about it.

Could Paul hear it? Because it was there in the car with them and the hope that Ruth would know what to do wouldn't settle in him. It wouldn't sit right and do its job because this fear had got in deeper, into his bones. His failure was a part of him now and everything else that came and went wouldn't change it. He didn't think about it but that didn't matter. His heart pumped blood, his lungs breathed air and his kidneys and liver filtered and processed, all unheard, unseen and unthought of, but that didn't mean it wasn't happening. That didn't mean they weren't there.

Ruth was annoyed. Paul could see it before he got to her. The two kids stood beside her, silent, and he could tell that something had happened. She had lost her temper and shouted or something.

'What happened?' she asked when he got close enough to hear. 'We've been waiting for half an hour.'

'I know. I know. I'm sorry.'

'I'd no money. We couldn't even go and get a coffee or anything.'

'I know.'

'What happened?'

'I'll tell you later. Let's go and pay for this.'

'Tell me now.' She looked behind him and saw Clare watching. 'What happened? Is something wrong?'

'Nothing. Just wait. OK? Jesus. I told you.' The three of them were looking at him. The younger two looked scared. 'It's nothing. I'll talk to you about it later. Come on.'

He took the trolley and pushed it to the shortest queue he could see, the others trailing behind him. When he looked around Ruth was asking Clare something. Clare shook her head.

They loaded up the car and drove home. Nobody spoke. Paul felt sorry for them. For Ruth and Fin and Lou, who would be worried that it was worse than it was. For Clare, who would be thinking that all of this was her fault, that this silence was the start of the punishment. For himself, for his own stupid self who didn't know what to do. Stop your whining and toughen up. It was Clare's fault and nobody else. They would sort it out. Fix it. Punish. Move on. No drama. No big story. They would all forget this short uncomfortable drive. Not his fault.

He told Fin and Lou to put away the shopping and sent Clare upstairs when they got in. He went into the living room with Ruth.

'I'm sorry,' he said as she sat down. 'Everything is fine. There's nothing to worry about.'

'Yeah? So what happened?'

'When I got back earlier, when I came in for my wallet,' Paul said, 'Clare had one of the young fellows from across the road in her room.'

'What? Who? What were they doing?'

'Nothing. I think. They were both dressed. I don't know.'

'Who is he?' she asked.

'Whelan. One of those ones that's always out there on the green. Dopey-looking guy.'

'They're all dopey looking.'

'He's taller than the others.'

'I don't know him.'

'Neither do I.'

'And they weren't doing anything?'

'Not when I came in. But you know, what if I hadn't?'

'And had she invited him over or what? I mean did she want him there?'

'I don't know. But she wasn't happy to see me.'

'So what did you do?'

'I kicked him out and asked her what the hell she was doing. What was going on. Then you rang. That was it. I wanted to talk to you about it.'

'OK.' She wasn't angry. She was thinking.

'But the thing is—. Right. Last week when I was coming in Joe Mitchell said something to me about it.'

'Said what? What did he say?'

'That when we were out Clare was having people over.'

'People?'

'Well, not people. Your man. This guy.'

'This same guy?'

'Yeah.'

'And what?'

'Well, I didn't know what to do. I didn't know if he was making it up or imagining it or what.'

'So you just ignored it?' Her tone was rising.

'No. I didn't ignore it. I asked Clare about it.'

'When?' she asked.

'A couple of days ago.'

'Why didn't you tell me?'

'What was the point?' he said. 'You know Joe is mad. He's not normal. I asked Clare and she said it was nothing. She said it wasn't true and I believed her. I just did. You would have too if you'd seen her.'

'But I didn't see her. I wasn't there. I knew nothing about it.'

'What was the point?'

'Oh, Paul.'

'What? No. I didn't believe it. I believed her. She told me it wasn't true. It seemed more likely that Joe was looking to settle some mad paranoid score, not that she would be having these secret liaisons when we were out. Why would I tell you about that?'

'But that's what was happening.'

'I didn't know that,' Paul said.

'Neither did I.'

'But you would have worried.'

'Rightly.'

'Oh, for Christ's sake.'

'What? What? We can't do things that way, Paul. We can't make unilateral decisions about the kids. It doesn't work. We both need to know what's going on.'

'But you do it all the time. You sort things out and take care of their problems and discipline them all the time without consulting me. And it's fine. I don't mind because you know what you're doing. Turn this one around. If Joe had had a rant at you and told you what he had told me, what would you have done? Would you have come running back to me saying the manic-depressive down the road says Clare is slutting around with some yob? The one who makes his life a misery? Would we have discussed it? Or would you have asked Clare about it and believed her when she told you that it was all just rubbish?'

'But I would have told you. I would have let you know.'

'Well, I forgot.'

'Forgot? How could you forget something like that?'

'I don't know but I did.' He paused. 'I didn't believe it was true. Maybe I got it wrong. I don't know. But you surely understand what I was trying to do. To avoid you having to worry.'

'I'm worried now, Paul. I really am.'

'Well, don't be,' he said. 'Because we have to sort this out.'

Neither of them spoke for a minute.

'I was trying to deal with it,' he said. 'I thought I'd sorted it out. But she lied to me.'

'You have to talk to me, Paul. You have to.'

'I do. I always have. But not this time and the reason it's turned out to be a problem is Clare. It's her fault.'

'Who cares whose fault it is, Paul? I'm not blaming you. But we have to try and stop this happening in the future.'

'OK. OK. Fair enough.' Again he waited. 'So what do we do?'

'We talk to her. We listen to her. We find out what's being going on. What have you told her already?'

'Told her?'

'What did you say when you found her earlier?'

Paul exhaled.

'Nothing. I don't know what I said. Nothing.'

'Well, that's good,' she said. 'It's good that you didn't overreact.'

Clare sat in front of them in an armchair, her face turned away, looking out the window. She had come in and sat down opposite Paul without looking at him. Ruth followed her in.

'So?' she started.

Clare said nothing. Paul sat holding his breath.

'Clare?' Ruth said.

'What?' Clare replied without turning.

'Do you want to tell us what's been going on?'

'Not really.'

'Well, I think you should.'

'Why?'

'Oh, don't be so bloody childish, Clare. You're old enough to talk to us about this now. This sulking pouting thing is beneath you.'

If she was trying to provoke a reaction, it worked.

'What am I supposed to do? How else am I supposed to behave?'

'What are you talking about?' Paul asked.

'Nothing,' Clare said.

'Hey,' he shouted. Ruth looked at him, just a look but he couldn't help it. 'You've got something to explain here. It's not about us. It's about you and what you've been doing. Don't try and turn it around.'

'This is it. This is exactly what I'm talking about. You tell me that you want me to talk and then as soon as I say anything, I'm told to shut up. So what's the point? I may as well just say nothing. That's what you want.'

'No, it's not, Clare,' Ruth said. 'We want to hear what you have to say. Your explanation. We want to know.'

'Do you? Really? Both of you?' Clare looked at Paul.

'Yes, of course we do,' Ruth said.

'Absolutely,' Paul said. His voice was feeble.

'We want to sort this out. OK?'

'What's to sort out?' Clare asked. Paul thought she was enjoying it. That the space that Ruth was giving her was being abused. But he had been silenced by the message in Ruth's tone and the words that she had used. He let her do it. Whatever she wanted.

'Who is this boy who was up in your room?' Ruth asked.

'Robbie. Whelan.'

'Who is he?'

Clare clucked. Paul bit his lip.

'I don't know. He's a guy.'

'I know that,' Ruth said. 'But who is he? Where is he from? Where did you meet him?'

'He lives across the road. I met him out in front of the house.'

'And has he been coming over here when we've been out?'

Clare shifted in her chair.

'Who cares?'

'I care,' Ruth said. 'We both care.'

'Yeah,' Clare said. 'Well, he has.'

'Since when?'

'I don't know.'

'This is going to be a long conversation if you're going to be difficult. I don't think any of us want that.'

'I don't know. He's been up a couple of times. I invited him.'

'Is he a boyfriend or just a friend.'

'Well, he's a boy.'

'Clare.'

'I don't know. Yeah. We were kind of seeing each other. But not now. That's why I asked him over today. To tell him I didn't want to see him any more. I was telling him that when you walked in.' She looked at Paul. 'So if you hadn't forgotten your wallet, everything would have been all right and we wouldn't be doing this.'

'Well, I did,' Paul said.

Clare smiled at him.

'Why didn't you ask him over when we were around?' Ruth asked.

Clare laughed. More of a snort. It was ugly, Paul thought.

'What? Why didn't you?' Ruth asked again.

'For what? So you could try and talk to him? What would you say? He couldn't even talk to me. It's just embarrassing. It doesn't matter now.'

'And what was he doing in your room? What were you doing when he came over?' Ruth asked.

Paul saw Clare redden. She looked different. Not the irritating young woman smart-arsing her way through the conversation. Gone with one question. The wrong question. It made Paul feel nervous.

'Nothing,' she said at last. 'Just hanging around.'

'That was all?'

'Yeah. Yes.'

Ruth was patient. She was in charge and she could see that Clare didn't want to talk about this.

'Really? Clare? Why did you need an empty house for that?'

'Who cares what we did?'

'We want to know what's going on in your life. We want to know if there's anything we should be worried about.'

'Worried about. It's all worry with you. You don't need to worry about me. I'm fine. I know what I'm doing. I can take care of my own business and I can look after myself. If you didn't know about this, would anything be different? Would it? Because I know that it wouldn't. Except for the fact that I wouldn't be here having to justify myself. How are things better with you knowing what's going on in my life? I don't need to be told or lectured or punished or any of it. I know you will anyway because that's what you do, what you have to do. But I'm OK. Everything is all right. So do you really want me to talk to you about this? What is the point?'

'The point is that you are seventeen years old,' Ruth said. 'And at seventeen everybody thinks that they know everything and that their parents are stupid and that they don't understand what's going on in their lives. They don't understand the pressures that they're under. But I was seventeen and I remember what it felt like. It wasn't that long ago and things weren't that different. OK? And I know that I would have told anyone who asked that I knew it all. But I didn't. There were all sorts of things that I didn't know—'

Clare laughed. She didn't mean to but it came on her so quickly that she couldn't stop it. Ruth stopped.

'What's funny?' she asked. Clare didn't speak. The two of them looked at each other.

'What's funny, Clare?' Paul asked. He'd had enough. When she didn't answer him, he spoke.

'I'll tell you what I see. I see you sitting here telling us that we don't need to worry and that you can look after yourself. But what I know is that you're too young to understand what people are like. You can't know. I'm not saying you're stupid but you just don't have the experience to deal with the kind of crap that life can throw at you. You don't know how vulnerable you are. If you ask a guy like that into the house when we're not here then you don't know what you're doing. You don't know what might happen. You're on your own in a detached house with a young fellow. Do you know what he could do to you?'

'Yes,' she said. 'Yes, of course I do.'

'Oh, you do? Because if you know that much and you still invite him in, then maybe you are stupid. Because he could kill you. He could beat you up. Rob you. Rape you.'

'Yeah, but he didn't.'

'Yeah, well you're lucky. He might have. How well do you know this guy? I mean, what does he do? All I've ever seen him do is hang around that rock, spitting and eating and shouting and laughing like an ape.'

'The point is—' Ruth said.

'The point is,' Paul continued, 'that a guy like that is going nowhere. You hang around with those guys and they will bring you down with them. How many of them are going to college after school? How many of them are even still in school? They're probably already on the dole and they'll be there for the rest of their lives. A brilliant career of arse-scratching and teenage fatherhood and alcoholism and bookies' shops and child support. You want to be a part of that? Do you? Is that what you want out of life?'

'The point is, Clare—' Ruth began again.

'Fuck off,' Clare said. She was looking at Paul, talking only to him.

'What did you say?'

'You know what she said, Paul,' Ruth said. 'We should calm down.'

'You think I'm that stupid?' Clare went on, ignoring Ruth, not hearing her. 'You think I don't know every stupid thing you've said? You think I hang around with these guys because I'm impressed or something? They live here. You brought me here. What am I supposed to do? They're our neighbours and they're nice guys.'

'They're wasters,' Paul said. 'They're nice to you because they think you might invite them over when your parents go out. And oh, amazingly, they were right.'

'What are you talking about? You don't know them. You've never even spoken to them. How can you say this?'

'Because I can see, Clare. I'm not blind. You forget. I deal with guys like this all the time and I know what they're like much better than you do. I can tell you what will happen to them and you can wait and watch it happen. You tell us you know it all? We don't need to worry about you? You're in control? That's why we worry. Because you think you are. Nobody could be more certain of anything. And yet it's so obvious that you're not. It pains me to see it. I hate it. You don't know what you're doing. Your judgement when it comes to male company is pretty bloody suspect.'

'Who told you this? Your paedophile mental friend?'

'Stop it. Just stop now,' Ruth said.

'Why did you bring us here?' Clare asked. 'For a bigger garden?'

Paul couldn't speak. Ruth stood up.

'Go upstairs, Clare. We'll talk about this later, when you've calmed down.'

'When I've calmed down? Me? You want to talk to him?'

'Who's him?' Paul asked.

'You.'

'Clare,' Ruth shouted. 'Go.'

She walked out and went upstairs to her room.

Paul and Ruth sat in silence. The room seemed to hold its breath. There was nothing. No sound. Neither of them wanted to start speaking again for fear of where it might bring them.

'Paul,' Ruth said eventually.

'I know,' he said.

'I don't think you do.'

'I do. I do. Honestly.'

She waited until she trusted herself enough to say what she wanted to say.

'What did you think you were doing?'

'I lost it,' he said. 'She laughed at you.'

'I know she did. But so what? She would have talked to us. She would have opened up. She was talking. She was getting there.'

'I don't know if she was. I thought she was out of line.'

'Yes, well. Look where we are now. What were you thinking?'

'I wasn't thinking.'

'Why were you so angry? So suddenly? It came out of nowhere. Seriously, Paul. I was worried.'

'So was I,' he said. 'Maybe that was it. I mean do you know what she's been up to? Because I don't. And when I saw her like that, so sure of herself, I just thought, this is our kid and she has no idea about anything. I had to say something.'

'No, you didn't. You didn't have to say anything because if you had let her talk, just been patient and waited, she would have told us everything. And now she won't. She won't and the whole thing will have to start over again. All because you lost your temper with her. Why?'

'Am I allowed to say anything in my defence?' he said after a moment.

'What?' She looked at him. 'Don't do that, Paul. Don't make out that I'm stopping you from speaking.'

'I have to have a role here,' Paul said. 'I have to feel that my opinion counts. It can't always be you making the decisions and being the voice of reason. Sometimes I have to be allowed to do what I think is right.'

'Nobody's stopping you. You can do what you want. You just did, though, and are we any better off as a result? She's upstairs probably crying and thinking that you think she's a fool and that her friends are criminals. What good is that? How much better are we now as a result of your need to express yourself? Tell me.'

'It had to be said. Somebody had to say something. There was not one word that I said to her that wasn't true.'

'Truth has nothing to do with it. There are lots of things we could say that are true but what good would it do us? It's not about truth, Paul, for Christ's sake. It's about feelings and support and comfort and confidence. The truth doesn't matter. Why do I have to tell you this? And, anyway, how do you know what those guys are like? They could be fine. Up until now she's been a good judge of character. She's always been sensible and much more mature than people her age. You have to recognize that.'

'Well, she can't have it both ways. She can't complain that we don't treat her like an adult and then when I'm frank with her, when I talk to her as I would to an adult and tell her what I think, she can't complain and say she doesn't like it.'

'Who would you talk to like that? Who would you speak to in the tone that you used with her? You're telling her that her judgement is useless, that she's naive and that her friends are bums. How can that possibly help her?'

'She was mocking you and your reasonable methods. She was laughing at you, Ruth, and you deserve more respect than that.'

'Well, I can live without it. And what we have now is a situation that's worse than it was before we started. We've resolved nothing. We clarified nothing. We've alienated her and now we're fighting.'

'I have to be able to do what I feel is right. I have to be able to express the doubts and fears and worries that I have, don't I? I mean I am her father. I do have a role here. I think she's taking stupid risks and she needs to be told that. She needs to hear what I have to say. I really don't want us to argue about it, Ruth. Not at all and I know that this isn't good, but it's because of what she's done. It's because of the lies she's told us. That's where the problem comes from. It's not a problem between us. We'll sort it out. We always do.'

'That's because we usually agree.'

'Usually. But sometimes I keep my mouth shut and let you get on with it because I know you're better at it than me. You know what's best for the kids. You understand them better than I do. But this time I think you're wrong.'

She looked at him, expressionless. He was right. He had to say it. He had to talk. To let her know.

And then he saw it. The rage passed and he was left in the room with his wife and his words still echoing in the room. He could hear his tone come back at him and he didn't like it. In a second the confidence left him. A combination of the silence, her expression and his doubt, and he was on his own on the wrong side of an argument that he knew he would lose.

'I'm sorry,' he said. He stood and walked to the window. Fin was out the front cycling in tight circles around the car. Paul could understand now how out of touch he must seem to her. He could feel her disappointment, understand her fear. Understand that this wasn't about Clare any more, that it was about them. He had talked himself to a point where he was at odds with her, with the whole lot of them. He was putting himself out of step with his own life. It was too much. He had to know what to ignore and what to hold on to.

'I'm wrong,' he said. 'I don't know why. I'm just thinking too much. It's not anybody's fault. We can get over it.'

'Why?' she asked him. 'What is it, Paul? You're not right in your-self. It's not like you.'

'I know. I don't know. It'll be all right. Won't it? I'm just worried.'

'Don't be. It'll be fine. We'll sort it out.'

'We will. We will.'

It became true between them. Paul felt it and he knew that her strength would carry them through, beyond this back to normality. He looked for it in himself. For the same strength that he needed to contribute and he thought he could find it.

11

An hour later in the same room Ruth was about to speak. Clare watched her, never turning her head. Paul could sense the strain in her neck that kept her from allowing him to slip into the periphery of her vision, as if he was something too awful to be seen. Something that would disappear and cease to be if she couldn't see it. He laughed then shook his head when Ruth looked at him.

'What do you think we should do?' Ruth asked Clare. 'How do you think you would deal with this situation? Putting yourself in my place. In our place.'

'I don't know.'

'Think,' Ruth said.

'It's not going to work. It's just not. I don't want to do this. Just tell me what my punishment is and let me go.'

Paul could feel a prickling in his arms and back. He said nothing.

'No, Clare,' Ruth said. 'That's not good enough. Can you not see what it is that we want? We want you to be happy. We want to be able to trust you and let you enjoy yourself. But you keep putting up barriers between us and we don't know what's going on. Maybe you are mature enough to make your own decisions but unless you learn to talk to us we can't be sure. We know that you're brighter than most people your age but that doesn't mean that you're ready for everything.'

'If I tell you what I'm doing you'll just try to stop me. He'll just try to stop me.'

'We won't,' Ruth said. 'Not necessarily.'

'You will. Did you not hear him earlier? You can say all you want about trusting me and wanting to talk to me, but there's no trust in him. There's just suspicion and doubt.'

'There's not,' Ruth said. 'Really there's not.'

'It's not true, Clare,' Paul said.

She sat there in silence. When he saw her smile Paul felt hope rising in him, that somehow Ruth's words had got through to her and that the end was in sight. He would have forgiven anything right then. He wanted her back. But when she spoke she sounded tired.

'I've had enough,' she said. 'I can't go on like this. I don't know how I'm supposed to live here. I'm sick of always being in the wrong. All the drama and rows and shouting over nothing. I'm sick of you not listening to me when I tell you that I'm all right. You can do what you want. Tell me whatever it is that you want me to do and leave it at that.'

'Clare,' Ruth said. Paul could see that she was trying to keep from breaking. He didn't know if it was rage or sadness. He felt powerless. Any natural reaction in him was gone. He was useless.

'I'm going to bed,' Clare said and she left the room. Neither of them tried to stop her. After a moment Paul spoke.

'So what now?' he asked.

'This is your fault,' Ruth said and the words hit him so hard that he couldn't breathe.

Two days later. Two days when nothing had changed. Life went on and they all knew that they were waiting until it would be all right again. Waiting until the house felt ready before dealing with anything. It was still too raw. Nothing could be done yet.

Clare walked into the kitchen between them. She could not be ignored.

'Am I allowed leave the house?' she asked, facing Ruth.

'Of course you are.'

'What for?' Paul asked.

In the pause before she spoke, Paul thought that every interchange between them in the future would be this loaded. He had killed normality for ever. The tension that gripped her on hearing his voice could be permanent. It was hard to remember that she was wrong.

'My Walkman is dead,' she said. 'I need batteries.'

'Fair enough,' he said.

'I am going to the garage,' she said, sing-song. 'I am getting batteries. I will come home afterwards. I will talk to no one.'

'I can't deal with this stuff,' Paul said, walking to the door. 'Let me know when you want to start being civil again.'

'Civil.' She spat it out.

'Yeah,' he said, stopping in the door, enjoying his exit. 'That's all. Nothing more. Not friendly or loving or affectionate. I'll settle for civil.'

'Get over it, Clare,' Ruth said when he was gone.

'It's not me.'

'It is you.'

'No,' Clare said. 'No. It's not. And you know it's not. You know he's in the wrong and you're not doing anything about it. I'm on my own and you won't do what you have to to sort it out.'

It was depressing. The truth was not something that mattered to Ruth any more.

'I'm tired of it all,' she said. 'I'm fed up with all of you.'

Clare looked at her. She needed to be held. She needed to be told that everything was all right and that they would get beyond this and life would return to normal. But she got nothing. She was given nothing. She left and went up the road.

Afterwards she thought that maybe he had been waiting for her. It was the first time that she had been out in three days and there he was as she was leaving the estate, suddenly walking beside her.

'Hiya,' he said.

'What?' she said, without looking at him. He didn't answer. 'Do you want something?' she asked, her tone less aggressive. She needed him to be gone.

'Are you all right?'

She laughed, hollow.

'Not really, no.'

'What happened with your old fellow?'

'You could have stuck around long enough to find out. If you were so interested.'

She kept walking without looking at him. He had stopped at her last comment. She knew he would come after her and he did.

'Hey. Here.' He ran up behind her. 'Hang on a second. What was I supposed to do? I thought you would have wanted me to go. I thought it would make it easier for you.'

'Right. And for you.'

'No.'

'Well, actually, yeah. Right? Really? Wasn't it?'

He looked shocked. He looked younger again. He didn't know what to say.

'No,' he said.

'OK,' she said. It was too easy.

He grabbed her by the arm.

'Hold on.'

She shook his hand off and looked at him.

'Don't,' she said. 'Don't you touch me.'

He held his hands up.

'Sorry, OK. But hold on. Will you stop for one fucking minute?'

She waited and looked at the ground.

'If I thought that you wanted me to stay when your father came in, I would have. But what could I do? He told me to go—'

'And you did. It's fine. I don't care.'

'No. Clare. It's not. I didn't want to go. I wanted to stay and tell him to fuck off and mind his own business. And I wanted to ask you – that stuff you were saying before, that you didn't want to see me any more – was it true? Did you mean it? Because I didn't know afterwards. I didn't know and I wanted to talk to you but I couldn't because I didn't want to go up to your house and make things worse for you.'

'Too late for that. Couldn't have been worse. Thanks, though.'

'Stop,' he said. 'Just stop being like that. I did nothing wrong. I did what I thought you'd want.'

'You did.'

He was trying to remember what he wanted to ask her.

'What I want to know is whether or not your father had anything to do with you breaking up with me?'

'That was before, Robbie. I told you before he came in. Do you not remember?'

'Yeah, I remember but I don't know. I thought maybe he was putting pressure on you before or something. I thought maybe that was it. Maybe that had something to do with it. Because he doesn't like me. I know that. The way he looks at me.'

Clare felt sorry for him, but what could she do? It wouldn't work. It never could.

'No,' she said. 'I'm sorry but it wasn't that. It had nothing to do with him. We can be friends or whatever but we can't go back to – ' she paused, unsure – 'whatever that was before.'

'I don't want to be friends,' he said.

'OK. Fine. Fair enough. Goodbye then. See you.' She moved to go on.

'What happened?' he asked. 'What did I do? I don't understand.'

'Oh here, Robbie. Just leave it.'

'No. I won't. You have to tell me why you're being like this. What did I do?'

'You did nothing wrong. I told you this the other day. You just weren't who I thought you were. That's all. There. Now you know.'

'But I don't know what you mean. I've been thinking about it for two days and I still don't understand.'

She started walking again. She didn't want to look and see the expression she knew would be on his face. Hurt, ignorant, bruised. Childish. Too young. Not up to it.

'What I mean is that it wasn't your fault. It was me. Not you. I have to go now.'

'But I love you,' he said.

Clare stopped. He would have said anything to keep her there talking to him, she thought.

'No, you don't,' she said. 'How could you? You don't even know me.'

'Yeah, I do.'

'No, you don't. Forget it, Robbie. I'm not interested.'

That was it. She kept walking and when she got to the traffic lights, she looked back. He was gone. She didn't want to be nasty but it was a cheap shot from him to say love. What was he trying to do? Anything to protect himself from rejection. She had tried to be nice. She had tried to let him down gently and he had stalked her. Take it like a man or else take worse. She knew enough to see through hurt pride. She knew what this was about. He had given her nothing. He couldn't talk to her. There was nothing there. Too late now to start talking and opening up about how he felt. She didn't believe it. It wasn't true. She didn't care enough now. She didn't need a nice guy. She had a kid brother already. Robbie could stand around and look as tough as he wanted and stare at the ground as a means of expression, but there had to be more and there wasn't. He should know what to do. Move on to something else. She would. Not her fault. She'd enough to be thinking about without him. Love? She wasn't stupid.

It was cold. That was what he thought first. It was cold and he was alone and he walked back down the road without seeing anything. She threw it back in his face. She told him that he couldn't talk and he told her everything, all that there was for her to know. That he loved her. And it meant nothing to her. His love meant nothing. His love wasn't real. So what was it, he wondered, that hurt him at night when he was in bed away from her? That pained him as only an absence could. What was it that silenced him when he was with her? What was it that made him think that he could only be happy with her and nobody else? That he would change anything to stay with her. The warmth that he had felt with her. If it was not love what was it? The combination of pain and fear and longing and complete happiness in her company. It could only be love. And how could he not know her? He knew enough. What else was there? He wasn't who she thought he was. But he was himself. He hadn't changed. Who did she want him to be? She couldn't turn on him. She couldn't talk to him like that. He deserved better. He deserved respect, but instead he had to put up with this shit. Why? What for? What was the point in any of it? He could go out tonight and get any girl he wanted. He could go into town and find the girl he wanted and get her. But he couldn't because the one girl he wanted didn't want him. She'd had him and had said no. She spoke in a language that he didn't understand. He said things that made her laugh and sneer and snarl. What was so great about that? Get over it.

He could do anything. Ring up Alan and go on the piss, go and get out of their heads. Get some money together and do something, anything, to stop thinking about this girl who could not be worth it.

Nothing could be worth this. Somebody had to pay. Go and get pissed and find some fucker who would say one wrong word, look at him for even a second and give him a hiding. She should pay. It should be her, for being a lying, cold bitch. The next time he saw her, if she had Alan's one, Emily, with her would they laugh at him? Would Emily say something to Alan? Robbie told Clare he loved her. Laughs. Robbie's a fucking sap. Robbie's losing it. That one had him wrapped around her finger. Did you see him? Did you see him running after her and her walking away from him, leaving him looking after her. Was he crying? Robbie loves Clare. She thinks he's an idiot. All of this for a stuck-up girl whose father was still in charge of her. She'd used him and he'd liked it. Tell her father that. Tell him what they'd done together. What she'd done to him, his nice little daughter. Think about that, you posh cunt, and think about who's the scumbag.

He wanted to go and lie down, go to bed and sleep because what was the point? Go to bed and get up in a couple of days when he felt OK again. When he'd got over it. He was going to get over it. He'd told her he loved her and she'd said no. I'm not interested. What could you do with a girl like that? He'd never said that to anyone before. He hadn't meant to but it had been there and when he had been looking for the thing to say, the thing that would make her look at him, make her see him and his pain, it had come out. He had thought for a second that that would do it, that that would be the thing that had been missing to make her stay with him. But he knew now that there was nothing he could have said. Ring Alan. Ring him before Emily did and get out. Go and drink until he forgot it all.

Close it down. Shut it all up. Lock it away because it had done him no good. He knew what he had to do. Back to the others. Back to how it was before. Harder and stronger than ever. It would all work again. He could get what he wanted back again.

*

At the dinner table, Lou could tell that there was a problem. Nobody was shouting and when her parents spoke to each other everything they said was normal, the words were all right, they were what they should be, talking about the house and what to do tomorrow and all that, but it wasn't right. She knew it was because of Clare. She had done something wrong and Lou didn't know what. Fin said it was something to do with a boy, something bad that Clare did. Or the boy was bad. Something was wrong and Lou didn't like it. She knew that Clare wasn't happy. She never talked to her any more, since they moved house and they had their own rooms. Lou liked having her own room. They let her do it the way she wanted with the right paper and the curtains that matched and nobody ever touched her things. Fin never came in. It was better but then sometimes it had been nice with Clare: when she woke in the middle of the night Clare would take her into her bed until she fell asleep and she would wake up with Clare holding her and Clare was very beautiful and she would joke with her and they would talk a bit and she would read to her. And now Clare wasn't happy. Lou watched her eating, not looking up, and she looked sad. She looked lonely and Lou wanted to do something for her. She wanted her to be happy and she wanted to say something but she didn't know what. It was very sad. She wasn't thinking about it really, she didn't know why but then she was crying.

'What is it, Lou?' Ruth asked her.

Lou shook her head.

'What?' Paul asked her. His voice was softer in his throat than he had heard in a long time.

'What's wrong with Clare?' she asked. Clare looked up.

'Me?'

'What's wrong? Something's wrong.' Lou was talking herself up, her voice getting thicker, her breathing less regular. The sadness of her situation struck her more and she knew that she could sort it out. She could see that she could make things better for them all. Maybe only she could make it like it should be. Like it normally was so that she didn't have to think. She let it come on her and found herself getting up and going over to Clare and standing beside her.

'What's wrong?' she asked.

'Nothing,' Clare said. 'I'm fine. Poor baby.'

'I'm not a baby. Why is everyone so sad? What happened? Tell me.'

'It's nothing,' Clare said.

'No, it's not,' Lou said. She was really crying now. She couldn't see properly and she could hardly breathe but she knew that there had to be something, that somebody would have to do something so that she would stop.

'I'm fine,' Clare said. 'Really.'

'No. No.' That wasn't enough.

'It's OK, Lou,' Paul said. She turned and looked at him when he spoke. 'We weren't very happy with Clare because of something, but it's over now and everything will get back to normal.'

'What was it?' Lou asked.

'It doesn't matter,' Paul said. 'It's over now.'

'What did you do?' she asked Clare. Clare smiled.

'Nothing,' she said. 'I don't know.'

'You were right, Lou,' Paul said. 'There was something wrong and things haven't been the way they should be, but I hope now they will be. I don't want Clare or you or Fin or anyone to be unhappy. OK?'

Lou looked at Clare. Clare was looking at Paul. She turned back to Lou and when she did Lou could still see that her face wasn't right. Her father was saying the right things but it didn't make anything better. She felt another wave of sadness pass through her and felt her body convulse with the same hiccuping crying. She pressed her wet face into Clare's neck, feeling the warmth and trying to hide from the table and the room and the whole house that she didn't want to go back to, happier to stay where she was. Across the table Paul looked at Ruth and saw her expression. He looked at his two daughters holding onto each other and didn't know what to do. The more he tried, it seemed, the worse this was getting.

Paul went out after dinner. The evening was warm and cloudy. It had rained that afternoon and as he left the house he could smell damp tarmac, honeysuckle and cut grass, barbecues lit by their neighbours out of habit and hope and determination that the good weather could not be over. He saw the younger kids with jackets for goals playing football on the green. This safe secure area full of suburban people doing what they should do. What was his problem? What had happened to him that meant that all he saw were the risks and the threat? Girls and boys. Boys and girls. It was never going to be right for him. There was nothing he could do about it. All this uptight need to be right. Now even Lou was noticing. He was getting it wrong, he was trying, but he was getting it wrong and Ruth was too kind to tell him.

It was the wrong time to meet Joe. There was never a good time, but this was just wrong. Had he been waiting? Paul wondered afterwards. There was no avoiding him. Joe was standing straight in front of him and when Paul was still too far away to hear him he began to speak.

'Sorry?' Paul said.

'What?' Joe said. He was smiling. He was happy. Paul began to hope.

'I didn't hear you,' Paul said. 'What did you say?'

'I was asking did you sort that out? With your daughter, I mean. Did you find out what was going on? I saw you sent him packing the other day.'

'Yeah, well,' Paul said. 'It's sorted out now.'

'He's worse than an animal, that fellow,' Joe said. 'You wouldn't know what he'd be doing. I had to tell you. I know it's not my business but I thought you should know.'

'Yeah, well thanks,' Paul said. Joe's mix of politeness, bitterness and excitement was unsettling him. 'I'd better go on,' he said. 'I've to get to the shops.'

'He's dangerous,' Joe said. 'The things he's done to me, to my car. I don't want to scare you but you have to be careful. Everyone thinks I exaggerate, but I'm telling you. You know now. I'd be scared of him. The wrong kind of young fellow for your daughter, for anyone's daughter.'

'Yeah. Thanks again.'

'Did you talk to him?' Joe asked. He had to talk, Paul thought. These words would come out of him and Paul could do nothing to stop him.

'Not really,' Paul said.

'No point. Did you see how he looks at you? How he looks at people he doesn't like? Not that he would be capable of liking any-thing. Not that he would have enough empathy for that.'

'I didn't,' Paul said. He tapped his watch and shrugged. 'I've got to go, Joe.'

'I think he could kill. I've never seen anything like it.'

Paul stopped and looked at him. He was connected to this man now. To this depressed, depressing man. They had something in common. He saw Joe's excitement tempered by fear and anger. They were in it together, bonded by a mutual enemy, and whatever Joe said he would have to listen. This was where he was headed. Neighbour-hood disputes and dramas could take him over and absorb him as they had this lonely bastard. He wouldn't let it happen.

'You can't say that,' Paul said. 'If you have anything to complain about, call the guards but don't be saying stuff like that. It does nobody any good.'

'I'm serious. I'm not joking. There's a . . . a disconnection.'

'I'll see you,' Paul said. He walked away, leaving Joe behind still talking. He was calling after him but Paul wasn't listening and he didn't hear. He kept walking, lost in his own world, in his fears and realizations and hopes. In the thoughts of that disconnection that Joe had planted and which he was trying to weed out before it took root. Because of this he didn't notice that Alan and Tim and Robbie were watching him from Robbie's front door step as he left the estate and turned up the road towards the shops.

Robbie had spent the afternoon in bed. His mother woke him for dinner and he came down, his head still foggy with sleep. He was trying to remember what was going on. His father was waiting at the table.

'All right?'

'Yeah,' Robbie said as he sat down. 'I don't know. I mustn't have slept properly last night.'

'How long were you up there for?'

'Four hours,' his mother answered.

'You must have needed it,' his father said.

'Must have.'

Robbie was beginning to remember. He wanted to get Alan and maybe even Tim and go into town. Get hammered. He was going to forget about Clare and all that bollocks. It was no good for him.

'I feel a lot better,' he said.

'Good,' his mother said. 'You haven't been yourself for the past few days.'

'Really?' Robbie was surprised. He hadn't known that it showed.

'You've been too quiet,' his father said. 'Not that I'm complaining. No cops or neighbours over giving out. I can't remember the last time. Must be at least ten days. I said to her there must be something wrong with you.'

'I've been all right,' Robbie said. 'Just taking it easy.'

'You didn't seem right to me,' his mother said. 'I thought you were getting something.'

'Sense,' his father said. 'Maybe. At last.'

'I don't think so,' Robbie said. 'I hope not anyway. I'm going out tonight and I'll see what I can do.'

'Don't,' his mother said. 'Please.'

'I'm joking. I'm only messing.'

'Well, it's good to see you back to normal,' she said.

'I don't know what it was. I was just a bit down. I didn't think you'd notice.'

'She sees everything,' his father said.

He felt different. It was gone, he thought, or it would be soon. He just needed to stop thinking about it. It was a warm evening. They would go into town and have a proper night out and when he woke tomorrow it would be over.

'Where are you going tonight?' his mother asked.

'I don't know. With Alan and them.'

'Don't be getting up to anything.'

'I'm not. I won't.'

'There's a few quid for you,' his father said. He held out his hand. Robbie took it. He didn't look down or count it. 'It'll get you a few pints or whatever.'

'Thanks,' Robbie said. 'You don't have to.'

'Oh, come on,' his mother said. 'Money for drink?'

'Ah what? Isn't he better off in a pub like a normal person

than out in the fields like an animal? He's on holidays. Where's the harm?'

'Thanks,' Robbie said again.

'But listen to me,' said his father, 'you have to watch yourself in town. There's some serious people around the place. Keep your head together.'

'I know,' Robbie said.

'I hope you do. Because it won't be black eyes or cut lips with some of these guys. It's not slaps in a shopping centre with a bunch of young fellows.'

'That wasn't my fault. And anyway I'm in town all the time. I know what I'm doing.'

'Just be careful,' his mother said. 'Walk away from trouble. Nobody will think the less of you.'

Robbie smiled.

'I don't know about that.'

'She's right,' his father said. 'There's a lot of arseholes around.'

'I know,' Robbie said. 'I've met most of them.'

It was better when it was like this. He could talk to them. When he left the room after dinner he saw that his father had given him fifty quid. They could go out.

The three of them went into town, Alan and Tim and him, to some new five-storey place. Fake IDs and pints of cider and shots and bottles of green stuff that would take your head off. The three of them, drinks on him, not saying anything, just buying and they were there and they listened to him and it was easy to forget her. They didn't ask and he wouldn't tell. He wanted to know. He wanted to ask Alan what he had heard but he wouldn't let him see. He wouldn't know what he might say when he was drunk or what he might do or what he might hear. Easy to forget when he was drinking and there were girls everywhere and then there was one who was looking at him and he went straight over and he didn't even speak. He didn't have to because she knew what was going on and it was OK. He just grabbed her and it was easy.

He didn't think about it again after that. Not when he was outside down a lane with this one. Not when he was waiting for the others to come out. Not in the taxi or in the chipper on the way home.

'That was the best night,' Tim was saying when they were walking down the road to the estate. He'd got some girl as well and she looked all right. Alan was drunker than the other two because he'd ended up at the counter on his own for most of the night while the other two were off doing their thing. It wasn't that late. Maybe two o'clock. Alan stopped and puked and they waited for him.

'Are you all right?' Tim asked as he joined them again.

'I'm too drunk,' Alan said.

'You're fine,' Robbie said. 'You'll be grand. I needed that. I needed to go out and get fucking messed up. And I'm glad you were there.' It was getting harder to stop himself. The words were coming and he thought they were all right but he had to be careful. He didn't want to start being a sap in front of these two, even though he had nothing to worry about. They were his friends and they'd always be there. What would he have without them? Where would he be? He was drunk and he wouldn't normally see it like this. But maybe this was better. To tell people what you thought of them. Not think too much about it and stop yourself so that they would be scared of you. Give you respect. Fuck it. He had enough respect. He could sort anyone out. But sometimes you had to tell.

'You're my best friends,' he said. Even then the words sounded wrong to him.

'Thanks,' Tim said.

'I'm going to puke,' Alan said.

'What?'

'Seriously.'

Alan walked to the side of the road and got sick in the gutter. When he'd finished, they sat on a low wall near the entrance to their estate and smoked cigarettes, the three of them, not talking. Alan was coughing and spitting, trying to straighten himself up. Tim said nothing and Robbie remembered what he had said to them and realized that it was stupid. It didn't need to be said and now they might remember. He might remember. What was it? What was it that he was trying to remember? Or forget? Then he remembered and he wanted it to be gone again.

It was sometime later and he was there on the wall on his own. He was drunker than he thought. The others were gone and when he tried he remembered the three of them walking into the estate and watching the two of them go off to their houses. Then he had turned back and come here to have a cigarette. Except that wasn't why. There was something else. He smoked and thought about it and then he stood up.

It was so clean, he thought, as he walked back in and passed the gate to his own house. It was so easy. It would put an end to it all. He had the brick in his hand. He had found it on the ground before he had even started looking for it. Onto the next one. A simple statement. The air was cool in the early morning, damp with the dew, and it was all so clean. He was so happy and excited. He understood it clearly now. What it had all meant. Now that he could smell the air in the morning it reminded him of a time when he was a kid, when they first moved to Dublin, how the air had smelt then, the things that he had been hoping for, which seemed promised to him in the air. All there again now in the cold and the darkness.

He stood at the end of Clare's drive. He looked at the whole house in darkness and swayed slightly as he turned to see was there anyone around. There was no one. He had to try not to laugh. The feeling in his stomach like nausea, but better. Happier. The bay window of the living room stood out from the house, black against the white of the wall. It was closer to him, inviting him in. What else could he do? For her, for her father, for the whole fucking lot of them. For the way he could see Clare in her father's face when he looked down his nose at him. For the way his own voice sounded when he spoke to her up there in her room, slow and awkward. To let them know that it wasn't always going to go their way. That he could do something. He could wake them and scare them and make them think like he had had to since they had arrived. If he was not good enough for her then this is what he would do. This is what they should expect. This is where it would end up and it wasn't much, it wasn't too much but it was enough.

He swayed again, steadied himself and then drew his arm back, holding the brick steady, and threw it. He watched the arc as it rose, then fell towards the window and the crash as it hit. He stood long enough to hear the noise and see the glass break and remember the perfect flight that he had produced and then, before he saw anything else, before he could think, he was across the green, trying to keep his feet off the ground as much as he could, stumbling and leaning forward to steady himself and then he was in and he closed the door behind him. He held his breath and felt his heart pounding in his throat, the pain in his chest as he tried not to breathe. He made his way upstairs quickly and silently, suddenly feeling as sober as when he had left the house earlier that evening. He took off his clothes and before getting into bed he pulled back the edge of the curtain and looked across the green. There was a light on now in one of the upstairs windows of Clare's house and downstairs in the living room. From this distance he could see no one. His window was open and as the cool air blew on his face from outside he listened and could hear nothing. Not a sound. No traffic on the main road, no sirens or shouting or distant voices. Nothing. He had done it. It was as perfect as he had hoped. From somewhere inside him it had come to him and told him what it was that would let him move on, make him forget about her and he had done it. He had been protected. Nothing could have happened to him, he realized now, when he was in the process of delivering his message.

She was in bed. She was asleep but she wasn't because she was awake and thinking about what that was. And what was that? Turn it back and listen again to the noise that had dragged her out of a dream. Who knew? But here she was with a crash. She lay in bed and now heard the conversation downstairs between her mother and father, his voice fast. Her mother trying to slow him down and make him think, make him wait and assess before he started shouting. Holding him back, like he needed to be. Her voice sorting him out. Straightening him out. Her tone that could be heard through the floor clearly in a way that words, syllables, vowels and consonants would never make. Reducible to a single noise. Reason. It was there and she could hear it and she knew then that it was about her. She didn't know how, what it was that she could have done from here in her bed, what she might have done in her dreams or sleepwalking or in memory. She had no idea what it was that could have wakened them all, that her mother was now trying to play down, but she knew for sure that it was all about her.

She was downstairs in the morning before she had even remembered. Easy and natural. A distant doubt that things weren't as they should be but that could just be morning. The fear of the new day. Nothing to worry about. All this in ten seconds walking down the stairs. And then into the kitchen, her hand on the door, and then she remembered and it all was different.

Paul could not be stopped. He had told himself that he would say nothing until Ruth had explained the situation, but when he saw her it came out.

'There she is,' he said. 'Do you know what he's done now? This friend of yours?'

'Who?' she asked.

'Who?' Paul said it back to her. 'Who, she says. Who else? Your boyfriend. The guy you trusted so much.'

Clare said nothing. She went to the fridge and took out milk. From the cupboard she got cereal. Paul stood still, watching her.

'Do you know what he did?'

'Paul,' Ruth said.

'No. No, Ruth. I'm going to tell her. I have to.'

'Paul. Don't.'

He stood in front of Clare.

'Do you know what he did? This guy? Threw a brick through our window.'

'When?' Clare asked.

'You didn't hear? Last night. In the middle of the night.'

'Did you see him?'

'Well, he didn't stand around waiting to be caught. He ran off. He's not so big when it comes to being caught.'

'So you didn't see him?'

Paul shook his head and laughed grimly.

'Don't you start with this,' he said. 'Who else would it be? He's dangerous, this guy. This thug that you were bringing into the house doing whatever you were doing. This is the result of all that. This is where your judgement brings us.'

'You don't know it was him,' Clare said. 'You don't know that for sure.'

'Oh, come on. The pair of you—' He stopped. 'Who do you think it would be? Who is most likely to do something like this?'

'Him,' she said. 'Probably. But I don't know.'

'So what now? Are you going to sulk for the next six months because he broke our window? Are you going to ignore me and pretend that I'm a bad smell around the place that you have to put up with? Are you going to punish me for being right? Punish me because you got it so wrong?'

'Stop,' Ruth said.

'No,' Paul said and he stared at her.

Clare looked up at him.

'I want to know,' he went on. 'She's spent the whole summer clicking her tongue at me and sighing and complaining that we don't understand her and that we worry too much when actually everything's all right. She can handle everything if we leave her to it. Well, what now? What happens now, Clare? You take over. You tell us what we should do. Because I don't know.'

He saw the tremor in her shoulders.

'If he broke the window, he did it because I dumped him. Because I'd had enough of him. How can you blame me for this? Whoever threw the stone or whatever. It's their fault. Not mine. I didn't ask for this. I didn't do anything wrong. Go and talk to him if you're so sure that he did it. Don't talk to me about it. What do you want from me? What do you want me to do?'

'I want you to realize that this is the direct result of you— of your—' Paul hesitated. He didn't know how to finish the sentence. He had lost his flow. 'I'm not blaming you, Clare. I don't want to be having this conversation any more than you. I just want you to realize what's out there. The danger that is waiting for you literally outside the door,' Paul said.

'There is no danger,' she said. 'He's stupid and he's pissed off but he's not dangerous. That's just ridiculous. I know what he's like. You don't. You've never even spoken to him.'

'I don't have to,' Paul said. 'I know.'

'Well, then you can sort it out,' Clare said. 'Seeing as you know so much.' She stood to go. It was a stupid thing to say. Childish. She should have waited for something better but she couldn't stay. She had to get out.

'Don't you walk away from this,' Paul said after her but he didn't do anything. As she slammed the door behind her she could hear the two of them inside starting to argue. She went upstairs to get away from it all.

'What has happened to you?' Ruth was saying.

'To me? To me? Jesus, Ruth. Look around you. There's a problem all right but it's not with me.'

'This thing with Clare. It'll blow over if you let it. If we work together but you don't seem to be interested in doing that and I don't know why.'

'Because I'm worried. I think you're wrong on this. I think she's at a critical point here and if we get it wrong, it could mess her up long term.'

'Why? Why do you think so? I don't understand. So she doesn't want to talk to us. She's moody all the time. She comes home late. She has a boy over to the house when we're out. That's it. So what? She's seventeen. She's completely normal.'

'No. There's nothing normal about this. Don't tell me that. Have you seen this guy? Have you seen what they get up to? You tell me that she's mature for her age and still she's drawn to an ape like that. He bricked our bloody window. And you're saying we should talk to her. Let her make her own mistakes. One mistake with this guy, Ruth. That's all it would take. He could do anything. She is getting in with the wrong people here and you want to let it happen.'

'Of course I don't. But you can't protect her from the world, Paul. She has to live and we have to let her.'

'No. We don't. We have to look out for her. We have to stop her from doing things that will damage her.'

She was looking at him. It was clear to him now. He knew what needed to be done.

'You were never like this before,' she said. 'I don't know where this stuff is coming from. What is it?'

'She's seventeen. The next couple of years matter. They're crucial.'

She shook her head.

'No. You haven't been right all summer. This stuff with Clare is just the latest. You don't talk to me. You're quieter. What is wrong with you? Is there something?'

'There's plenty.'

'So tell me.'

He sighed. She was waiting. He wanted her to know everything. To stop holding back.

'I hate this place,' he said and as soon as it was out he realized that it was true.

'What?' she said.

'I don't like it here. I don't feel right. I don't like these people. It's not a good place to be. And things are beginning to go wrong. I don't know. I don't know what to do. I don't feel in control.'

'Jesus, Paul. What am I supposed to do about that? We're here. We have to make it work. You were happy to move. You were fine when we got here. You can't start into this now.'

'You asked me and I told you.'

'You're not one of the kids, Paul. You're my husband. Their father. You have to be stronger. I need you to be stronger.'

He looked at her. She had brought them here. It was her idea. But what was the point in that? What good was there in complaining? She was right. He had to think, to decide and to do. To be stronger. To make it better.

12

Clare had to wait. It was three days later and in that time she had come to understand what needed to be done. Too angry with her father. Betrayed by her mother. It required energy to keep the fight going. She had had enough. It wasn't supposed to be like this. She could change it.

It was ten o'clock in the morning when the others left. All of them into the car and gone without saying a word to her. When she came down there was a note saying that they were shopping. Her father had written it. It said 'Gone shopping'. She smiled when she saw it. They would be away for hours.

It didn't matter now. It wouldn't make any difference. Clare walked across the estate without looking around her. She didn't care who saw her. She had to do it. She stood on his doorstep for the first time and rang the doorbell. She didn't know who would come. It was late morning. When the door opened it was him. She saw it in him straight away. That he had done it. That he thought he had her now. Stupid.

'What were you thinking?' she said.

'Come in.'

'No. I'm not coming in. I didn't want to come but I had to ask you—'

'Come in,' he said again, calm, confident. Different. 'I need to talk to you.' He turned and walked from the hall into the living room, leaving the door open. Clare stood there thinking but it was no good.

She couldn't think. There was too much going on. She had to ask him. She had to tell him. There was no choice. She realized that she was out of control when she closed the door behind her.

He was on the couch when she went in. She stood in front of him, the door behind her and she spoke. She could do nothing about the warble in her voice. She hated it but there wasn't time to sort it out.

'What the fuck did you do that for? Are you completely thick?'

'What? Do what?'

The smirk. The enjoyment. She could hit him.

'Do you not see how pathetic it is? How sad it makes you look? I tell you I don't think we should go out or whatever and you break my parents' window. Did you think I'd be impressed? That it would make me change my mind? Make me love you?' She knew it was cruel but it wasn't her fault. He had done this. 'Or were you just trying to scare me? What were you thinking? Did you think at all? Did you just do it without thinking like a stupid fucking animal?'

He was still sitting. He looked up at her, his expression unchanged as if he hadn't been listening. But he had heard and he was thinking now. He knew what he wanted and this was it. He wanted her here in front of him shouting and really upset and angry. Maybe even afraid. He wanted her in a place that he had never seen her before and he had got it. He had made it happen. He was winning.

'What happened?' he asked. 'A window?'

There was no doubt. They both knew that he'd done it but Clare was lost for a second. She didn't know what he was doing. Pretending? She didn't know how to react.

'You know,' she said and stopped. He smiled up at her.

'I know.'

It was then that Clare began to feel scared. He couldn't deny it, she knew, but when the words came out of his mouth they were so unexpected that she believed at that moment he could do anything. That was why she didn't move.

'You knew it was me straight away, didn't you?' He looked at her and laughed. 'I bet you didn't feel so clever then.'

'Why would I feel clever?'

'Because I'm me and you're you and you were the one telling me how it's going to be. Like you controlled me. You told me that you didn't want me, that you didn't love me. I said it to you. I said, I love you. And you laughed at me. What did you think I would do? What could I do? What did you expect?'

He sounded like he needed her to say something but Clare didn't trust herself. She didn't know what he would do.

'Do you know what that feels like? What it feels like here?' With a clenched fist he punched himself in the chest. The echo rang in Clare's ears. 'Or do you have anything in there? Are you empty inside? Because you should know that you can't treat people like that. You can't treat me like that. I didn't know how to tell you what I thought about you but I did, I tried, and it's not my fucking fault that I got it wrong. You can't blame me. You can't laugh at me when I tell you.'

Nobody knew where she was, Clare realized then. He was still sitting, eyes lifted to her, reddening and filling as she watched.

'Robbie—' she said.

'Shut up. You wouldn't let me talk before, so I'm talking now. I am saying to you that that's not something you should do. Because you will regret it. You will be sorry. And that's why I broke your window. To let you know that you can't do that and get away with it. You're a nasty fucking bitch and you had it coming. You need to learn a few things about other people and what they can do to you.'

Clare turned and walked out the door. He was up in front of her. She didn't know how.

'Wait,' he said. 'You can't go.'

'Get out of the way,' she said. She couldn't even pretend to be calm now. 'Robbie, please.' He grabbed her by the arm and pulled her back.

'Don't touch me,' she said.

He smiled, laughed, smirked. She didn't know. She was looking at him and she didn't know.

'Don't you tell me what to do,' he said. 'It doesn't work like that now.'

They tried not to react when they realized that she wasn't there when they got home. As they unpacked the bags and Fin and Lou ate lunch, Clare's name wasn't mentioned. Paul tried not to think about it, tried not to let her take over his thoughts again. Ruth didn't want to say anything. They had talked enough. It was nothing. She was out. She would come back. They could ring her if they were worried. Ruth could pick up the phone right now and call her on the mobile and ask her where she was and it would be all right. But she didn't. She stopped herself because it was nothing.

At six o'clock Paul came in from the garden and said, 'Is she back?'

In that moment Ruth felt close to him again, reconnected. 'Not yet,' she said. 'Will I ring her?'

'I think we'd better.'

Ruth dialled and heard Clare's message. She hung up.

'No reply.'

Paul shrugged.

'She's probably in town.'

'She should let us know. I don't know if she wants dinner.'

'It's annoying,' he said and he went back outside.

At seven o'clock Ruth rang Emily, but she hadn't spoken to Clare all day. She rang Emma and Caroline's houses and nobody knew anything. She rang Clare's mobile and left a message. She tried to sound normal and not let her fear come through. She asked her to give the house a ring when she got the message. She heard herself say goodbye in a voice that sounded like someone else. They ate dinner and when Lou asked where Clare was Paul just said out.

Time slowed down for Ruth. She looked at the clock and watched the hands stay where they were, forced herself to look away, fighting her urge to look again a minute later. Every second increased her pain, the voices getting louder in her head and slowly, slowly, time was passing. Making it later but bringing closer the moment that something would happen.

'What do we do?' she said to Paul at eight o'clock.

'Will I go out and look?' he asked.

'Where?'

'I don't know. Drive around. Just in case. Before it gets dark. Better to do something.'

'OK. I'll wait here in case she rings.'

'She'll turn up,' he said, trying to smile and showing only strain.

'Where is she?' Ruth said.

'She's teaching us a lesson,' he said. 'That's all it is. It'll be fine.' He went outside. As he unlocked the car, he changed his mind and walked down to Joe's place. He rang on the door and tried to calm down.

'Hello,' Joe said when he saw him. 'What's wrong?'

'Hi,' Paul said. 'Nothing's wrong. You didn't by any chance see Clare today? She's not home and we're just wondering.'

'Who?'

'Clare. Our daughter. Our eldest one.'

'Right. Yes. Yes. I saw her this morning. She was going across to Whelan's place.'

'You saw her.'

'Yes. I don't know when. In the morning. After you went out.'

'And did she come back?'

'I don't know,' Joe said. 'She could have.'

'But you didn't see her.'

'No. But I had a bath then.'

'What?'

'I wasn't around. You should ask him. The young fellow. I wouldn't believe a word, but you should ask him. See what he says.'

'You're sure it was her?'

'Your daughter. Yes.'

'Thanks,' Paul said and he walked away, leaving Joe talking after him.

He hadn't let himself think it. He couldn't believe that this was going to be the answer, that he was going to have to talk to these people about Clare. He was walking out of Joe's driveway and across the green. It was a still, cloudy evening. The sky came down low, hovered above the roofs and participated in Paul's drama. The sky that had spent the summer elsewhere leaving vacant space, came down now and watched as things began to go wrong, the air warm and short, letting him know that it too understood that something was going on and that suddenly, malevolently, it wanted to take part. It wanted to see what was happening.

They were there in front of him. Four of them. Not her. He couldn't see Robbie from here, the one he needed. He began to feel sick. It was happening very fast. He was closer now and he saw Robbie. Robbie looked back at him and he said something to the others and Paul heard the laughter, too hard and cruel. They stopped and Robbie was waiting for him, staring. As he arrived Paul saw a moment of fear that seemed to tell him something and that was it.

'You,' he said.

'What's your problem?'

There was no thought. No time or room. The information was all.

He pushed him, an open palm on Robbie's chest. He could feel how skinny he was under the T-shirt, how light he was. Robbie fell back, stumbling, trying to stay standing. Paul didn't see the others.

'Here,' Robbie said. 'What are you fucking doing?'

Paul stood beside him, face to face. Paul was taller, wider, heavier. He was using it without even knowing. He wanted this guy to be scared.

'Where is Clare?' he said.

'I don't know where she is. Mad fucking bitch.'

Paul hit him. Open hand, slap on the ear. Loud and hard. He grabbed Robbie's T-shirt at the back of his neck and shook him. Robbie struggled, waved his arm around to try and shake Paul loose but couldn't.

'Shut up. Where is she now? You fucking know and if you don't tell me I will kill you. I will kill you. Where is she?'

'I don't fucking know. Get your hands off me,' Robbie said. Paul hit him again, twice, cuffed him hard across the head to stop him struggling. Because he could. He had control and he would get what he needed but he was afraid now of what it was. He was afraid of what he might have to do.

'She was with you today,' Paul said. 'What did you do to her?'

'Nothing,' Robbie said. 'She just left.' There was something in him. Paul could see it. He could get it out. There was only time between Paul and the information.

'Where is she now?'

'I don't know. She came over. I talked to her for five minutes and she left. That's it. You can't fucking hit me.'

'I'll hit you if I want,' Paul said. 'I'll fucking hit you until you can't speak. Hard man. You little animal. Where is she?'

Robbie said nothing. He looked at Paul. He was trying not to break. Trying not to show what he was thinking and Paul knew it.

'I know what you're like,' Paul said. 'I know the kind of things you do and I hear the lot of you laughing and I'm telling you, you are shit. You are the shit of the world. You're dirt and if you touched her I'll get rid of you.'

The words came out of him. He didn't hear himself. He wasn't thinking. He was trying to find out what had happened and this was what he was saying. This guy could do anything. Joe said that. He put bricks through windows and vandalized cars and houses and spread filthy rumours and maybe he fucked Paul's daughter. Now what? What had he done now? Paul would say anything to scare him, get the truth out of him. Robbie looked scared now. He looked terrified and young and nothing like the same guy who a minute previously was joking with his mates. Paul was forty years old and he had him.

'Where is she?' Paul said again, calmer now.

'I don't know. I don't fucking know. I swear to you. I swear to God. Now let me go.'

'Here,' a voice said behind them. Paul turned and as he looked around Robbie broke free. He took a couple of steps away but he didn't run. Paul was looking at a man he didn't know. He saw now the other boys standing around him, motionless, shocked, silent, waiting.

'What are you doing?' the man said.

'Who are you?' Paul asked.

'I'm his father,' he said, pointing at Robbie. 'What do you think you're doing? Hitting a boy of seventeen years of age?'

'He's done something to my daughter. I don't know where she is. He's done something and I'm going to get it out of him.'

'What are you talking about?'

'She's not come home. She went into your house this morning and now we don't know where she is. And it's him. It's this scumbag son of yours has done something. She never does this.'

'Watch what you're saying,' Whelan said. He stood in front of Paul, one step too close. He was short and solid. Not like his son. He wouldn't move. Paul could see it.

'Watch your language or you're going to have a problem.'

'Where's my daughter?' Paul said. 'That's all I want to know. And he knows something.'

'Where is she?' Whelan asked Robbie.

'I don't know,' Robbie said. 'I told him. He fucking slapped me around. I know nothing about it. She came over this morning and started giving me a whole load of shit. And then she left after five minutes. That's all I know. I've been with Alan and the others all day since. You can ask them.'

'So?' Whelan said to Paul.

'I don't believe him,' Paul said. 'I'll get it out of him.'

'You won't. There's nothing to get. You heard him. And if you touch him again, lay one finger on him, you'll be dealing with me. A man like you fighting a boy. You should be ashamed.'

The threat was so casual, so unemotional and calm that Paul hardly noticed it.

'You're the one should be ashamed,' Paul said. 'Do you know what your son is up to? How he's ruining people's lives around here? He put a brick through our window last week. He's a thug.'

'No, he's not.'

'He is.'

'Who's the thug? How old are you? What are you doing? Roaring and shouting and slapping a child. He may do some stupid things but he'll grow out of it. Not like you. It's a disgrace. Go home. I don't know where your daughter is. But with a father like you it's no surprise to me she's gone missing. God love her.'

He turned away slowly and walked towards his house. Robbie followed behind him, silent without looking back. Paul realized that there was a small crowd of people watching them now at a short distance. They stood, still looking, and Paul felt his face get hot as he realized what they had seen. He started to walk home.

It was wrong, Paul thought now. It wasn't this boy. To see him with his father. To hear his father talk and watch the two of them walk away. Paul knew he was wrong. It was a mistake. He thought how quickly Robbie had broken, bravado and poise and swagger gone in an instant when Paul slapped him. All that he had been trying to hide was his fear, Paul thought now. He could feel himself shaking as useless adrenalin pumped through him. He thought about what he would do now. If she wasn't there when he got back, he would ring the guards. He would tell them what had happened, how they had been having problems with Clare, and that now she was gone. He would tell them about Robbie and how she had broken up with him recently. He would tell them all this and they would come and check it out. They would deal with it and find her and it would be all right. She was just making a statement. She was showing what she could do. It didn't mean anything. It would be fine.

He was at the bottom of the drive. She would be there when he got back, he thought now. It was hope. It came on him suddenly and it felt as sure as fact. When he opened the door in twenty seconds, she would greet him in the hall and say she was sorry for all the trouble but she had just forgotten to call and she was back now and she was sorry. He would tell her then that he was sorry, too. That all he had wanted was for her to be happy and safe. He wanted her to grow and live and be happy. He had made a mess of it but he had been trying. He had tried. That was all it was and now, at the end, they could start again.

She was moving now. The ground dropped away, the lights glowing orange in the evening sky. She watched as black space opened up between her and the people, the buildings, the cars and buses. She watched it all, watched them all as they blurred and blended. Shrank and faded. Slowly disappeared until all she could see was a line of light and above it the dark outline of the hills that stood behind the city. She stood and watched and then she went inside because she was getting cold.

Inside she was hit by a wall of noise and heat and smoke from the bar. Everybody seemed to have started shouting since they left the port. There was music playing and as she went to buy a drink she heard the mix of accents around her. People were going home after holidays, trying to keep the mood going still before they had to settle down again. Back to normality. Not for her.

She took her drink and left the bar. She wandered past tables of men playing cards, backpackers sitting in groups along walls, drunk guys on their own, until she found a free seat opposite an English family. The mother smiled at her as she sat. Clare smiled back quickly and took out a magazine. She opened it and stared at the page. She listened as the two children whinged about everything, squirming and flapping. They wanted to see the boat. They wanted to go upstairs, outside, and see the sea. They were both exhausted and their parents knew it but the kids didn't and they were keeping each other awake.

She had enough money for a couple of weeks. She knew where she was going. She knew what she was doing. She knew what time the train left Holyhead and what time it arrived in Euston. She knew how to get to the hostel on the Underground. She had been in London before. It was bigger. That was all. That afternoon she had bought a book and checked out the Internet. There was work that she could do. Not great work but enough to get her started. The hostel she had picked was friendly. It said that in the book. That it was a good place to meet people. Meet new people. Start working. Earning. Maybe share a flat. See what it was like. She could do it.

It had started when Robbie broke the window. She had felt it then. She couldn't handle it any more. It was too much. She just realized that she could never be happy there, with her parents on top of her all the time and Robbie across the road. All that she could see in the future was conflict. Over who she wanted to see, where she wanted to go, what she wanted to do. Who she wanted to be. At what point would she be free of it? She had another year in school. Another whole year before she could do anything. Her father was getting worse. Angrier and harder and more and more mistaken. It wasn't her. It was him. Paranoid. Freaking out over everything. He didn't know how to deal with her any more. Another year of that.

And Robbie was a psycho. He had scared her that morning. When he grabbed her, she thought he was going to do something. He was wild. She saw the expression on his face when he saw the fear in her. He was enjoying it. He could have hurt her. She didn't scream though she wanted to. She waited a minute and said his name one more time and looked at him. This time he let her go but he was smiling at her. She ran from the house and didn't look back. When she went into town later she walked as quickly as possible to get to the main road. It could never be normal living there with him.

Why would she stay? For school? She could go back next year and finish. For her parents? Not for her father, who had no respect for her, no idea what her life was like. Not for her mother, who tried but couldn't make him listen. She would understand. She would know that Clare had to do this and that she could make it work. They would be worried of course, but she would ring them when things settled down and she would tell them the truth. She would miss the others but what difference did it make to them? She would have left in a year anyway. It was hard to think of them. She had been happy with them. With them all. Even her father. She remembered a time in the car with Paul, just the two of them, and they were laughing so hard that he nearly crashed. It wasn't long ago but she couldn't remember what it was that had made them laugh.

She was going to London. She was leaving behind the worries and the life she had lived as a child. She was growing up. She was making her own space, making new friends, starting to work. She had always told them that she could look after herself and now she would prove it. She would make her own life. She would be able to breathe again, away from the claustrophobia of that house, those people, that town. It was a bigger world.

She was getting tired herself now. Across from her, the children lay sleeping in their parents' arms. Clare lay back in her chair and made herself as comfortable as she could, using her coat as a pillow against the wall. She closed her eyes. She could still hear the noise from the bar, the music and shouting, the electronic bells and beeps of the slot machines, the low growl of the engine coming from beneath as it took her away. She was asleep in minutes.

She had rung when she arrived at the hostel that first morning. She rang because she didn't want them to worry. She wasn't trying to hurt them. She just wanted to get away for a while. That's what she said. Ruth spoke to her. It was the first time Paul had heard her say anything through that horrible night of waiting. He watched her relax and stood beside her, listening, trying to hear but getting nothing. When he tried to speak, Ruth put her hand up in the air to quieten him. Her voice was calm, not even hinting at the expression that dragged at her face. Paul couldn't do anything.

'Where are you?' Ruth asked her eventually, then over and over until she got the answer that she needed. After that everything happened quickly. She said goodbye and hung up before Paul could speak to Clare.

'Where is she?' he asked.

'In London.'

'Is she all right?'

'She's fine. I'm going to go and get her.'

'When?' Paul asked.

'Now. We can go now.'

'OK.'

'If I get on a flight straight away, I can be with her in four hours,' she said. 'I can see her in four hours.'

Paul drove fast. It was after the morning rush hour and they got onto the motorway quickly. They travelled in silence, each too tired to deal with another conversation, concentrating on getting there. There was no point in talking about what might happen. They would find out soon enough.

'Should I come with you?' Paul asked as they were getting near.

'Probably not,' she said after a moment. 'It's just easier.'

Paul nodded.

They got her onto a flight that left forty minutes later. He walked her to the gate.

'I'll ring you and let you know when we'll be back. It shouldn't be too long.' She tried to smile at him.

'And you're sure I shouldn't come? Let her know that it's OK?'

'I'm sure,' she said. 'I can talk to her. I can let her know. It'll be fine. I'll give you a ring later. OK?'

'OK.'

She turned and left. Nothing else. She was gone.

Paul went home. The house was empty. The children were with his parents. He sat on the couch in the living room with the phone in his hand, so tired that he couldn't think. There was no making sense of it now. It had happened. That was all he knew.

He wouldn't have made the mistakes that he had if he hadn't been trying. He had to look out for her. He was her father. He couldn't stand by and watch her fuck her life up. That's what he thought it was and he knew that he had got it wrong. It was an issue of trust. An issue of consultation. Belief. Space. Forgiveness. Understanding. If he'd talked to Ruth. If he'd trusted her. If he'd trusted Clare. If he'd ignored Joe. If they had never moved. All the ways that he could have avoided it. The past months grew into a maze, infinite paths that led nowhere, that never seemed to bring him closer to finding the moment where it began to unravel. Every day a tiny instance. A thought. Something that barely registered but contributed in some way to the end result. An expression on Clare's face. The tone of her voice. The way she looked away when he spoke. They felt like signs to him, signs of something bad that would bring them down. But now he had to believe that they had never been there.

He was wrong. It was his fault. That's what he kept coming back to. It wasn't Clare or Ruth or the boy. It was Paul and the pressure he had brought to the situation. Every time he thought about it the debate opened again in his head. What if? Wasn't she? Didn't he? But Paul had been there before. He knew to get out before he went too far because it offered him nothing. It was his fault. He was sorry. In the future it would be better.

He was dozing on the couch that evening at seven o'clock when Ruth rang to say that they would be on a flight arriving at nine.

'How is she?' Paul asked.

'She's absolutely fine.'

'Is she there?'

'She is.'

And before he was ready, he heard Clare's voice on the other end. She was saying hello, sounding nervous. As if she didn't know what to expect. He had to say something.

'Clare?' he said. 'You're OK?'

'Yeah, I'm fine.'

'You're coming back.' He said it like a statement, when really it was a question. He couldn't pull it back. 'Aren't you?' he added to soften it. To make it sound the way he meant it.

'Yes,' she said. He waited but she didn't say anything else.

'It'll be all right,' he said. 'You know that, don't you? It will be better.'

'I don't know,' she said.

'But I do,' he said. 'I'm sorry, Clare. That's all.'

'Thanks,' she said. The phone was beeping. 'We have to go.'

'I'll see you later,' he said but she was gone.

Paul was standing among a crowd looking up at the screen. He would be waiting for twenty minutes. He went to the cafe and bought a takeaway coffee and sat in the arrivals hall. Halfway through drinking it, he realized it was making him edgy and he put it in the bin.

Nobody there would have noticed anything different about him. He looked tired, he was sure. He'd hadn't slept but apart from that he was the same as everybody else. He showed nothing of the pain and worry that he had brought there with him, though it had been all that he had lived with for twenty-four hours.

Everybody was waiting for someone. He watched the reunions and the eyes of the people as they walked through the sliding door, searching. Sad cold outside faces transformed into something almost beautiful by the presence of another person. Families, boyfriends, girlfriends. Businessmen and drivers shaking hands without stopping or looking at each other. Tourists walking out not knowing where they were going, knowing that there would be no one there for them but still looking. Still hoping for somebody who couldn't be there. All these lives coming together and passing each other by. Nobody knew about him. Nobody knew what had happened to him. Nobody even saw him because he wasn't who they were looking for.

He got up and walked over to look at the screen. Their flight had just landed. It was early. He walked to the barrier directly across from the doors so that they would see him as soon as they came out. He stood there and waited.